THE FEATHERS OF DEATH

Simon Raven

The Feathers of Death

THE GAY MEN'S PRESS

First published 1959 by Anthony Blond Ltd
First Gay Men's Press publication 1998
GMP Publishers Ltd,
P O Box 247, Swaffham PE37 8PA, England

World Copyright © 1959 Simon Raven

A CIP catalogue record for this book is available
from the British Library

ISBN 0 85449 274 7

Distributed in Europe by Central Books,
99 Wallis Rd, London E9 5LN

Distributed in North America by InBook/LPC Group,
1436 West Randolph, Chicago, IL 60607

Distributed in Australia by Bulldog Books,
P O Box 300, Beaconsfield, NSW 2014

Printed and bound in the EU by WSOY, Juva, Finland

INTRODUCTION

This republication of Simon Raven's first novel could hardly come at a more appropriate time. When it first appeared, all homosexual activity was unlawful in Britain, even in private, as it had been since the passing of the 'Labouchere amendment' of 1885, generally known as the Blackmailer's Charter. The early 1950s in fact saw an intensification of gay prosecutions, with traditional British moral hypocrisy reinforced by a new paranoia against 'deviants' washing over from McCarthyism in the US.

The catalyst for change came in 1954 with the Montague case. Three men from highly respectable backgrounds, including the present Baron Montague of Beaulieu, were convicted of sexual offences with national servicemen. Public disquiet was especially aroused by the methods employed by the police in their pursuit of the defendants. These were then convicted largely on the testimony of two of their sexual partners – described by counsel as 'vastly the social inferiors' of those whom they denounced, and in fact browbeaten by the police into turning Queen's evidence, though this was not known at the time. In 1955 one of these three, Peter Wildeblood, a professional journalist, published a harrowingly frank account of his ordeal when he came out of prison. *Against the Law* was a bestseller, and is rightly seen as a seminal document in the history of gay emancipation. The author made a significant contribution to the findings of the Wolfenden Committee which investigated the state of the law relating to homosexuality, and led to the Sexual Offences Act of 1967.

Published originally in 1959, *The Feathers of Death* thus appeared in a period of uneasy flux. It was at this time that novels and films began to appear which tried to treat the subject of homosexuality openly and candidly. Yet the strength of the taboo was so great that these early efforts were almost all nervous and awkward. The rule was for a gay character to be portrayed as fathomlessly unhappy; and if he obligingly committed suicide by the end of the entertainment, that was simply par for the course. To be sure, gay men in those times had ample cause for misery. Yet this misery had to take a specific and precise form. As Simon Raven described it to me: 'The homosexual character had to be portrayed as continually clutching his brow and wailing how he desperately wished he could find true fulfilment in getting married and having a family...' He described it

i

thus with a rich Simon Raven chuckle, but the truth of what he says is easily observable in such typical novels of the period as *No End of the Way*, or even pioneering films like *Victim*.

Into this atmosphere of fervid doubts, phobias and bewilderment stepped Simon Raven. He is an extraordinary writer, and his prose style seems to have sprung forth like Athene from the head of Zeus, for it is there complete in this first novel. And if the inimitable prose style is already fully developed, so too were the attitudes that helped to shape it. The first characteristic one notices is the outspokenness. Simon has never been one to mince his words: indeed, one wonders whether he is actually capable of it. For those of us who love him it is his readiness, nay his clamorous eagerness, to say the unspeakable, if not unthinkable, that makes us feel as we do about him. Yet there is far more to this than an enfant terrible setting out to shock with what would nowadays be termed 'politically incorrect'. If he hates a great deal about the modern world, there is one thing that he detests still more, and that is hypocrisy. Every single one of his books, fiction and non-fiction alike, abounds in scathing references to weasel words, mealy-mouthed unction and other variants on the theme. This is no enfant terrible showing off in order to be noticed. It's just Simon telling it how it is – or, at any rate, how he sees it – because he's constitutionally incapable of doing any other.

His other great attribute, especially striking forty years ago, is the ability to write plainly and straightforwardly about sex. Even now, this is still a rare quality among British writers: the old attitude: 'No sex please, we're British,' dies amazingly hard. When the two attributes are combined, it makes for an explosive mixture. Thus it was that soon after the publication of *The Feathers of Death* he could cheerfully write of his expulsion from Charterhouse school for homosexuality – with law reform still five years and a change of government away. And his jaunty description of his first novel as 'a story of homosexual romance in the army' must have sent appalled shivers down the spine of, say, Viscount Montgomery. In the novel itself, I suspect there is no single passage that more emphatically sums up his approach than this early one in which his hero, the army officer Alastair Lynch, is speaking of one of the enlisted men in his troop. In doing so he incidentally defines not merely which manner of young man takes his fancy, but which manner of young man takes Simon Raven's fancy also:

'...if there's one thing I can't resist it's a combination of softness and masculinity. Like those boys at school who are all fair hair and enormous blue eyes but nevertheless lead the scrum or score dramatic centuries. I could never resist them at Harrow and I don't seem able to now.'

You just didn't go around saying things like that in 1959, even if you felt them (especially if you felt them?), not even through the mouth of a character in a novel. Except that Simon did say them, and has gone on saying them ever since. When all this is said, gay rights have had less unlikely advocates: one friend of mine who is emphatically of the politically-correct tendency told me that he would admire Raven as a prose stylist but could not accept, or forgive him for, his 'gamey right-wingery'. I suspect that he would not be found dead on a Pride march or any other overt demonstration: it would offend profoundly against his loathing of all forms of 'enthusiasm' – in its earlier meaning of zeal or fanaticism – which is how he would regard such things. That is of a piece with his fastidious disdain to apologise for one's private tastes. He takes the very eighteenth-century attitude that one's private life should be one's own affair – though he is certainly willing to explain: indeed, his entire canon may legitimately be described as an extended explanation of what makes him tick.

Just to be sure, though, I asked him if he could define any specific points he had wanted to air in *The Feathers of Death*. He suggested, a little tentatively, two, which seem on the face of it to be contradictory. (Tentatively, I think, because he would subscribe, quite properly, to the view that the primary intention of the novelist must be to tell as good a story as he can devise, as well as he can tell it.) First, he said, he felt a voice ought to be raised against the trend of those films and books of which we have spoken, in which it's okay to have a gay hero provided he doesn't have any fun. 'I thought homosexuals ought to be shown as potentially able to have as good a time as anyone else.' He said this without heat; but as a definition of true equality it seems to me a very fair start. Second, he said, he had wanted to make the point that after the first objective was said and done, 'you can't have that sort of thing going on in an army. It's simply too dangerous, too destructive of discipline and good order.' This is plainly another example of where he is likely to offend today's gay sensibilities as he has habitually offended a lot of non-gay ones. But it must be understood in the context of his attitudes towards the army, which we must briefly examine, for they are crucial to an understanding of the man.

Simon Raven was a soldier twice, once as a national service conscript and then, after a series of the disasters which he has chronicled for his admirers' delight ever since, as a regular, with a commission in the King's Shropshire Light Infantry. Indeed, it is an important fact in his life story that it was only after a further, final disaster, occasioning his precipitate and premature departure from the army, that he finally discovered his true calling as a writer. I shall not say any more about that, because if you are encouraged by this novel to read more of his work you can hear his own version of events, and he tells it far more entertainingly than I could begin to do. But it is worth pointing out that he volunteered for the army as a career.

Simon Raven is a deeply romantic novelist. That becomes apparent once one has become familiar with his prose style. To begin with he gives indications of cynicism; there is also an element of upper-middle-class, public-school hauteur to be coped with. But these are layers to be peeled off his writing: the cynicism reveals itself, when one gains a deeper insight into his work, as mostly a defensive, self-protective carapace; the apparent arrogance is in reality more the effortless, triple-armoured self-confidence that is those schools' greatest gift to their alumni. Once the layers are peeled away they reveal the much gentler, altogether more human and likable persona beneath the self-protective carapace. And as one begins to penetrate to this truer perception of him, one begins to see that he is also a profoundly romantic man. It is essential to appreciate this to understand his feelings towards the army.

He has devoted several of his novels, apart from this first one, to stories of the army, and in all of them he is at times excoriatingly critical of it. He can ridicule it so hilariously that one would be forgiven for imagining that he saw it himself as no more than organised lunacy, with occasional intervals for farce. But it takes very profound knowledge and, much more important, understanding of an institution to make effective fun of it, and that is the secret here. Simon loved the army, and it was his love of it that gave him the true understanding that enabled him to poke fun at it. At the bottom of all the ridicule is the affection of son for mother. He saw the army as a measure of protection against all that he loathed and feared in the changing world outside. It gave him tolerable comfort, fine comradeship, an intimate world of male-bonding (how he would detest that expression!) and a great deal of fun. He criticises it and ridicules it; but he is entitled to do so, because he is part of it. He belongs.

This same profound romanticism colours, indeed shapes, his attitudes to much more than just the army. It affects his view of Charterhouse (all the schools in his work are in fact Charterhouse), to love, to comradeship and to sex. But nothing demonstrates it more comprehensively than his loving portrayal of the army. It takes the supreme confidence that love alone, perhaps, can engender, to show something warts and all. *The Feathers of Death* is as good an exemplar of all this as any other of his books.

It is ironic that its reappearance comes just at a time when the long-running debate about whether homosexual activity should be legal in the armed forces has had one of its periodic airings; but by its open espousal of a point of view opposed by most gay people, it may even contribute helpfully to the debate. Indeed, posterity may find that its author has made some contribution to the whole matter of gay emancipation in general. But no one can know what posterity is going to find, and in any case it doesn't matter much. The main thing about *The Feathers of Death* is that it is a very fine story, superbly told, and as good an introduction to Simon Raven's work as any. If you are coming new to him, I hope it will awake in you a desire to go on to his other books, many of which are also being currently reissued. If you will forgive the cliché, you have a treat in store – and I envy you.

Mike Seabrook
December 1997

CONTENTS

'The wings of man's life are plumed with the feathers of death'

Elizabethan seaman in a plea to his Sovereign

PROLOGUE

IF THERE IS one thing which I shall remember until I die, it is the day Duthwaite and I set off into the hills to relieve Alastair Lynch. Why I should remember this ride so clearly, I do not know, for in itself it was, like all journeys, only an interlude; and for that matter, you would have thought that the horrible scene which was waiting for us at the end of the journey itself would have driven out any other memory of that day. But this is not the case. I can still see, as though it were just at the other end of this room in which I write, Duthwaite talking in that grimly efficient way of his to Sergeant Major Mole, giving precise and sensible instructions about the composition and the mounting of the little party that was to come with us; I can see poor Mole looking forlornly at the pitiful gaggle of spare signallers, batmen and native policemen who made up at least half of our expedition.

'I don't know what Captain Duthwaite's going to think of this little lot,' he said to me.

'He'll think what I think – that there isn't any choice.'

'Wish he'd let me come. Can't sit still for thinking of poor Mr Lynch up there with those black bastards all about, murderous swine . . . Do you suppose, Sir, that if you had a word with Captain Duthwaite . . . ?'

'No, C.S.M.,' I said; 'Mr Byrt will need your help if anything crops up here.'

Mole grunted and ambled off without saluting. He had a soft spot for Alastair Lynch, who, among other things, had lent him money for his daughter's wedding. I knew how much he wished that it was Duthwaite or myself up in the hills, that it was Duthwaite, with his prim manner, who was up there wondering if his throat would be cut in the night, that it was I who was waiting in the forest rain for the help that took for ever to come. Not that Mole disliked either of us : it was just that he yearned, in his rotten and loyal old heart, for Alastair to be safely back at Company H.Q., laughing at the feeble jokes Mole loved to tell him or pulling Mole's leg about the precision and punctuality of the Company returns. As it was, the poor old man must simply sit and wait, though Michael Byrt, I thought, would be kind to him, would listen to his stories and see that he had enough whisky to make him sleep . . .

And then there was the first stage of the journey, along the track to the bottom of the escarpment, where Mole was to say good-bye to us and turn back to camp.

'You'll see that Mr Alastair's all right, Sir?' he said to me.

'We'll do our best.'

He watched us make our way up the narrow track which led to the top of the escarpment, a lonely, stupid, sad old man sitting on his sad old horse. When we reached the summit and were about to disappear from his sight, he drew himself up and saluted, with great smartness and precision, and then lifted his cap and waved it above his head before he finally turned his horse away. It was a gay and gallant gesture; even Duthwaite was touched, and smiled as he returned the salute. But he meant all that for Alastair, I thought to myself; none of it's for us.

And so we rode off through the scrub towards the Hills. Away on our left, beneath the escarpment, was Lake Philia and beyond that, many miles across the plain to the north, the twin snow-capped peaks of Mount Eirene. The natives said that God lived on Mount Eirene, an assertion which seemed quite credible that afternoon; for this was the first time in weeks that the weather had been clear enough for one to see the twin peaks plainly, even from the escarpment, and I had almost forgotten the magnificence and brilliance of the sight when seen against a clean blue sky. Alastair had once made some comment about Castor and Pollux, referring to an alternative native legend that the peaks were in fact twin gods. I was just thinking about this, and how Alastair had gone on to quote Homer's account of Helen on the walls of Troy, when Duthwaite beckoned me to join him at the head of the column. He looked furtive and confidential. Having turned his head to confirm that the two files immediately behind us consisted of native policemen, whose English was rudimentary, he started talking, low and urgently, about Alastair and the young soldier, Malcolm Harley. It seemed that Corporal Killeen had been telling Duthwaite about this in the private interview he had asked for a few days previously. I suppose I had always known that this affair would come out sooner or later, but I had hoped it would come out to anybody rather than Duthwaite. At any rate, here he was talking about it, quiet, controlled, but evidently excited; talking and talking, intensely and fiercely, on and on through the afternoon, as the lake disappeared beneath the escarpment and Mount Eirene faded with the day and the hills in front of us came steadily closer.

Perhaps it was Duthwaite talking like this (on and on about the man we were going to rescue, his manners, his morals, his career, his money and his love) which made me remember that afternoon so clearly afterwards. Duthwaite wanted to know where it would all end, how it had all begun, why, when. He always wanted to know things of this kind. It was no good saying that such matters begin, spontaneously and almost unnoticed, like seasons of fair weather (so that afterwards, when the rain comes again, no one can

14

really remember the exact day on which he first took his work into the garden or sat talking to a friend beneath the trees) : it was no good saying that all such matters start like this, vague and unobserved, and only end where and how the gods ordain. Duthwaite had a tidy mind and expected tidy answers. And so, since he had obviously heard enough already to be dangerous if he so wished, I told him everything I knew, just as I am now going to tell you : how we came to the country of Pepromene and the city of Eirene : how Alastair Lynch met the soldier Malcolm Harley, and what passed between them : how the native rebellion started, and Alastair's Troop was sent into the hill country : and how it was that Duthwaite and I, with our pathetic little band, came to be riding through the evening towards the shadowy mountains of Dis.

PART ONE

PEPROMENE

CHAPTER ONE

THE EVENING BEFORE we were to disembark at Port Ulysses, they
put up the boxing ring on deck for the Finals of the Inter Company
Competition. There were armchairs in the front row for the officers,
hard chairs in the second row for the sergeants; while everyone else
had to sit about on bits of nautical equipment and watch as best
he might. Robin Hathaway was refereeing in the ring, for he, being
the youngest of us, had been made to give up four days of his leave
to attend a course about boxing before we left England; Major
Sinclair, with a sour yet self-satisfied expression on his face, was acting as time-keeper; and Duthwaite, with a similar expression of acid
self-approval, was one of the three judges, who sat at various points
round the ring and kept the score, blow by blow if they could
manage it.

'Robin has got himself up daintily,' said Alastair Lynch.

Hathaway was wearing white trousers, a white silk shirt and a
black evening tie.

'It's obligatory,' I said. 'The Army Boxing Association insists that
referees dress like that.'

'I only hope they taught him what to do as well as what to wear.
I've seen some very muddling situations in these boxing affairs. Man
gets an accidental and harmless blow beneath the belt, pretends to
be half dead, claims the fight on a foul ... Referee says he's sham-
ming, orders fight to continue, man drops dead from sheer resentment ... Referee lynched by crowd or court-martialled for negligence
... Very troubling.'

Hathaway, blushing furiously, climbed up into the ring to get
things started. C.S.M. Mole, who was to announce the fights and
in general act as master of ceremonies, shambled up after him, stood
to attention facing Colonel Sanvoisin, and then conferred with
Hathaway.

'A fat lot of help old Moley will be if they do start lynching
Robin,' said Alastair.

'Moley's a loyal old number,' said Michael Byrt. 'He'd do his best.'

'How erotic those white shorts are ...'

For the first two contestants, dressed in clean white shorts as befitted the finals, and without vests since we were in the tropics, had

17

now appeared in opposite corners of the ring. As usual the white shorts, especially provided by the Q.M. for such occasions, had been lobbed out without regard to suitability of size or cut. One man was baggily covered to almost below the knee, the other was bursting out of a kind of loose and totally inadequate jock-strap.

'Up the bikini, come on the plus fours,' yelled the good-natured crowd, happily anticipating an hour's free entertainment, forgetting the early Reveille and sweaty bad temper that must inevitably attend tomorrow's disembarkation.

'Cut that out,' snarled Duthwaite over his shoulder.

'Quiet,' said C.S.M. Mole, and blew his whistle. 'The first fight, which is in the featherweight division, will be between Mounted Infantryman Baines in the red corner and Mounted Corporal Soley in the green. Baines, Soley, forward to the referee.'

Another yell from the audience, a brief word to the boxers from Robin Hathaway, an ill-tempered clang from Major Sinclair's gong, and the whole thing was under way. For a long time nothing of note occurred. Fight succeeded fight in good order, no troublesome situation arose to perplex Robin, and the one knock-out which happened was a straight-forward affair, the victim of which was instantly whisked off by the medical orderly for attention. It was only towards the end of what might have been a very ordinary and even rather dull evening's boxing that a cause of real excitement and emotion suddenly appeared.

Into the ring stepped a stocky, tough, hairy little brute of a man, seemingly about twenty-six years old, with a furtive, vicious and resentful face. He went to the red corner. Up the steps into the green corner came a taller but very much younger man, of far slighter build, loose and gangling in movement, with a fair skin and a lazy, smiling face.

'Light-welterweight,' said Sergeant Major Mole. 'The finals in the light-welterweight division will be between Mounted Infantryman Beatson, of "C" Company, in the red corner, and Drummer Harley, of the Corps of Drums and "H.Q." Company, in the green corner. Beatson, Harley, step forward to the referee.'

'Trouble for Robin,' said Alastair, as the two opponents went into the middle of the ring to receive the usual exhortation to stage 'a good clean fight'. 'That little brute Beatson is twice as strong as the other one and knows every dirty trick that ever there was. Even if the fight's fair, he'll make mince-meat of the Drummer, and Robin will have to stop the fight. I only hope he does so before any damage is done . . . What did Moley say that boy was called?'

'Harley,' I said. 'Drummer Harley. I see him in H.Q. sometimes. He's not long been in service as a man. He joined as a band-boy some years back, but spent a long time trumpeting at the Depot.'

'Well, they've no business to let him get cut about by Beatson. No wonder mothers don't want their sons in the Army. Sinclair's organised this competition, and he's old enough to have more sense.'

But all this was interrupted by Sinclair slashing at his gong to start the first of three rounds. From the beginning it stood fair to be a fierce battle, for Beatson had a very nasty look on his dark, mean face and started after Harley with both his thick little arms jabbing and swinging without a pause. However, Harley had the wit to know that his height gave him some advantage, for he retreated slowly round the ring keeping Beatson away with occasional punches from his left, thereby catching some heavy blows on his left shoulder and upper arm but without suffering serious harm or even being scored against. This went on for about a minute and a half, and then suddenly one of Harley's lefts went properly home on to Beatson's nose. Beatson stepped back with his eyes watering, muttered something under his breath, and then rushed at Harley with such speed and concentrated malevolence that he swept the Drummer's guard aside and bore him up against the ropes, where poor Harley flinched and bucked unguarded and helpless while his opponent hammered at him with both fists on the face and chest – with a kind of clawing motion, yet without, as far as I could determine, striking foul blows with the wrist or palm. For a few seconds more the terrible, scrabbling blows poured on to the tormented Harley, who was then rescued by the gong. (The first two rounds were to be of only two minutes, the last of three.) He went back to his corner flushed and quivering, though apparently not badly damaged. When he sat down on the stool, he leaned right back against the corner pad and stretched his legs out in front of him, so that, from where I was sitting, I could see right up his shorts to the groin. Alastair had noticed this too; he sat by me rather stiffly, but then seemed to relax a little, and remarked :

'So far, so good, if he can keep himself away from the ropes.'

'If,' said Michael Byrt.

'I don't know. Beatson is a beery little man. He may not be capable of any more efforts like that last.'

But Beatson showed no signs of letting up at the beginning of the second round. He came straight out of his corner at Harley, who squared up bravely this time, standing toe to toe with his opponent and sending in straight, graceful punches at about half the rate Beatson put in his vicious swings and hooks. Many of these missed or crashed pointlessly but painfully on Harley's arms; but many more struck home, and already Harley's nose was streaming blood and the tears were brightening his eyes. For they were the heavy, grinding blows of a mature and muscular man; and the face behind the blows showed hatred, impersonal because the two soldiers hardly knew each other, but assuredly hatred. After about forty seconds of this courageous but very ill-advised close fighting, Harley stepped away

19

to the right, receiving as he went a sharp blow in the stomach, which seemed to wind him, for he sagged back heavily against one corner. Seeing his opponent trapped and weakened, Beatson leapt furiously toward this corner; but Harley somehow pulled himself together, and though he flinched away with his body straining back over the ropes, though the blow he made was nothing more than a blind, childish, terror-inspired chop, he did catch Beatson heavily on the ear, causing the older man to reel and collapse.

Beatson got up after a count of five, by which time Harley was apparently recovered and safe in the middle of the ring. But there was something strained and uneasy about his bearing, something not to be associated either with exhaustion or with the damage to his face. As for Beatson, he was evidently rather disconcerted, and for the remaining forty seconds of the round he responded only half-heartedly to a series of equally half-hearted long-range blows from Harley – blows stiffly delivered and seldom coming within inches of their target. But despite a lame ending to this round, there was much applause when the gong went : for the crowd appreciated Harley's courage in standing up to Beatson at the beginning of the round, and everyone had been glad to see Beatson, a well-known canteen bully, put on to the floor.

It was when Harley turned to go back to his corner at the end of this second round that I noticed two thin brown trickles dripping down the back of his right thigh. Robin Hathaway had also noticed this. He glanced nervously at Colonel Sanvoisin as if seeking help, but the Colonel went on calmly talking to his neighbour. He was not a man to interfere with his officers on their ground; Hathaway was referee, let him do as he thought fit. So Robin went over to Harley's corner and whispered to him and his second, Sergeant Royd. Royd shrugged, but Harley shook his head violently from side to side. This time, so far from stretching out, he was sitting almost doubled up in his corner. Royd had improved his face, but his nose was swollen and the nostrils encrusted with blood, while his left eye was nearly closed. Nevertheless, it was clear that he was firm in his refusal to give in. Robin touched him on the glove and walked away. The gong went for the last round.

I suppose Harley reckoned that if he was going to make a Roman holiday of himself, it might as well be a memorable one. In any event, he went straight for Beatson with a ferocity that shook the spectators, who had been accustomed hitherto to see him either retreating or standing his ground, mild, agitated and brave by turns, but in no way taking the offensive. He certainly took it now, thrashing at Beatson with all the strength in his slender arms. But a chance blow from Beatson had already started his nose bleeding again, the brown trickles on his thigh had become large patches of filth, some of which was dropping on to the boards, and, worst of all, he was really achieving very little; for Beatson had a way of contracting himself into a kind of muscular and invulnerable ball, so that the blows, thudding on to his strong sinews or the top of his skull, did little except drain away Harley's remaining strength.

'He can't keep this going,' whispered Michael Byrt.

And indeed, after about a minute, Harley stumbled back a pace or two and just looked blankly and despairingly at Beatson, who, uncoiling from his shell, came whipping back at the Drummer and sent him shambling and groaning across the ring with a series of vicious punches in the ribs. Harley was now up against the ropes again, making only the feeblest efforts to guard himself, but writhing and twitching in a futile attempt to evade the short-armed but immensely powerful jabs which Beatson was directing at his stomach and his face. He was sobbing openly now, the dirt was pouring down his legs, and there was no question but that Robin ought to have stopped the fight at once. This he was probably just about to do. But at that moment Beatson stepped back for an instant and paused, obviously measuring up his kill for the most brutal method of despatch he could contrive. Before he could come in again, however, or Robin could raise his hand and shout to Beatson to stop, Harley gave a great blubbering howl and with all his remaining strength lurched forward and struck at Beatson with both fists together. Had this blow ever landed, it would undoubtedly have been judged a foul; as it was, Harley missed by about a foot, fell forward on to his knees and then collapsed completely on to his stomach. Robin sent Beatson to his corner and beckoned for the stretcher bearers; and meanwhile, for about twenty seconds, there was absolutely complete silence in the crowd, a silence broken only by the breeze picking at a loose piece of canvas on the deck and the stretcher bearers fussing towards the ring. But as the bearers climbed between the ropes, Harley stirred and lifted his cheek from the boards. When this happened, a great shout of cheering thundered out, wild and deep and warming to the heart, so that Harley might know, then and for ever, how his comrades felt about a man who, beaten, humiliated, self-defiled and terrified, could yet come back out of the depths of defeat with a final, hopeless and splendid effort of the will.

While all this was going on, Alastair disappeared. I did not see him again until just before dinner, when I found him in the Officers' Saloon drinking with Robin Hathaway and Colonel Sanvoisin. Robin was evidently in a great state because he had let the Harley fight go on for so long, and the other two were doing their best to calm him down.

'My dear Robin,' the Colonel was saying, 'I grant you it was a very open question whether you ought to have let the thing continue after the second round. But you weren't necessarily wrong about that, and it was very plain that Harley wanted to go on. Once you decided to let him, wherein are you to blame? Harley took the offensive early in the third round : no question of stopping it then. After that, Beatson got him on the ropes and it was obvious that something would soon have to be done. However, just at the stage when something *would* have been done, Harley pulled off his final attack and passed out. So the matter was settled for you.'

This was Colonel Sanvoisin's way. Once a thing had fallen out, for good or ill, he expended effort and intelligence on reassuring people that they had taken a reasonable course and that he himself was as happy as possible about the outcome. If things went consistently wrong, and this was consistently attributable to one person, then he would try to find that person a different and more suitable job within the Battalion. Once, however, that an officer had arrived in the Regiment and been accepted, there was no question, unless an outright scandal occurred (and not always then), of getting rid of him altogether.

'One is stuck with one's friends,' Colonel Sanvoisin used to say, 'and one must accept both them and their deficiencies and make the best of it. There are, after all, worse things in the world than incompetence.' ·

It was this sort of remark which made me love him and others, like Sinclair (our recently imported second-in-command), despise and even deride him. Nevertheless, whatever degree of tolerance or even laxity Sanvoisin displayed towards others, it was impossible to impugn either the gallantry or competence of the man himself. His record was sound and in places distinguished ; and it was clear that his conception of his officers, whom he saw and treated as a body of old and trusted, but human and therefore fallible friends, made for more good will, ease of mind and loyalty than Sinclair, for example, could have inspired in a thousand years. Just now Sanvoisin was having considerable success with Robin, though the latter was plainly still troubled by the earlier events of the evening.

'It must have been so humiliating for Harley,' Robin said. 'Like a child . . .'

'The men made it plain what they thought,' Sanvoisin answered. 'I'd put up with a lot for a cheer like that.'

'He was quite pleased with himself once they'd cleaned him up,' said Alastair, 'though at first he seemed to think that the cheers were for Beatson for knocking him out. I put him right about that.'

'You saw him?' Sanvoisin asked. 'I didn't know he was one of yours.'

'He isn't, Colonel,' said Alastair evenly. 'I thought someone should make sure he was all right.'

'I suppose so.'

Sanvoisin looked briefly at Alastair and then smiled at us all.

'Once we get off this damned boat,' he continued, 'things are going to be very tiresome for a week or so. We've got to settle in at Eirene. We've got to see what arrangements the G.O.C. has made for us. General Peterson is a fair man but he's hard. Another thing – he doesn't take easily to people enjoying themselves. It may be some time before we can have much amusement without Peterson coming nagging into the Mess and wanting to know why we're not all in bed or else out doing a night exercise. He's a great one for sumptuary laws, and if he doesn't like what we're up to, he's quite capable of saying that conditions do not permit of our having more than one waiter in the Mess or of any transport being used to collect drink from the N.A.A.F.I. Depot. He could hardly say that at the moment because Pepromene isn't yet an operational station; but they're having trouble, it may be made operational at any time, and this kind of thing is meat and drink to Peterson. He was one of Montgomery's finds in the war – advertisingly democratic, single-minded and a damned busy-body. So I'm telling you this to warn you, with my condolences, that pleasure,' and here he smiled particularly at Alastair, 'will not be plentiful for a bit. *Integer vitae,* whether we like it or not, is what each of us is going to be.'

'In which case, if we are to believe Horace, we shall at least have nothing to fear from the wild animals.'

'Do not rely too much on one of his less happy efforts. I suspect that ode of having been written by Dr Arnold and smuggled into the canon by way of a school edition. But what I'm leading up to,' said Sanvoisin, 'is this. For all there must be an early start tomorrow, I thought we might have a little party tonight, if only to make up for our depressing future. I've squared the Purser and the stewards, there's plenty to drink, they say we can have until three a.m. to drink it, and we might even have a little game of something later on. So tell all friends to be here after dinner by about ten ... And as for you, Robin, you're to stop worrying. You behaved very reasonably in what was an unimportant but nasty predicament.'

Lieutenant Colonel Lord Nicholas Sanvoisin detested fuss or panic of any kind and in any circumstances. Again, being something of a scholar by training (he had spent three years at Trinity College, Cambridge, and entered the Army from the University) and very much a pagan by inclination, he had long ago adopted the sound ancient custom of anticipating any event which was likely to require disagreeable effort by holding a tremendous entertainment in the hours immediately preceding it. It was therefore typical of him to give a party at this juncture. Most C.O.s, faced with a disembarkation into new country and being about to join the command of a notoriously savage G.O.C., would at best have sent everyone early to bed and at worst have kept everyone up all night, holding a series of last minute inspections and making countless futile and muddling adjustments to the existing arrangements for the morrow. Lord Nicholas merely held a party. Adequate orders, checked and signed by himself, had already been issued; no one had complained that he could not understand them; and it was therefore to be presumed that everyone would get off the boat without difficulty. If the worst happened and there was a shambles, well, disembarkations had ended in a shambles before now and the Devil had stayed in Hell for all that. And if General Peterson came nosing on to the dock and didn't like what he saw, let him choke over it if he would; for Colonel Sanvoisin had £3,000 a year of his own, was in any case going to retire when his tenure of command was done, and, for all his loyalty to the Army and love of our own Regiment, he was not going to put his Battalion or himself into a sweat for Peterson before the man actually had us in his clutches.

So a party there was, and later on Sanvoisin himself took the bank at Baccarat. Again, it was typical of the man to take the bank; for this meant that he himself could pay out the winners at the end of the game and that all losses would be directly due to him. Thus if someone made a fool of himself and could not pay up for some time, only Sanvoisin would know about it, and the officer in question could be confident both that his secret was safe and that he would not be disagreeably pressed for the debt. C.O.s are expected to discountenance gambling because it leads to debt and disaster; Sanvoisin, who enjoyed gambling and knew his officers did too, countenanced gambling but insured against disaster, a manner of dealing with the question nicely calculated to affront his seniors and to enrage moralists.

This particular game was certainly enraging James Sinclair and Richard Duthwaite. They were talking together some way from the table, sourly and without drinking. Sinclair, the second-in-command, was an ambitious soldier who had recently been transferred to us from another and very different regiment. He disliked these rather disreputable manifestations of Sanvoisin's robust and pagan attitude to life, considering them to be both immoral and bad for discipline. Had Sinclair had his way, we should all now be standing on troop decks making sure that the men's kits were packed and assembled in precisely the specified manner, tiring the men and ourselves with sheer nagging interference. Duthwaite probably felt the same as Sinclair. Duthwaite came of a lower-middle class family and had been commissioned on a temporary basis at the end of the war. He had then applied for a permanent commission, which he had very properly received, for he was a conscientious and persevering man, shrewd and, in the last resort, fair. But it was something of a mystery that he had been allowed by our Colonel-in-Chief to stay with our Regiment after the war; for though we were not exactly 'smart' in the sense that the Household Cavalry was 'smart', there had always been a rather snobbish insistence that our regular officers should have 'public school' status and preferably some private money as well. Duthwaite had neither – and was very conscious of the fact; but of course this only increased his determination to maintain his grinding day-to-day efficiency and reaffirmed his dislike of such frivolous scenes as the present one. A soldier was there to soldier, in Duthwaite's view; there was always work to be done. This was all too true in his own case, for he was second-in-command of 'D' Company, an organisation blithely and ineptly presided over by Major Percy Berkeley, who had not had a thought in his head for twenty years that was not connected with his own immediate pleasure or comfort.

Percy Berkeley was sitting on Sanvoisin's right. Beyond him was Alastair (who commanded a troop in Percy's Company and was a great favourite with him because of his tolerance and knowledge of Burgundies), and beyond Alastair again was Giles Bancombe, the Adjutant – a weak-minded, fatuous, conceited ass, who was well known for his concern with the niceties of good-form military behaviour. A fondness for gambling was Bancombe's one rather surprising departure from the official military norm. I myself was sitting opposite Colonel Sanvoisin, between Robin Hathaway and Michael Byrt. Robin, I remember, was very uneasy – it had taken a iot of persuasion to make him join the game. But Michael Byrt, whose acute mathematical intelligence led him to prefer Bridge to pure gambling such as this, was nevertheless taking his usual lazy but shrewd interest in the run of the play, waiting for the time when the laws of chance or averages seemed to indicate a long reverse for the bank – the time to pounce and grab with both hands. It was surprising how often Michael was right about this – and just as well, for he had little enough money to throw away. Alastair used to say that Michael was just extremely lucky, and that if there was one thing certain about the laws of chance and averages it was that they could not be applied to short games lasting only a few hours. Or perhaps, said Alastair, it was intuition Michael had. Whatever it was Michael had, Alastair himself did not. Known for wild and ferocious play, he occasionally achieved, by the sheer amount of his stakes and persistence of his betting, some dazzling periods of success; but these seldom lasted more than a few minutes, and there were few evenings when he left the table a winner. There had indeed been some trouble about Alastair's gaming debts before we left England. He owed nothing to any of us, but it seemed that several London bookmakers were looking down their noses and that the organiser of a well known London Chemin-de-fer game was getting restless. However, Alastair's father, reminded by Colonel Sanvoisin that Pepromene should prove an economical country even for Alastair, had come to the rescue and even found a bit extra as a going-away present; so that tonight Alastair was as reckless as ever in indulging what he called 'the Irish side of my character'.

'The Russian side of your character, if you ask me,' I said. Alastair had just called a £20 bet against the bank. This was doing well, and I supposed that Colonel Sanvoisin must be a good £200 in hand, though since he was obliged, if the table wished it, to take as much as £50 against his bank at any one *coup*, a bad run would soon see him stripped. However, few of us were likely to bet more than £5 or £10 on any *coup*, and for this particular one, on which Alastair was risking his £20, there was besides only a sprinkling of bets for a pound or two. Robin risked ten shillings – the minimum stake permitted.

'*That's* no good,' said Michael. 'Lord Nicky is due to win seven times in ten over the next twenty-five *coups*.'

'Why?' said Robin. 'He's been winning steadily.'

'I know. But people have been playing foolishly. At this moment there have been only fifty-one *coups* in favour of the table, and nine cases of *égalité*. However, much the heaviest betting by the table has always been when the bank happened to win. Hence Lord Nicky's up-money. But on the average showing, he's still due to receive the advantage in *coups* for some time.'

At this point Alastair turned up a natural nine and won outright against Sanvoisin's six.

'I told you,' said Alastair. 'Your averages only apply in the very long run, over days, not hours.'

He turned to the banker.

'I'd like to leave the whole forty in for the next.'

'All right,' said Sanvoisin, 'if the rest of the table is content with ten.'

We were content with ten. Michael again abstained, Robin left his previous ten shillings and the ten he had just won to make up a stake of a pound, and Percy Berkeley, taking a very long swig of brandy and going rather red, put down a counter worth £5.

'I'll bet two,' said Bancombe.

'£48 against the bank,' remarked Sanovoisin. 'Who'll make it a level fifty?'

Two players further down the table put down a sovereign each. Sinclair glanced at Duthwaite. Sanvoisin fingered a card out of the shoe and pushed it across to Alastair, flicked out one for himself, another for Alastair, another for himself. (Since there were only eight players, he was playing only to the right.) Alastair examined his cards, and then turned them up to show a natural eight. Sanvoisin turned his up one by one, a four and then a five.

'Napoléon,' he said, 'a natural major of nine.'

This was cruel for Alastair, as he had been losing heavily and it is irritating, to say the least, when one's minor natural of eight is confronted, against all the odds, with the only thing that can beat it. However, he pushed his counters across with a pleasant enough smile. Robin heaved a sigh and parted with his pound. Bancombe looked cross and unwillingly allowed his two counters to be swept away from him by Alastair towards the Colonel. Fat Percy Berkeley registered nothing, but drank a lot more brandy.

These had been the last few cards in the shoe.

'Remake the shoe please, Robin,' said Sanvoisin. 'I shan't be gone two minutes.'

He left the room.

'I thought you were in for one of your runs,' said Giles Bancombe to Alastair.

'I expect you corrupted my luck.'

'What do you mean by that?' said a thin voice behind him. James Sinclair was now standing right over Alastair and looking down at the top of his head.

'Mean by what?'

'Saying that Bancombe had corrupted your luck.'

'Don't be silly, James,' said Percy Berkeley, 'no one meant anything at all.'

'I asked Lynch.'

'It's as Percy says, James. A mere meaningless gambler's pleasantry.'

'I wouldn't know about gamblers' pleasantries. I've other things to occupy me. I thought it was a rude and uncalled-for remark. I suppose you blame Bancombe for all that money your father had to pay for you in June?'

'Of course he doesn't,' said Bancombe. Normally subservient to his seniors, he could hardly desert Alastair in this very plain situation of ill-tempered and irrelevant fault-finding.

'I asked Lynch.'

'Lynch says,' said Alastair, 'that he passed a meaningless joke to Captain Bancombe, and that he does not require Major Sinclair to interfere in that or in any other part of his business.'

'Insolence won't help you. We're just getting to a country where there's proper soldiering to be done, where there'll be discipline and hard work and no time for this kind of messing around. But it looks as if all you're fit for is getting rid of more of your father's money.'

'Now look here, James,' said Percy Berkeley, 'we're only trying to have a pleasant evening before all this work and discipline you talk about gets going. You might at least—'

'You might at least go and put your bad-tempered face where it will be more welcome,' said Alastair, who was sweating with anger. 'Go and lick General Peterson's rump. He'll like you from what I hear. Go and get ready to grovel in front of him when we get off the boat tomorrow.'

'That's enough,' said Sanvoisin, who had returned unnoticed to the room. 'Alastair, apologise. James, if you drank a little more at parties, you might not get so cross when you were meant to be enjoying yourself.'

'I'm sorry, James,' said Alastair politely.

'I'll need more than an apology for what you've just said.'

'Come, James,' said Sanvoisin equably, 'you're surely not going to challenge poor Alastair to a duel.'

'I was thinking in terms of discipline, Colonel.'

'You should know by now, James. In this Regiment nothing that happens between officers who are not on duty could possibly lead to disciplinary action.'

'My rank—'

'Your rank is, at this minute, the same as Alastair's and my own. We are three gentlemen spending the evening together. If you choose to dislike the activities of the rest of us, then you should leave us. If, on the other hand, you see fit to make unpleasant personal remarks, you may expect them to be returned in kind.'

'You're not going to support a subaltern against your own second-in-command?'

'I'm doing no such thing. Merely telling two friends of mine that I do not want a pleasant evening spoilt by senseless bickering ... So we can now get on with our game.'

I thought Sinclair would leave after this, but in fact he went back to Duthwaite and continued to talk to him in the background. From time to time, I heard rather venomously mouthed phrases like 'disembarkation', 'fit for tomorrow', 'all the things to be seen to'. But if this little scene had not improved Sinclair's temper, neither had it helped Alastair's. He was now quiet and disgruntled. Obviously he was ashamed of himself for having spoken in such crude terms. I happened to know, too, that he did not like it being generally known that his father had had to pay his gaming debts, although, perversely enough, he was proud of the size of the debts and of the fact that he had, in whatever fashion, achieved their settlement. Now he was playing with sulky concentration, betting in large amounts and losing steadily. Michael Byrt's prediction was confirmed by the event: Sanvoisin was winning two *coups* in three on the average, and once he won seven *coups* in a row. I wondered how Sanvoisin would react to Alastair's losses. It had, after all, been he who had finally persuaded Lynch senior to pay up in June, so that he could scarcely sit there, almost in *loco parentis*, and allow Alastair to work up large debts, this time to himself. But I suppose he thought that Alastair had to work off his bad temper, not to mention his passion for gambling, in some fashion or other, and this was as good and safe a way as any. There would be many months in Pepromene during which Alastair's pay and allowances, to say nothing of his private income, would mount up almost untouched; and in any case Colonel Nicholas could always devise some scheme by which honour would be preserved on both sides. However this may be, he made no comment as Alastair continued to lose money, which he did in a manner at once attentive and casual, at once careless and yet bitter, playing persistently and yet evidently without any hope, taking no joy in the drink or the game. He smiled now neither when he won or lost, but just sat woodenly at the table, occasionally sipping a glass of champagne or glancing over his shoulder to the Mess Sergeant by the door, summoning the man to bring him some more counters and the necessary chit for him to sign in exchange.

As was usual with Sanvoisin's entertainments, this party went on long after the time originally stipulated. At four o'clock there was a faint lightening of the sky behind the uncurtained windows of the saloon; but no one showed any signs of leaving the game.

'Colonel Nicky's due for a set-back now,' said Michael Byrt. 'I'm going to start putting good money down.'

It fell out as he said. *Coup* after *coup* fell to the table, and Michael and Bancombe started to win considerable sums. Percy Berkeley, long since drunk, was sprawled asleep in his chair; since he was the only man who ever punted sums commensurate with Alastair's, and since Michael and Bancombe, though now winning regularly, were still betting in reasonably cautious amounts, Berkeley's defection from the game in fact left Alastair free to make large bets at each *coup* without breaking the table limit of £50. This was a privilege he had used freely when Sanvoisin was winning. But now that the luck of the game was turning with the dawn, he ceased to bother. Had he continued to bet as before, he would have regained the bulk of his losses; but it seemed almost as though he was deliberately abstaining from so doing, as though he was determined to leave Sanvoisin safe with what he had lost to him; and although he occasionally put down £5 or £10 simply to show he was still in the game, and so, despite himself, recouped a fair sum, he continued in his conscious disregard of the opportunities given him, until finally the busy sun shone through the window and Sanvoisin called for the chits we had been signing through the night.

'You were kind to me at the end,' he said to Alastair. 'Why didn't you follow the others in against me?'

'I lost interest.'

'You lost money.'

A survey of the chits and counters revealed that Alastair was almost the only loser. Sanvoisin produced his cheque book. Michael and Bancombe received over £100 each, Robin and I between £15 and £20, others had slightly larger sums, and then it was the turn of the losers to pay in to Sanvoisin. Percy Berkeley was woken up to be told he owed £40 odd, and was treated to a description of the long run in the table's favour, of the enjoyment of which his incontinence had deprived him.

'You might have woken me,' he mumbled.

'We hadn't the heart to disturb you,' they said.

'You've found it now.'

'A new day, Percy,' said Sanvoisin. And then, turning to Alastair: 'Yours is £550. Don't bother now. There's plenty of time.'

But now Alastair was entirely happy and at ease, for the first time since his quarrel with Sinclair.

'But this will be a pleasure, Colonel Nicholas,' he said.

'No sarcasm.'

'Sincerity.'

Alastair fiddled in his pocket for a moment. Suddenly the whole table seemed to be covered with five-pound notes, piles of them, wads of them. New notes. White, crisp, glistening in the morning sun.

'I wouldn't have minded a cheque, Alastair.'

'Settlement in new money,' said Alastair, 'to celebrate our arrival in a new country. If we go out now, we shall see it.'

We all rose and went towards the door.

'I wanted you to have that money,' said Alastair very quietly and stepped aside to let Sanvoisin through the door and out on to the deck.

Then he saw Sinclair, dressed now in boots and breeches and a light service dress tunic of gaberdine. He too seemed in a better temper and smiled as he saluted Sanvoisin.

'There it is, Colonel,' he said.

And there it was. Port Ulysses, a mile away over the sea, dishevelled and vulnerable in the early morning, cowering between the ocean and the desert; and beyond it just sand and scrub, stretching without welcome to a low and distant line of rocky hills. Port Ulysses, where we must now land, and where a mad old man had first landed a hundred years ago, naming the place Ulysses because, he said, this country must be the end of his wandering.

'What is that mountain?' said Alastair. 'The one beyond the hills, with the two white peaks.'

'I can see no mountain,' I said.

CHAPTER TWO

AT THIS STAGE, I think I should say something of the Regiment to which we all belonged; what kind of Regiment it was, and how regarded by ourselves and by the world.

To start with, then, our Regiment was one of mounted infantry. Of cavalier and west country origin (and thus much older than most regiments in the British Army), it had been raised by a certain Lord Martock during the Civil War. Lord Martock had demanded the privilege of raising a mounted regiment, but although he had no difficulty in finding men, he could not for the life of him find enough horses. The result was that his Regiment was accorded mounted status but had to proceed on foot. Later on, long after the Restoration, some pardonable confusion in the matter led to the Regiment being accorded infantry status but instructed to proceed on horse. The reason for this was that it had been in the past derisively nick-named by better equipped cavalry regiments, 'Lord Martock's Foot Jockeys' or, for brevity, 'Martock's Foot' – a name which, though originally a sobriquet, had an official ring about it. When, therefore, the Regiment was officially absorbed into the British Army, the pundits in charge of the arrangements had assumed that it was a normal infantry regiment. The commander-in-chief of the day was thus much confused, on arriving at Yeovil to review the Regiment, to find 400 impeccably mounted men led by the Lord Martock of that time, who had had better fortune than his grand-father in procuring horses. Confusion was followed by indignation, indignation by approval. The horses, accoutrements and men were all that could be desired. Colonel the Lord Martock himself was a young man of education, good humour and good sense, who surely knew how to provide dinners and explanations acceptable to commanders-in-chief. The end of the matter was, since it was now too late to take the Regiment out of the Line, that it received in compromise the title of The 21st Mounted Infanteers (Lord Martock's Regiment), and was instructed to retain its horses. (Despite which, the traditional and convenient appellation, 'Martock's Foot', was by this time there to stay for all but the most formal usage.) Its rôle was that of an infantry regiment, in that it actually fought on foot, but that of a cavalry regiment in that it was expected to use its horses in order to move swiftly from place to place before dismounting to engage. Once or twice it charged as cavalry, once or twice it marched long distances as infantry; but normally it was denied both the former distinction and the latter inconvenience.

It was, of course, very convenient for commanders in the field to have a trained regiment of infantry which could be whistled up from the reserve at ten times the speed of a normal infantry regiment. Thus the habit grew of leaving Martock's Foot well behind the lines at the beginning of engagements and only calling upon them when, at the end of the day, a force of infantry was quickly needed in an unexpected quarter. This had two results. Firstly, neither the officers nor the men of Martock's Foot ever rose early from their beds, justly observing that they were seldom required to be anywhere before the dinner hour. (Even to this day, we have Reveille an hour and a half later than anyone else, thus enraging general officers, who, arriving at early hours for unexpected visits, are courteously told that the men will not be mustered for another hour and that the officers are at breakfast.) Secondly, and of rather more importance, Martock's Foot, by virtue of their swift and late appearances on the field, took part in some of the most vital and most bloody encounters that have ever undone empires or thrilled the hearts of men. It was said that whenever the great Duke of Wellington called out, 'Send for Martock's Foot', the faces of his attendants grew pale with fear and their eyes bright with anticipation; for they knew that this summons had so often indicated the approach of defeat and yet had so often resulted in a victory snatched before evening.

'Your Grace is very good,' said one Lord Martock, on being congratulated after another such engagement.

'I'll tell you this, Martock,' said the Duke. 'I would rather see a company of those damned lay-a-beds of yours than any two battalions of the Line.'

After this, our Regiment was for some time known as 'Martock's Lay-a-beds', until a humourless colonel-in-chief (long after the Martock family had died out) ordered that the phrase was to be forgotten for ever.

When mechanisation came, Martock's Foot were easily able to preserve their traditional rôle. They still fought on foot, being quickly carried to their business in lorries or armoured carriers. It was still customary to keep them in reserve and then rush them in transport, at the last minute, almost to within spitting distance of the enemy. It is perhaps true that this treatment resulted in Martock's Foot becoming rather pampered on the one hand (not for them the long marches through the rain) and rather inclined to regard themselves as indispensable on the other. However this may be, their repute had in no way diminished up to the very day we left for Pepromene. We had received a fine send-off at Liverpool and much publicity in the Press; for it was rumoured that not only might there be trouble in Pepromene but also, of rather more curious interest this, that the rough nature of the country and the shortage of proper military supplies might actually mean that Martock's Foot would once again be seen on horses. As to that, we had yet to see.

Certainly, we should be easily able to contend with such a situation, for like cavalry regiments proper we had, since the war, kept many horses and encouraged riding among all ranks. Several of our officers were well known as steeplechase riders, while many of the N.C.O.s had been in the Regiment before mechanisation; so that instruction and supervision would be amply available to prepare the men for what, in any case, would clearly be more a matter of sitting a walking horse for long hours rather than of performing complex equestrian manoeuvres. Again, our organisation and customs, now as ever, owed as much to the cavalry as to the infantry. Like the infantry, we spoke of battalions and companies : but within a company we had troops and not platoons. All officers (again much to the annoyance of post-war generals) habitually wore service dress with riding boots, breeches and spurs, while other ranks wore tight trousers and spurs with full dress and number one dress. Our full dress, which we were one of the few regiments outside the Household Brigade to retain for certain occasions, was of scarlet, as for the infantry, but the head-dress to go with it was a busby worn with a plume of feathers of royal purple. (The feathers of death, as the French had called them long ago.) Normal dress for the men was of course battledress, though serjeants and above often appeared in the old rough service dress with breeches and puttees. Head-dress with khaki, for all ranks, was a fore-and-aft cap of royal purple, not worn on the side of the head in the deplorable war-time fashion, but dead centrally. These were highly practical (contrary to general surmise), as a little fiddling with hooks and folds would convert one of them into a kind of Balaclava helmet, which had a soft strip of felt to hold it firm under the chin and gave good protection to ears and neck against dust, rain or cold. (They were always worn this way on the march.) Ranks and appointments were equally derived from the background of a mounted past. Officially the prefix 'mounted' was used before all non-commissioned titles (mounted corporal, etc., etc.), though in practice this was too onerous for normal speech. Like the cavalry we had trumpeters, but in fact we called them drummers; thus Drummer Harley had probably never sounded a drum-beat in his life. We had a 'riding master', commissioned, like the quartermaster, from the ranks; but his inevitable task these days was not so much to supervise riding instruction (though he did this) as to organise and maintain the battalion's transport. As final points of detail, our motto was 'My will be done' – that of the house of Martock; and our cap badge repeated the motif of the purple feathers in our busbies, being a plume of feathers worked in silver, the regimental motto inscribed in gold on a silver scroll thereunder.

From all this, it will be seen that not only were we more or less ready to be mounted again, but that we were, by post-war standards, 'reactionary' to say the least. In fact, of course, like many regiments who preserve a 'reactionary' frontage, we ran our internal affairs far more easily and more flexibly than many 'up-to-date' regiments, who may have abandoned old-fashioned types of dress and privilege but still treat their men in a harsh and unsympathetic manner. This is because such regiments draw their officers from the professional middle class and often from the lower middle class; and such officers, having no status in the world other than that conferred on them by the Army, are intensely conscious of their military rank and prerogatives. But in our Regiment, although we were by no means among the smartest, officers very much tended to enjoy money or social position in their own right, so that they were not compelled to reassure themselves of their importance by bullying their men. Our men came largely from the south-west, and were by nature respectful, docile, loyal and, above all, responsive to kindness : so that a very easy relationship could and did exist between commissioned and 'other' ranks. (This fact Sinclair, who came originally from a 'town' regiment, could never get into his head.) Furthermore, as is usual in regiments where most officers have reckonable social standing quite apart from their Army rank, relations between officers themselves were very informal. It was unthinkable, except on certain strict parade ground occasions, that any officer, however junior, should call a senior officer 'sir'. (The Colonel was usually called 'Colonel' or 'Colonel Nicholas'.) It was equally unthinkable that any senior officer should try to discipline his juniors when off duty or to interfere with their private affairs – unless his advice was called for. Thus we had none of the prying into Mess bills, complaints about gambling, or investigations of sexual morals so common in the dowdier regiments. In all matters, moral or otherwise, our standards, I like to think, were liberal, tolerant, civilised and worldly; though for the matter of that, I suppose that these days such a statement is about the most 'reactionary' one could make.

At this time, when we came to Pepromene, Lord Nicholas Sanvoisin commanded us, and would continue to do so for another two years. The Martock family had long ago expired and with them the long line of Martocks who had always served with us. But Lord Nicholas came from a west country family that had at one time been closely connected with the Martocks, so that his colonelcy in our Regiment was apposite and pleasing. Major Sinclair, the second-in-command, had been seconded to us, for no very clear reason, from a north country line regiment which did most of its recruiting in an industrial area. Himself a man of education and means, Sinclair nevertheless entirely failed to understand our methods with our men or our behaviour amongst ourselves. Giles Bancombe, the Adjutant, was a harmless but often pompous fool. I myself am called Andrew Lamont. Being at this time Intelligence Officer, I normally worked in Battalion Headquarters and close to Lord Nicholas. But most of my friends were in fat Percy Berkeley's 'D' Company, in which Alastair Lynch, Michael Byrt and Robin Hathaway all commanded troops. Percy's second-in-command, Richard Duthwaite, was neither my friend nor anyone else's; but despite his sourness, his grinding insistence on tedious points of detail, his disapproval of our attitudes and amusements, there was a quality in the man which I admired; and I had never known him unjust. For the rest, we will speak of them as we come to them, whether in the city of Eirene or the country beyond.

The first thing that happened after our arrival in Eirene was the visit of the G.O.C., General Sir Stewart Peterson. Peterson nominally came under the direction of the Commander-in-Chief, Far East Central; but in fact Pepromene was so far from Far East Central Headquarters, and so very clearly an entity on its own, that for all practical purposes Peterson had an independent command, and indeed was officially instructed to act in consultation with the Governor General of Pepromene rather than by reference to an impossibly distant field-marshal. His visit was anticipated without pleasure on our side and passed without pleasure on either, though profit there was in the shape of some definite information about what we might expect to be doing. It was planned that the General should take luncheon with us in the Mess and that after this, during the heat of the afternoon, he should address the officers as a body. There was to be no formal parade review, for whatever you might say about Peterson, he loathed parade grounds; but he was going to 'have a look round' in the morning before lunch, and this in itself seemed likely, from what Sanvoisin was saying, to lead to more trouble than ninety parades. Meanwhile, the prospect of sitting on hard chairs after lunch, with the sun beating through the tenting (our camp was entirely of canvas) and being exhorted to hard work and discipline as predicted by Sinclair, was corrosively disheartening.

The General made no comments during his morning 'look round', though it was generally suspected that he was saving them all up and meant to torment us with them later. Luncheon too passed off all right. There was a bad moment when Michael was clearly heard, during a silence in the ante-room, to be ordering 'a quadruple gin and tonic, Corporal Griffiths, to stave off death by boredom'; but as Alastair afterwards opined, 'Peterson just won't have believed his ears when he heard a *quadruple* gin being ordered, and in any case the extreme nastiness of the lunch will have reassured him.'

Still, this was edgy work, and the afternoon did not improve matters. The plan was that Sanvoisin should say a few introductory words, that I, as Intelligence Officer, should then say something of the history and background of the country, and that the General should then address us on the military position and our probable function in the near future. My part had been put in because the General was known to like the idea of units under his command giving anticipatory and unprompted consideration to the problems they were likely to encounter. Sanvoisin thought a speech from me would give the impression that we had done so. This seemed to me unlikely; for my knowledge of Pepromene was of a very general order and the idea of 'wide open spaces' and 'pioneering prospects', an aspect of the place which any general might find sympathetic, was to me distasteful in the extreme. However, there was plainly no help for it; and when Sanvoisin had concluded a tactful enumeration of Peterson's campaigns and distinctions, I rose at his bidding to say my piece.

'May I begin, General?' I said.

'You may begin by calling me "Sir",' said Peterson.

'If you wish it,' I said.

'I order it.'

'As you say, Sir.'

There was plainly something about me which did not appeal to Peterson. I determined not to be downcast by this inauspicious exchange, took a good hold on myself, and started off.

'I shall not keep you long, gentlemen,' I said, 'as there are others to follow me. But Colonel Nicholas thought it would be helpful if I outlined to you something of the historical and racial background of Pepromene. The important points are as follows.

'The place was originally explored by a nineteenth century eccentric called Ezra Popperwell. He is politely referred to as a geographer, but he was in fact a bankrupt confidence man whose considerable charm and learning had not prevented him from being expelled from all his London clubs for cheating at cards. Furthermore, writs were out for him in substantial sums of money, and Popperwell, seeing travel as an agreeable alternative to the Fleet Prison, proceeded slowly east, living by his ingenuity, plausibility and the shifts of an undeniably resourceful and adventurous disposition.

'He was an old man when he first came to Pepromene. However, he liked the look of the country (though God knows why, since he first saw only the arid tracts by the coast), and with the help of his three or four Levantine confederates he collected a party of native guides and bearers and set out to explore. When he finally reached the relatively temperate uplands in the region of what is now Eirene, he realised two things: firstly that the land in this region was very fertile and was to be had from the natives for next to nothing; secondly that the Mountains of Dis, as he himself named them, might well, both according to native legend and geographical configuration, contain gold. Either way, the country could well be opened up and might provide a plentiful if rather crude living for those who found it advisable to leave more traditional regulated locations.'

The General, I noticed with a mixture of apprehension and satisfaction, was looking both puzzled and displeased.

'So Ezra got back word to friends in Europe, many of whom saw possibilities in all this. However, Ezra's chums were not necessarily very respectable, and the mixed crew of Greeks, Italians, cashiered Irish officers and whatnot who eventually turned up, while of interest to students of the curious, did no conventional credit to Europe or to the human race. They were here for easy living and made no bones about it; and since the natives were simple and unsuspicious people, ready to trade their land for beads and their labour for bread, Ezra's friends made a very good thing out of them without having to undergo the severe privations and struggles which are the normal lot of colonists. But I should add that those either adventurous enough or greedy enough to look for gold in the Mountains of Dis all came to a sticky end – which brings us to the serpent in this paradise.

'The mountains proper begin about fifty miles north-east of where we are at this minute. Now, although most of the tribes, whether down by the sea or here in the uplands (and all of whom are known as plainsmen or farm-men) are feckless, peaceful, generous, indeed rather Latin in their outlook, the mountain tribes might belong to a different race and by origin probably do. They are hunters and warriors, hard, austere and honourable by their own lights, barbarous, unsympathetic and cruel by ours. At first they confined themselves to killing prospectors : later they took to making occasional raids, when they wanted a fillip, from the mountains into the farmlands : and finally these raids became so numerous and well organised that a police force-cum-army had to be raised, officered by white men and manned, *faute de mieux,* by the placid and unwarlike plainsmen. These latter were probably the worst soldiers in the world; their officers were the scum of European armies or the most hopeless bad hats (and in this respect at least Pepromenean standards were high) from the local white families.'

The General was now looking so restless that I hurried to my conclusion.

'Pepromene was made a colony of the Crown in 1889. By this time the bulk of the settlers was British. But it cannot be said that either their methods or their manners were any improvement on those of old Ezra's original gang; and such was the cruelty and exploitation in this country that, had it not been for the good nature of the farming tribes, there would assuredly have been a revolt long since. As it was, when the place was made a colony, it became the custom to keep two or three British battalions here, and these of course provided the settlers with adequate protection against the only real menace – the mountain tribesmen. When, during the last war, it was decided to keep a whole army in Pepromene, as a reserve in case anything went wrong with British interests in this corner of the globe, the settlers were delighted with this guarantee of security. Since then of course this Army has shrunk to a division; but the G.O.C. and his staff are still of rank and complexity sufficient to deal with an entire army should it ever be necessary to send heavy reinforcements here.

'The final stage is very simple – at least on the surface. The common mountain tribesman is convinced that the white is (a) still after his gold, and (b) has usurped the land that he could have usurped himself. The gold, as far as we know, only exists in legend; the land of course belongs neither to the settlers nor to the mountain tribes but to these sympathetic plainsmen – who are much too flaccid ever to claim it back. As is usual in such quarrels, both sides are in the wrong. The fact remains that there is a quarrel and that it is likely to become a serious quarrel. For of recent months the mountain tribes have become increasingly restless because of unscrupulous agitation of a partly military and partly religious nature. They also have a leader of great charm and ability, an Oxford graduate of princely status called Karioukeya – the Lion of Judgement. Karioukeya has strong political ideas about native independence and indeed is a man of great integrity. But for the time being he is content, as he must be, to use the less respectable elements of resentment, greed, restive militarism and religious hysteria to further his political ends.'

'Thank you, Andrew,' said Colonel Sanvoisin, 'that was extremely interesting. And now, gentlemen, General Peterson is going to be so kind as to tell us the details of the military situation.'

Peterson stood up and surveyed us. He was a 'lean' general, if ever I saw one : handsome, fit, assured, aggressive.

'Pay attention, all you officers,' he said. 'What you have just heard may or may not be of interest to you. You are not here to be amused : you are here to listen to me. Firstly, let me set you right on one or two things. Popperwell is admired by the settlers as a pioneer and as the virtual founder of this colony. For the sake of good relations, you are to forget Captain Lamont's remarks about his early life.

'The original settlers were pretty tough people – otherwise they would not have come here. Their descendants are still in the country, but the white population has been greatly increased by the addition of many sound British families of good stock and high principle.

I therefore wish to hear no more fancy talk about cruelty and exploitation – or, for that matter, about the sympathetic nature of the local natives. They are idle, dirty and shiftless. They owe every- thing they have to the settlers – who very properly make them work for it.

'As for the mountain tribesmen, they are fine fellows but misled. Karioukeya, whether he went to Oxford or not, is the Queen's enemy. For the rest, this country is part of the British Empire, and a fine fertile healthy country it is for those that like an open air life and are not afraid of roughing it. This, I hope, means all of you. And that is all the background you need.'

Alastair grinned sideways at me.

'Let me have men about me that are fat,' he whispered.

'Stand up, that officer,' said Peterson.

No one stood up.

'Stand up that officer who has seen fit to interrupt me.'

Alastair stood up.

'Now, Sir,' said the General, 'if you have something important to say, perhaps you will say it aloud.'

'I was merely saying, Sir,' said Alastair equably, 'how much I look forward to roughing it in this fine, healthy country.'

'No doubt, Colonel Sanvoisin, you will know what to do with this officer. Sit down, Sir. Intelligence Officer, bring me that map.'

I came forward with a large map we had made up the day before and hung it over the blackboard frame. It showed Eirene in the bottom centre and a road leading due north from there for about fifty miles to a twin-peaked mountain – Mount Eirene. Two thirds of the way up the road, on its right, was a lake of about ten miles in diameter; and at a point where the road nearly touched the lake was marked a small town called Nike. From Nike a dotted line indicated a track, which proceeded absolutely due east, for a time skirting the southern shore of the lake, and ended about fifteen miles from Nike and the main north road at a small village called Gikumo. (It was a relief to find that old Popperwell had not got around to renaming every place in the country from Liddell and Scott.) A few miles east of Gikumo a long line marked 'escarpment' ran across the map in a roughly north-westerly direction. The 'escarpment', I had been told, was a sort of cliff, at places perhaps 1,000 feet high, but in the south, near Gikumo, only 200 or 300 feet, which separated the plains round the lake from a large area of scrub or veldt which reached right up to the foot-hills of the Mountains of Dis. A section of these latter was prominent at the top right-hand corner of the map.

The General surveyed my work inimically.

'Not much on it.'

'Not much to put on it, Sir.'

He let this pass.

'Pay attention, all of you. Here in the north-east are the Mountains of Dis. In these mountains live the tribesmen who, as you have been correctly told, have made a tradition of conducting raids down over the escarpment – here – into the farmlands near Lake Philia and even almost up to Eirene itself.

'For a variety of reasons, as you have also been told, these tribesmen have recently become increasingly disaffected and there is a distinct possibility of trouble. This is the greater, as we know now that Karioukeya has been successful in smuggling quantities of small arms into the mountains. He is believed to possess not less than 1,000 standard Army rifles, perhaps 100 light machine guns, and small numbers of sub-machine guns and hand grenades. No doubt his Oxford contacts proved useful in helping him to obtain these.'

A nasty look for me.

'Our information is that Karioukeya has been training his men intensely in the most remote parts of the mountains for the last four months. He has what he calls a "brigade", which is divided into three "battalions" of about 500 men each. Thus there are enough weapons for perhaps four men in five; but he is known to be short of ammunition, and it is probably only this factor which has kept him inactive for so long. However, his persistence and efficiency will doubtless remedy this in the near future. When this happens, we can expect to be opposed by 1,500 men, 1,200 of whom will be armed with up to date weapons; men of great physical powers; men reared from birth to endure hard living and to make do with scanty provisions for weeks at a time; men with a military tradition strengthened, in many cases, by fanatical religious conviction. Any questions so far?'

'Yes, Sir,' said Michael Byrt. 'If all this has been known for so long, why have no steps been taken to seek out Karioukeya's men in the mountains and to confiscate his weapons?'

I thought this amounted to a direct criticism of the General's competence and awaited his reply with pleasure and interest, confident that his ill humour would at any rate be diverted from myself.

'Good question,' said Peterson.

I remembered that Sanvoisin had called him fair. An uneasy respect for the man formed a tenuous skin over my dislike.

'The reason is, in part, that Karioukeya is in such a remote and unknown region of the mountains that we might get ourselves into serious difficulties if we went after him. Much of the range is unexplored and uncharted to this day : we should be risking our necks on his ground – ground that might in itself prove so treacherous and unfamiliar as to finish us off without any help from Karioukeya.

'But the real reason is that political pressure is being exerted – from London. I originally suggested that a small armed force should be sent at any rate to the foot-hills and outlying villages, as a kind of warning and to see what we could find out. But the Governor General was told by London that on no account must "any action be taken such as might alienate the mountain tribesmen or be construed as aggressive by political interests whether in the U.K. or any other country". You know the sort of thing. Some of them in Westminster wouldn't let us move if we had proof positive that the mountains were crammed with atomic cannon. This brings me on to the plan that I have had to adopt instead.

'If we must wait inactive, if we are not allowed to seek out Karioukeya, then there is only one thing to do : we must contain him. Any action he takes will almost certainly start in the form of the traditional raids – but more violent, better organised, far more elaborately equipped than ever before. The favourite ground for these raids has always been the plains round Lake Philia, but tribesmen have made raids from the mountains in all possible directions – to the north and the east, as well as to the south-west by the lake. I must therefore endeavour to cordon off the entire range, so that wherever raids may happen there will be men nearby to deal with them, or at any rate to give the warning and summon help if necessary.

'At the moment I have only a division. I need hardly tell you that I should only get reinforcements six months after anything had actually happened. But it is true that a division is just sufficient for me to place detachments of company strength round the perimeter of the mountains at intervals of about twenty-five miles. These detachments can patrol their areas and make plans against the event of those areas being raided – though on no account must they go near the mountains, or the whole Labour Party will set up a whine we shall certainly be able to hear in Eirene. But even as it is, we should be able to receive sharp warning of any attack and therefore contrive to resist such an attack; thereafter, when adequate excuse has been given us to assume the offensive we can use these detachments as supply bases for sending more concentrated forces into the mountains – when and if we get enough troops to send. Meanwhile, the mountain cordon is the only thing. All right so far?'

One had to admit that this seemed clear and reasonable. It was a salutary reminder that people did not become generals simply because they were good at echoing the 'no more cakes and ale' cry that had been so popular with Lord Montgomery and the war-time Army Council. The prospect was as uninspiring as the General's manner; but in a certain fashion it made sense.

'This,' he went on, 'is where you will come in. I am giving your Battalion the area to the south-west of the range. Your Battalion H.Q. will remain here in Eirene. Your company detachments will proceed, in a few days, to the various positions which I and your C.O.,' (notice the order, I thought) 'will decide in consultation. One such position might well be Gikumo, another by the escarpment – here,' and he pointed to a position about fifteen miles northeast of the lake. 'But these details will be told you when they are settled. Your job, as I say, will be to patrol your areas and consider how best to defend them in the event of a raid. They are areas particularly well populated by settlers with rich farms, and correspondingly vulnerable.

'One more thing. I am, as you may know, short of wheeled transport. Therefore, while I can allow your battalion enough of this to send supplies to company detachments by truck there will be none for use *forward* of the various company headquarters – and in any case the ground would not encourage you to use it. Nor is it possible to take wheeled vehicles up the escarpment. So, after long thought and having regard to your traditions and capabilities, I have decided to mount you on horses. These will be useful for patrolling; useful to move you quickly to the scene of trouble; and later on, perhaps, to get you quickly into the mountains, *if* we are ever allowed to go there.'

There was no doubt that this statement had given genuine pleasure. In fact General Peterson might have left us with our blessing had it not been for his concluding remarks.

'I must tell you before I go, however, that there are things about this battalion which have given me displeasure today and which I will not tolerate in any unit under my command – let alone if that command becomes an active one. There are evidences in your camp of slackness, untidiness and a thoroughly casual attitude to military concerns. This morning I saw a warrant officer smoking while talking to an officer. The interview was conducted laxly, and the two of them parted without exchanging compliments. This is only one example. I know that this is a moneyed and worldly regiment by comparison with many; that is not to say that I approve of subalterns drinking spirit before lunch – a thing forbidden in my own regiment – or even of more senior officers drinking brandy after it, when they have an important conference to attend. You officers are here to get fit and properly trained to lead your men in what may be a tough and demanding situation. You are not here to condescend to your G.O.C. by calling him "general", to discuss or ride race horses, to give dinner parties, play Canasta, or indulge in Mayfair tittle-tattle . . . I even saw a bottle of scent in one officer's tent. I threw it away in disgust. So just remember this : I want hard work, hard training, and devotion to *the job* – my job and yours. No doubt you have much to do, and I will keep you no further. Colonel Sanvoisin, you will kindly accompany me to your office.'

Later that afternoon, Alastair and I took up a discreet position behind my intelligence office, from which we could watch Peterson being sent on his way by a guard of honour. Little as the man liked parades, we could hardly let a full general depart without ceremony of some kind. The guard of honour was a captain's guard of two troops with trumpeter. Giles Bancombe was commanding it, and was at this moment having a last minute inspection. There were five minutes to go till Peterson should appear, and his car was already waiting at the guard-room by the gate.'

'An intelligent man,' I said, 'but hardly sympathetic.'

'Not sympathetic at all. It was my bottle of "scent", by the way, that he chucked into the bushes. Only it wasn't scent. It was plain but expensive Eau de Cologne. I think I shall instruct my lawyers to sue. I thought "Montgomery generals" were supposed to be liberal in outlook.'

'Not in the sense you mean. Liberal in pretending not to like formal parades and in not wanting officers to have privileges. But not liberal about things like Eau de Cologne – or, apparently, about the native populations of colonies.'

'The man's just a jumped-up Malvolio,' Alastair said. 'Isn't that Harley doing trumpeter?'

'Yes.'

'Well, there's a good advertisement . . . I wonder they don't put him on a recruiting poster. Here comes Peterson with Colonel Nick.'

Giles Bancombe called his guard up to attention and gave the order for a general salute. This went well at first: the men presented arms sharply and in perfect time, while Bancombe made his sword salute with panache. At this stage, it was Harley's job, while Bancombe and the men remained at the present, to play the 'General Salute' on his trumpet. I saw him swaying slightly, put this down to nervousness, and watched him raise his trumpet to his mouth. A noise like a legion of starving cats came out. Harley stopped, tried again, and succeeded this time in producing a parady of 'Cook House'.

'Third time lucky,' said Alastair.

But Giles Bancombe evidently felt that enough had been heard already: he shouted to his men to order arms and himself went forward to announce his guard to the General:

'The guard of honour is present, Sir, and ready for your inspection. There is one officer on parade, one warrant officer, five non-commissioned officers and fifty-seven private men.'

Bancombe and the General, accompanied by Sanvoisin, started their inspection of the front rank. Harley was at the far end of this, stationed some ten yards beyond the left-hand man, in the partial isolation always enjoyed by trumpeters on such occasions. He had gone very white and was still swaying a lot.

'What a dramatic life Harley seems to lead,' said Alastair.

'Pure bad luck,' I said, 'it often happens with trumpets. I once heard the soloist at the Albert Hall make a far worse noise slap in the middle of the Hallelujah Chorus. Wind control goes wrong. Nerves too, I expect.'

'I think he's drunk,' Alastair said.

The General had now reached the end of the front rank and was going on towards where Harley stood. He had a pleasant enough smile on his face and started to talk in a friendly way. He too obviously knew about the vagaries of trumpets and was being nice to Harley about it in the fashion which appealed so much to the popular press. But Harley faced him with a glazed and totally incomprehending stare, then muttered something and keeled back a pace or two. The General's expression changed.

'This man is drunk,' he said.

'Corporal Killeen, escort,' shouted Bancombe.

A tall, dark and rather oily looking corporal doubled up from the edge of the parade ground with the two 'waiting men' who were in his charge.

'Put Drummer Harley in close arrest.'

The two men took an arm each and started hauling Harley away. It was plain now that he really was either drunk or very ill. His feet hardly moved after the first few steps, they just trailed along the ground; his head lolled; he dropped his trumpet, and the tall corporal, who was bringing up the rear of this unedifying group, stooped to retrieve it. The General started back, poker-faced, between the front and middle ranks.

'You're certainly right about Harley's dramatic existence,' I said. 'How did you know he was drunk?'

'Intuition. Like Michael playing cards.' But he didn't smile. 'Killeen's one of mine,' he went on.

'Killeen?'

'The Orderly Corporal in charge of the escort. He's in my troop. I might get him to say that in his opinion Harley had just fainted. That would save trouble.'

'The General said he was drunk. He must have smelt it. I shouldn't interfere.'

'The General won't appear to give evidence. Giles Bancombe can't have smelt it on his preliminary inspection.'

'Giles is so batty about niceties of dress that he doesn't notice anything else. Don't interfere, Alastair. It'll only mean more trouble in the long run. Besides, your man Killeen doesn't look very reliable to me.'

The General had now finished his inspection. After the Harley incident, he had neither stopped to talk to any of the men or even troubled to look at them. He just walked straight up and down the ranks and was now heading fast for his car with Sanvoisin at his side. Giles Bancombe ordered another present arms, and then had to chase after the General to attract his attention. He gave a sword salute to Peterson's retreating back, and then called out,

'Permission to dismiss, Sir, please?'

'Yes please, Captain Bancombe. I do not congratulate you on the condition of your guard.'

This was clearly heard all over the small parade ground. Bancombe went scarlet. The General just climbed into his car and drove away.

'This is going to be unpopular,' I said. 'You mustn't interfere.'

Alastair said nothing at all and walked away.

CHAPTER THREE

IN THE EVENT, preparations for our departure to the various company positions started even sooner than General Peterson had indicated. I was told by Sanvoisin to go with any company I chose, base myself at its H.Q., for a fortnight, and spend my days surveying the ground in which the Battalion was responsible and consulting with local district officers and policemen.

'For heaven's sake be polite,' he said. 'Colonial servants are as touchy as provincial dons.'

I chose to go with fat Percy Berkeley's 'D' Company, for this meant being with friends; and since Percy had been assigned Gikumo as his company H.Q., it also meant that I would be somewhere near the centre of the Battalion's terrain. ('B' and 'C' Companies were to be north of Lake Philia, 'A' and 'Support' Companies down to the south-east of Percy.) Furthermore, 'D' Company was within quick striking distance of Eirene if I wished to return there to consult Sanvoisin or merely to find amusements more elaborate than those likely to be provided at Gikumo.

These arrangements were decided on two days after Peterson's visit. We were actually to leave Eirene after a further four days, which meant that time was very short. Quite apart from the normal administrative details, which become unexpectedly complex when companies are to be completely detached and the administration of the Battalion thus to a great degree decentralised, we had to deal with the 600 horses which Peterson had produced for us, not to mention the problems of scratching together and refurbishing the necessary saddlery. Some of this we had already, some was provided by the ordnance depot in Eirene, but most of it had to be borrowed from the local police or private stables. This meant scouring Eirene and the local countryside for hours on end, and I had good cause to thank heaven that I was only responsible for myself and the very few men in the Intelligence Section. As for the question of the men's ability to ride the horses at such short notice, this was being left in the knees of the gods; but it was thought that the ride to the Company position could proceed at a pace slow enough even for novices – who would get benefit along with sore behinds from the experience. Once arrived at their positions, the men could soon be given adequate instruction to enable them to carry out the wearing but probably straightforward mounted patrols on which they would shortly be sent.

'Since you are honouring us with your company,' said Alastair, 'you had better come with me to Percy's office and hear about the arrangements he is making. They are rather confused.'

This was three days before we were to leave.

'I thought you'd be spending the day finding saddles for your splendid troop.'

'We've sent Robin off to do that. He looks so pathetic that no one in Eirene can refuse him. Not even inspectors of police.'

Percy was bouncing up and down behind his table. Duthwaite, armed with mill-boards, pencils and maps, was doing some grim calculations, while Michael Byrt was hanging rather glumly about occasionally making a sensible suggestion. Company Sergeant Major Mole kept popping in and out to explain that *all* the tinned meat he had been issued with was bully beef, whereas some of it was meant to be spam and some steak and kidney pudding.

'Go to the Quartermaster,' said Duthwaite.

'I've been, Sir. He says it's my fault for not checking the tins when they were first issued. I should have complained then, he says.'

'Why didn't you?'

'I was rushed, Sir. "Here's your lot, Mole," the Quartermaster says, "and bleeding well get out of my stores and sharpish."'

'You've been in the Army too long to be caught like that. You should have insisted on checking the tins.'

'Never mind, C.S.M.,' said Alastair, 'there are plenty of recipes for corned beef. And I expect there are things round Gikumo we can shoot.'

'Command Standing Orders say that in no case will military personnel shoot game,' said Duthwaite. 'It annoys the settlers.'

'It'll annoy them more if we're all too weak from malnutrition to protect them from Karioukeya,' said Michael.

'Oh, stop it, all of you,' said Percy. 'Michael, go to the Q.M. with the Sergeant Major and see if something can be fixed up ... It's all too exhausting.'

'Andrew and I have come to hear about the arrangements,' said Alastair.

'The arrangements?' said Percy guiltily.

'For getting to Gikumo.'

'Well, Richard Duthwaite and the Sergeant Major are going on with the advance party thirty-six hours before the rest of us. Then we're all going to start at about ten o'clock on Tuesday morning and should be there in nice time for tea.'

Percy sat back heavily. He seemed to feel that he might have missed something out.

'That's right, isn't it, Richard?' he said.

'Up to a point,' said Duthwaite thinly. 'I'll give you the details later,' he said to Alastair.

'Nonsense, nonsense,' said Percy. 'We must all go into the details

47

now. What, for example, is going to happen about my three cases of burgundy?'

'That will go with the main baggage party by truck. This party leaves on Tuesday at midday, will pass the Company column on the road, will stop to give them a hot drink of tea from containers, and will then go on to reach Gikumo at 1400 hours.'

'But this is no good,' said Percy. 'The wine will be all shaken up and undrinkable for Tuesday's dinner. No, Richard, you must take my burgundy up with your advance party, and then it will be nicely settled by the time the rest of us arrive.'

'I shall have no room for non-essentials.'

'Non-essentials? What can you be thinking of? How are we to endure Gikumo unless—'

But at this stage we were interrupted by Sergeant Royd. Royd was Alastair's Troop Sergeant, a loud-mouthed, drunken and entirely amiable man.

'Heard about the rations, gentlemen?' he said.

'Mr Byrt's fixing that,' said Duthwaite.

'Oh, is he, Sir?' said Sergeant Royd with relish. 'Well, he's got a lot of fixing to do yet. Him and the C.S.M., they went to the Quartermaster's stores with all those tins of bully and said they wanted some spam and things instead. See?'

'Yes, yes,' said Percy wildly.

'Well, the Quartermaster looks old-fashioned but he says he'll see what he can do. And sure enough, he gets up some crates of stuff saying "Spam" and "Irish Stew" and "Kidney Pudding" on the out-side, and Mr Byrt and the Sergeant Major comes back chuffed. O.K.?'

'It seems very satisfactory,' said Duthwaite.

'Ah,' said Royd. 'When they get back, they open up the crate marked "Irish Stew" just to make sure. And stroke them dead, but every bleeding tin has a label round it saying "Lunching Sausage". Not "Irish Stew", not even honest bully, but "Lunching Sausage" the labels say. So then they start smarting round the tits and open up all the other crates, and what do you think they find? Nothing but lovely lunching sausage in every bleeding one of them. So what do you think of that?' he concluded in savage triumph.

Percy gave a little screech and slumped in his chair.

'Poor Moley,' said Alastair, 'I can see we shall have to come to the rescue. Now, Percy, if I promise to straighten out this business of the lunching sausage, will you support a little enterprise of mine?'

'I suppose so.'

'Well, it's to do with Drummer Harley. He's the boy who fought so well in that boxing match on the boat.'

'The one who was arrested on the guard of honour?' said Duthwaite.

'Exactly so. And that's just the point. After this business on the guard of honour, whatever else they do, they'll suspend him from being a trumpeter for some time. He'll have to go somewhere else, and I want him to come here – to my Troop. I've spoken to Sergeant Royd about it, and he agrees with me that Harley would fit in. So with your permission, Percy, I'm going to the Adjutant to ask for Harley to be posted across to us.'

'I don't see why not,' said Percy, 'if you and Sergeant Royd are happy ...'

'And if the poor little sod can stay alive on lunching sausage,' said Sergeant Royd.

'Just a moment, Percy,' said Duthwaite. 'I know it's quite common for officers to request that certain soldiers be posted to their sub-units, but in my experience this is never a good thing. The other men always get to know when an individual has been definitely asked for by a certain officer, and it makes for bad feeling. They think that the man in question has in some way been singled out for distinction; they are continually on the watch for acts of favouritism in his direction. Even if these do not occur, the men imagine them or invent them. Either way it's bad for morale.'

There was a lot in this, and none of it calculated to please Alastair.

'I don't see that you need interfere,' he said. 'Harley won't be in your way.'

Sergeant Royd withdrew.

'I dare say not. I am merely speaking in the best interests of the Company.'

'So am I. Harley's a good man with plenty of guts. We can do with that where we're going.'

'We can do without drunks where we're going.'

But Percy was on Alastair's side. He always was, and in any case, had not Duthwaite made difficulties about the burgundy? After a little wrangling, all was decided: Alastair would see to the tinned meat crisis; Percy's burgundy would go with the main baggage party, but Duthwaite would take up three bottles in advance and in his own personal care, so that they would be drinkable on Tuesday night when Percy arrived; and Alastair was to go to the Adjutant, with Percy's blessing, and ask for Harley to be transferred to 'D' Company. The only thing that was not discussed was the organisation of Tuesday's move to Gikumo; but as to this, I reflected with relief, Duthwaite would have made a competent plan which he would communicate to Alastair and Michael in good time. Nobody would need to trouble Percy, who, now that the burgundy question was settled, had gaily shed all the cares that had sat so heavily upon him earlier in the day.

After lunch that day I accompanied Alastair over to the line of tents which housed the offices of Battalion Headquarters.

'Did that corporal of yours prove helpful over the Harley business?' I asked.

'Corporal Killeen? No. He put on an injured air and said that he could only tell the truth. That Harley was drunk.'

'So that when Harley comes in front of the C.O. he'll be well and truly for it?'

'I dare say. That's one of the things I'm going to find out now.'

I went to my Intelligence Office and Alastair went on to see Giles Bancombe. Later on I found out what happened.

First of all Alastair had spoken with Bancombe, making his official request that, if Harley were to be suspended from the Corps of Drums, he should be sent to 'D' Company.

'And this is all right with Percy Berkeley?' Bancombe asked.

'Most certainly it is.'

'Well, it's perfectly true that Harley will be kicked out of the Drums, at any rate for the time being. But how soon he'll be available to come to you is another matter. He's due to come up in front of the Colonel this afternoon. I wouldn't be surprised if he were sentenced to detention – at least a fortnight.'

'Detention.'

'It's no joke when people get drunk on a guard of that kind. It didn't do *me* any good for a start.'

'But how was it,' Alastair asked, 'that you didn't notice he was drunk before the General came round?'

'Not clever of me, I admit. He seemed all right when I did my inspection. It's possible the drink only really took after he'd been standing there in the sun for a while.'

'You're sure it wasn't just an ordinary fainting spell?'

'The General didn't seem to think so. And when the Regimental Police went to Harley's quarters to fetch his kit to the Guard Room, they found a lot of empty beer bottles under his bed.'

'I see.'

'It's a thing we can't overlook.'

'All right, Giles. But since he's coming to my Company and to my Troop, I take it I can stand in on the Colonel's Orders when Harley comes up?'

It was our custom for an officer from the accused man's company to be present whenever such a man was tried by the C.O. Before sentencing the man, the Colonel would ask this officer to give an opinion and where possible to speak in mitigation.

'I don't see why you shouldn't,' said Bancombe. 'Of course, James Sinclair will be there as O.C. Headquarter Company. But you can appear as well if you wish.'

The officer normally commanding Headquarter Company had

developed dysentery a day or two before, and Sinclair, for the time being, was doubling these duties with his own.

'Thank you, Giles,' said Alastair. 'What time?'

And so it had come about that both Sinclair and Alastair had been standing behind the Colonel when the charges against Harley were read out. These alleged simply that he had been drunk on parade and incapable of performing his duty. Bancombe himself gave evidence, stating in what circumstances he had ordered Harley's arrest. He was followed by Corporal Killeen, who said that Harley had had to be dragged off the parade ground and had afterwards vomited. Harley had smelt strongly of drink, Killeen added. This was gratuitous and malicious, but the evidence of a regimental policeman about the empty beer bottles would probably have clinched the matter in any case. Harley did not bother to cross-question the witness, as he was entitled to do, and indeed made a bad impression by looking sullen and bored throughout the proceedings.

'What have you to say about this, Harley?' asked Sanvoisin.

'Nothing, Sir,' Harley had mumbled.

'In that case I have no alternative but to find you guilty and proceed to sentence. You will speak first, please, Major Sinclair.'

'I'm afraid I know very little about this man, as I am only acting temporarily as his Company Commander. But it would seem to me, Colonel, that an exhibition of the kind described here can only merit the most severe sentence of detention it is in your power to give.'

'Thank you, Major Sinclair.'

'With your permission, Colonel,' said Alastair.

'Mr Lynch?'

'I have taken some pains to find out about this man, and as a result I have asked, with Major Berkeley's support, that he be posted to my Troop in "D" Company. For I am assured that whatever else happens to Drummer Harley, he will be dismissed his post as trumpeter.'

'That is certainly true.'

'I do not see that this is Mr Lynch's concern,' said Sinclair. 'Whatever may be the case in the future, *I* am at present in command of this man.'

'*I* am at present in command of this man,' said Sanvoisin. 'I take it, Mr Lynch, that you wish to speak in mitigation?'

'If you please, Colonel.'

'Very well?'

'You are no doubt aware, Colonel, that Harley has been with this Regiment since he was sixteen. He spent most of his boy-service at the Depot, where his record was spotless. When he became eligible for man-service, he joined us in this Battalion. During his short time with us, he has had a good record until this current charge, and you will certainly remember his courage in the boxing finals on the boat. Since this is his first offence, I ask, with the deepest respect, that he be warned or lightly punished.'

'This Regiment takes a clement view of first offences. But this was a grave offence and was committed on a particularly ill-chosen occasion.'

'Clemency, Sir, is not to be qualified in this fashion. The offence itself was drunkenness, which you may well be ready to pardon in an inexperienced boy. As for the occasion, it was, to say the least, unfortunate. But I would suggest, again with the deepest respect, that we can hardly accuse Drummer Harley of deliberately choosing the day of the General's visit to make a spectacle of himself. He is no doubt sufficiently ashamed of the discredit he has caused us without being further accused of having done so with purposeful malice. He was clearly both thoughtless and weak. But that a very young man should act thoughtlessly and weakly does not justify those responsible for him in condemning him to a savage and humiliating punishment. Detention for Harley would expose him, in all his weakness, to the influence of seasoned bad characters. It would spoil and embitter him at the very outset of what I believe to be a loyal and promising career. It would be a cruel and disproportionate punishment, one which I cannot believe could be awarded in a regiment in which we pride ourselves on our humanity and justice. To imprison Harley will not mend what has happened. But to let him go free will be to make possible a reward out of all proportion to the clemency of the action; the reward of commanding a man who, grateful for kindness and conscious of just dealing, goes on to repay his creditors with loyal service and fair regard.'

In this manner had Alastair Lynch pleaded, and pleaded successfully, for Malcolm Harley. How much better for them both if he had only held his tongue.

'So Colonel Nick warned him,' Alastair was telling me later in my office, 'and told him that if anything of the sort happened again, he'd have him torn apart. He also said that he regarded me as responsible for seeing nothing of the sort did happen. Harley was coming to my Troop, he said, and it was up to me to accept the responsibility which I had now doubly incurred – both by asking for the man and achieving his pardon . . . James Sinclair looked a bit sick about it all.'

'Im not surprised. . . . Your speech sounded rather dramatic.'

'In the world of drama, the only way of conveying sincerity is by underplaying. But in real life, and particularly in the Army where we all underplay the whole time, to dare to be dramatic is to convince everyone you're almost out of your mind with sincerity. Otherwise you wouldn't dare behave in such an unseemly way. Anyhow, as I told you, Harley leads a dramatic life.'

'His dramas seem to me to be rather adventitiously thrust upon him. I only hope there won't be any more of them, Alastair.'

'Meaning?'

'Meaning what Colonel Nicholas said about you being responsible for Harley. And that the situation in this country could be quite dramatic enough without any of us devising anything extra.'

'You sound like James Sinclair. "Eye on the ball . . ." '

'Do I?' I said. 'I'm sorry. But there is in this file a great stack of reports, compounded by area intelligence officers from the information of their agents in the mountains. It is all as Peterson says. The arms, the training; the military background, the religious fanaticism; above all, Karioukeya.'

'You seem very impressed with Karioukeya.'

'I've heard a lot about him from friends I had at Oxford. He's the real thing. A leader. A man of charm and enterprise and ruthlessness. Intelligent, informed, determined, knowing he's right, knowing the times are with him. He's no jumped-up, flashy nigger boy, with an American tie round his neck and a chip on his shoulder because they wouldn't have him in Vincent's. He's big medicine. A killer.'

'Do you think he's right?'

'No. But he does. And he will convince a lot of other people – not only his own people.'

'Tea?' said Alastair abruptly.

'All right.'

Harley was waiting outside my office.

'I saw you go in, Sir,' he said to Alastair. 'I wanted to thank you.'

'You'll be able to thank me by behaving yourself in the future. And there's one thing you can do now. Tell me why you got drunk when you knew you were on guard of honour.'

'I didn't mean to get drunk, Sir. I just wanted to show them I could drink like the rest.'

'In the middle of the afternoon?'

'Any time they'd be watching. They all said I was milk and water, see? Never no women, never no beer. But I knew all about women and beer, only they'd never seen me.'

'Why should they? You only joined us a few weeks before we left England.'

'That's just it, Sir. "Sweet eighteen from the Depot", they said. "Bet he's never been tight in his life." "I'll show you", I said. So I sneaked some bottles out of the N.A.A.F.I. and drank them that afternoon, while we got ready for the guard.'

'You certainly did show them. But you'll have no need to show them again, will you? Because if you do, you'll go to a detention camp. And then *I* shall look a fool. I don't want to look a fool on your account, Harley.'

'Don't worry, Sir. Anything you say, now. Anything you say after what you did.'

'Anything?'

'Anything, Sir.'

'Well, you can begin by reporting to Sergeant Royd tomorrow morning. He'll show you where to sleep and tell you who's who in "D" Company. Then you're to come and see me. All right?'

'All right, Sir. Good night, gentlemen.'

Harley saluted and walked away. Alistair was clearly pleased by his gratitude.

'What a nice smile that boy has,' he said.

'West Country charm. Rich yet simple, like butter. Smooth and golden. Spoiled,' I said, 'if handled with hot hands.'

'What can you mean?'

'Just a train of thought. Here comes your C.S.M.'

And round the corner came C.S.M. Mole and Sergeant Royd, heading hard for high tea in the Sergeants' Mess. Anxious though they obviously were to get there, when they saw Alastair they came across to talk with us.

'The R.S.M. says you got young Harley off,' said C.S.M. Mole reproachfully, rather as though it were Alastair himself who had been in trouble and narrowly escaped the consequences.

'That's right, C.S.M. He'll be reporting to Sergeant Royd in the morning.'

'A real lovely speech you made, the R.S.M. says,' remarked Royd. 'Makes one proud to have an officer in the Company with such a tongue in his head. Happen you'll use it on my behalf one day?'

'Happen I shall.'

'Well, it seems to me,' grumbled Mole, 'that we've got enough on our plates already without all making speeches and getting beery little boys sent to "D" Company. What are you going to do if he turns up tight tomorrow, eh, Sir?'

The mental picture of Harley arriving drunk the next morning plainly gave Mole much satisfaction. He stood there smiling his silly and gentle old smile.

'String him up off a tent pole,' said Royd. 'But he's a good lad, that. That boxing match ... now that made me think ... There's been nothing like that since 'thirty-eight, when Burney Jackson upped every gut he had into his second's pail and then knocked Smiler White as cold as death. They do say that Smiler got one whiff of Burney's breath after his lights come up and fainted with the horror of it. Good lads, those. Burney, now, he's out and lives in Taunton. But Smiler, well, he drunk his last drop in Normandy, gentlemen, and he's there yet, is Smiler. Farmhouse do it was; so we buried him in an orchard when it was all done and hardly had time to say a prayer over the poor bleeder's grave ... But young Harley, he's all right, Sir. Though you do seem to have taken a lot of trouble.'

'I suppose I have.'

'Trouble for everyone,' mumbled the C.S.M. 'Why were you so keen to get him, Mr Alastair? There's Captain Duthwaite, he wasn't pleased, and then you go talking your head off like Romeo in the Colonel's office. Not that I don't admire you for it. But it seems a lot of trouble.'

'It's as Royd says. That boxing match ... But he's ours now, Moley, and you must make the best of it.'

'And don't go calling me Moley, Mr Alastair. It's bad discipline. When Lord Nicholas was young, he called someone by their nickname, and the Adjutant heard him, and you'd have thought he was going to be orderly officer for ever. But I suppose that's all changed .. '

'For Christ's sake,' said Sergeant Royd, 'if I don't get the miserable old brute off to his tea, he'll fall apart. Excuse us, gentlemen, and good night.'

Alastair and I wandered on to the officers' mess.

'I hear we're getting Harley,' said Robin Hathaway, 'the one in that frightful boxing match. You seem to have been to a lot of trouble.'

'If anyone else says that,' said Alastair, 'I shall faint. I've had Moley moaning at me for hours. He seems to think that Harley's a dipsomaniac and that the whole Company will now become a kind of honky-tonk.'

'It's your little effort on the Colonel's Orders,' said Michael Byrt, 'that has really hit the headlines. Sinclair is furious, Giles Bancombe is stupefied, and the R.S.M. can think of nothing else. He says it's the most remarkable thing he ever heard in all his service, and he says it ten times a minute to anyone within range.'

'Oh, God. It's all so simple.'

'Simple it may be, but there's no denying the pains you went to.'

'Why not? I happened to like the look of Harley, I want him in my Troop, and I don't want him to rot in detention first. After all, in a place like Gikumo's going to be, it's important to be with people one wants, to have people about who—'

'Yes?' said Michael Byrt.

'Well, who one hopes will be suitable.'

'Granted. After all, even if he *does* turn Gikumo into a honky-tonk, I expect we shall all be very grateful.'

'That wasn't what I meant at all.'

'I don't understand all this,' said Robin Hathaway. 'After all, one has certain people in one's troop, they're there already or get posted in from somewhere, and that's usually the end of it. I sup-

SIMON RAVEN

pose some are nicer than others, some more reliable and so on. But this business of deliberately getting a certain soldier because in some way it will make things easier when you get to Gikumo...'

'Would you understand, Robin,' said Alastair, 'if I told you that I was glad you're coming to Gikumo because you're someone I like to have around?'

'Yes, I would. We're friends and we've known each other for some time. I'm glad *you're* coming to Gikumo. But then, we're both officers.'

'One is only to take pleasure in the company of officers?'

'Well, not exactly... But when it comes to the evenings, or whatever amusements there are, I suppose the officers will be more or less together. I mean...'

'Come along with me, Robin,' said Alastair, 'and I will try to explain. You can walk with me to the Q.M.'s stores. I'm still exercised over Moley's tins of meat.'

They went off together.

'I hope he doesn't try to explain too much,' said Michael.

'I don't think there's anything very serious to be explained. Alastair has just taken a mild fancy to this boy. He likes the idea, as he says, of having him around. I've dropped some broad hints and there's been no real reaction.'

'Perhaps you're right. But he has been rather sticking his neck out over all this. Tell me, can you remember anything... similar ... coming up with Alastair before?'

'Not really,' I said. 'Though he's always taken trouble for people he likes.'

'And he's now – what? – twenty-three?'

'Yes.'

'Women?'

'Casually. The usual kind of thing. Dinner and the "Four Hundred". Here today and very much gone tomorrow. Occasional women off the street as well.'

'But when he goes on leave – on those trips to France and Italy – who goes with him?'

'Well, you and I both have, as you very well know. Friends in general. No one very special.'

'Exactly. In other words, his life still centres on a small group of male friends, though there are occasional and rather squalid "bachelor adventurers".'

'Why not? In the nineteenth century circles the same applied to every man under thirty. Read your Trollope.'

'The emphasis has shifted a bit lately. These days girls are no longer hedged about with chaperons and mama's ideas on what would be a suitable match. Correspondingly, men are expected to take a more positive interest in them at an earlier stage. Everyone,

56

even in what we might call "our class", is getting married very much younger.'

'So much the worse for "everyone". Thirty is quite early enough. Allow us all a little freedom, Michael.'

'Gladly. I'll allow anyone anything he wants. I'm just speculating. Trying to discover a pattern.'

'Well?'

'I don't really know. But it would be a nuisance if the first real passion Alastair was to develop was for a soldier in his Troop. It makes things very difficult in a regiment like this.'

'Infatuation at worst,' I said.

'I hope you're right. Infatuation at worst. Passing fancy. Here today and very much gone tomorrow.'

CHAPTER FOUR

THE NIGHT BEFORE we were to leave for Gikumo, Alastair, Robin and myself had dinner with Colonel Sanvoisin and Percy Berkeley in the Pepromene Club. This club existed for the benefit of wealthy settlers, but all officers of British regiments were admitted as temporary and honorary members. It was a well-run establishment, staffed with silent and efficient native servants, furnished comfortably and in heavy bad taste, and provided with a bar of inordinate length at which settlers and a few high-ranking police officers consumed round after round of long gins and whiskies. Drinking customs in Pepromene were similar to those in most colonies, consisting in the main of drinking spirits on an empty stomach from six p.m. until about nine, so that by the time people came to dinner they knew neither what they were eating or what they were saying. Since the food in the Colony was usually atrocious and the mentalities of the diners both limited and tendentious, this could scarcely be said to matter very much; but the Pepromene Club had a well-deserved reputation for its cuisine, and so our little party, to the surprise and contempt of the local drinkers, merely ordered a single round of Dubonnets and then went straight to the dining-room.

'This,' said Sanvoisin, 'is said to be the only place in Eirene where one can dine as you and I understand the word. So let us see. Oysters from Port Ulysses? They take twenty-four hours from the coast, but I think we can assume they are safe here. Crawfish, also from Port Ulysses? As indigestible as lobster, I always think, and with an inevitable suggestion of staleness, however fresh. Burgundy snails? Tempting but presumably tinned. And now an Italian flavour. Veal *al Marsala*? Always welcome in Italy, where the recipes are so dull, but I see we are also offered *Coq-au-Vin* and even *Suprème de Volaille sous Cloche*. The trouble, in either case, will be the extreme scragginess of the native chickens. Not, it is true, as pronounced as that of the native children, but I cannot imagine a child or a chicken in all Pepromene with a breast abundant enough to yield a decent *Suprème*.'

In the end we settled for snails, fish soup and *Coq-au-Vin* ; the wines to be a non-vintage Chablis followed by a Nuits St Georges 1947.

'Now in England,' said Alastair, 'all the forty-sevens have long since disappeared. Thank God for the whisky-drinking settlers. Just imagine, if there's another war in Europe we shall have to come and live in Pepromene because it will be the only place with any decent wine left.'

'You'd live in a place just for the wine?' asked Robin.

'I was being a trifle hyperbolic, Robin.'

'Why not?' said Percy, and sucked the butter out of his snail shell with a noise like a fire hose.

'Why not, indeed!' said Sanvoisin. 'Who was it who was so happy to be exiled, even from Rome itself, to Marseilles, because, he said, the oysters were of such high quality? And wine is far more important than oysters. It is like a civilised culture – one of those things which are conventionally regarded as extras, but without which life would be a barren and meaningless affair. Wine, that maketh glad the heart of man. Eirene with wine might well be preferable to Athens itself without. Though one must admit that cultural standards here are rather doubtful,' he said, surveying two settlers with cummerbunds and high-voiced, prod-nosed wives.

'Don't let General Peterson hear you say that,' said Alaster.

'He is unlikely to come here, my dear Alistair. He is sitting at home with his ambitious and cheeseparing wife, eating the rations the Army allows them and drinking water. His heart is not being made glad. When he goes to the Governor General's reception later tonight, he will be sober, punctilious and barely able to conceal his contempt for the company. Not that he will despise them as colonials, as you or I might in a naughty moment, but he will just be puffed up with hatred at the idea of so many people coming together in search of enjoyment – even so little enjoyment as an official reception is likely to yield. He will probably take his ill-temper out on me, and rebuke me for wearing a black tie instead of uniform, though the invitation distinctly says black ties. Peterson, you see, comes from one of those regiments where people are always appearing in uniform – they get married in it, like the Navy.'

Meanwhile Percy had had one of the three bottles of Chablis almost entirely to himself.

'Sex,' said Percy, 'is going to be a problem in Gikumo.'

'Sex,' said Sanvoisin, 'is a problem everywhere.'

'But what are they all going to do, Colonel? It's all right for you or me, we're getting on . . .'

'And always mindful of your marriage vows, Percy,' said Alastair.

'Always mindful of our marriage vows. It's all right for old Mole. He's dried up. He may even be mindful of his marriage vows too. But the young men? What are they meant to do? Brothels are out of bounds – and in any case there won't be any up there. And if there were, they'd be full of clap or worse. So answer me that,' said Percy, tucking in to his *Coq-au-Vin* like a professional wrestler.

'Local women?' I said.

'No fraternisation allowed,' said Alastair. 'Command Orders lay

59

down that any man seen talking to a coloured woman outside the proven course of duty is to be arrested forthwith and charged with failing to obey orders, since this order itself is to appear weekly and prominently on company notice boards.'

'White women, I meant.'

'Very few, and all married or firmly booked. By people with far more money than mounted infantrymen.'

'There is such a thing as self-control,' said Robin.

'There is indeed, Robin,' Alastair answered, 'but it is not widely practised, least of all among soldiers. No, the official answer, Percy, is that we are to organise endless games of football, discussion groups, ping-pong competitions, sing-songs, even occasional beer-ups, to keep the men's minds healthily occupied. We shall have a darts league, a chess ladder. Officially, it seems, that settles the whole thing. *Sex est mort*, vive the Company debating society. So polish up your A.B.C.A. patter and hope for the best.'

'When I was a young man,' said Sanvoisin, 'and we were serving in places like this, a battalion or a company arriving at a new station would take over an existing brothel or, if there wasn't one, call for volunteers among the local natives and establish them in comfort with excellent rations thrown in. The medical officer would then make a thorough check, and would continue to do so every three days thereafter. This place would become the semi-official unit brothel and was open for stated and generous hours to any man in the unit who could muster half-a-crown. Everyone was happy. The girls were well fed and well paid, for the half-crowns were subsidised from the unit funds. The men were solidly contented and did not often get V.D. The C.O. was pleased because the men were pleased. Higher commanders were delighted because the venereal returns were negligible. Many regiments habitually did this and went on doing it right through the war.

'But of course it was too good to last. A solution which combined, as this did, economy with plain good sense, and also gave a lot of pleasure to a lot of people, was equally certain, as soon as it was known about, to give a lot of displeasure in quarters where envy and traditional morality were alike confounded.'

'But how *did* it get known about, Colonel? In the old days there was no trouble.'

'In the old days, all soldiers were regulars and knew how to keep their mouths shut. During the war there were ways of keeping things quiet. But after the war you would get, say, some young national serviceman who was either genuinely shocked by this or just plain bloody-minded and determined to make trouble. He told his parents, they told an M.P. or the newspapers. The bishops heard. No question now, remember, of quietly asking politicians or editors to suppress something "in the national interest". So articles were written and questions were asked. "Our young men are being deliberately incited to immorality." Rectitude loomed like a cloud. "Army brothels must go." And they did go. Men like Peterson saw to that. Eminent psychiatrists opined that all the men needed was more care and attention – more ping-pong competitions, as Alastair puts it. Eminent moralists said that any soldier should be content "with the memory of his sweetheart or his dear ones at home". So there was much ping-pong, and everyone was encouraged to put over his locker a photograph of his sweetheart or dear one. Result? Dissatisfaction, restlessness, breaking of bounds, picking-up of street women, long sentences of detention and rocketing V.D. returns. Public reaction? Officers to blame for still not organising enough ping-pong. Further result? More ping-pong than ever and more V.D. than ever. Conclusion? Chaos in the returns, bitterness and frustration among the men, anger at Divisional H.Q., blame recklessly apportioned by panicky C.O.s among helpless regimental officers. Nature, as always, had come back with a bang, leaping over ping-pong tables, roaring through evening discussion groups. And the resentment of the moralists is so great that they writhe and spit at us like snakes.'

'Bravo,' said Percy. 'Bravo, Colonel Nick. But you still haven't said what we're to do about it.'

'What can any of us do? All I ask is that you do your best to avoid scandal. I don't see Duthwaite allowing you to set up a brothel, no matter how well organised and hygienic. And I am not supposed to encourage you. So perhaps you'd better confine yourself to filling in the V.D. returns. These will be so enormous that you'll have to get Robin to help you.'

'Why me?'

'Because, Robin,' said Sanvoisin, 'a little dose of reality would do you good. Because you can't go on for ever being Head Boy and improving the tone of the House. In this House, which we call the World, the tone can no longer be improved. The boys and most of the prefects are totally incorrigible; the Housemaster has long ago locked himself despairingly in his study and is not interested either in your suggestions or your complaints. He has ceased to be concerned ... And here is James Sinclair to take me to the Governor General's reception. A brandy before we go, James?'

'Not for me, thank you, Colonel.'

'Wait for me then while I pump.'

'Brandy for me,' said Percy 'an *immense* brandy. *Immense* brandies for everyone except James. I hope you have a lovely time, James, at the Governor General's booze up.'

'It isn't a booze up. It's a reception.'

'You make it sound like a church social.'

'What time do you leave in the morning, Berkeley?'

'About ten, I expect.'

'So you're taking a company off on detachment tomorrow, yet you're sitting here half-drunk within twelve hours of doing so and with no exact idea of when you actually leave?'

'Percy's only teasing,' said Alastair. 'The arrangements are quite clear.'

'They'd better be.'

'How aggressive James is getting,' said Alastair after Sinclair and Sanvoisin had left. 'I almost think he must be in need of one of Lord Nicky's brothels.'

'More immense brandies,' said Percy to the waiter.

'You know,' Alastair went on, 'I think we really ought to have a look at one of the brothels in Eirene. This would give Robin a dose of reality, if nothing else. Percy can lend respectability to the party.'

'Brothels out of bounds,' said Percy.

'I know, Percy. But we're going to do a little field work. In the men's interest, as it were. And we can always say we heard that Moley or someone had gone there and we've come to arrest him and take him away.'

'I don't think I'll come, thank you,' said Robin.

'Nonsense, my dear. Of course you must come.'

'Black lollipops?' said Percy.

'Black lollipops.'

'Sticky black lollipops. Not for Percy. Percy wants more brandy.'

'Percy can only have more brandy if he promises to come with us to the brothel. Waiter, take that brandy away.'

'Oh, please. Percy *does* want more brandy . . . All right, Percy will come to the knocking shop to look at the black lollipops, but only if he can have *three* more brandies.'

'Two,' said Alastair.

'All right. Two. But *immense* ones.'

'I think perhaps I'll be going now,' said Robin.

'No you don't,' Alastair gripped his arm. 'You're going to stay with your friends.'

'You're hurting.'

'I'll hurt more if you try to leave again.'

'But I promised my mother . . .'

'Never mind that. You needn't do anything. But you'll have to come in.'

'You'll be all right,' I said.

Myself, I rather liked the idea of this expedition. For one thing, I had never had a coloured woman. And then the drink was obscuring any misgivings that might otherwise have arisen.

Percy's last brandy arrived.

'Just one more for Percy,' he said when it was finished.

'No, Percy. Time to move. You promised.'

So we got into a taxi, and Percy went straight to sleep. Robin looked white and unhappy; had I not been half-drunk, I hope I would have realised what a cruel thing we were doing to him. For that matter, Alastair was not exactly radiant. It was his idea, he had shepherded us all to the taxi, he had given the instructions to the driver; but he looked drawn and nervous, and I was sure that he would gladly have been back in the Pepromene Club, feeding Percy with brandy and teasing Robin but it was clearly too late now. We had left the suburbs and were heading fast by the central government buildings towards the east end of the city; at any moment now we should be in the brothel quarter.

When the driver stopped, I saw that we were by a small open square of rough ground, marked off on one side by the road and on the other three by long buildings of one storey with barred windows. It was rather as though we had come to a barracks. Percy would plainly have to be left in the car, but would provide the expedition with all the respectability it needed, Alastair said, by so doing. Robin's offer to stay and take care of him was fiercely rejected. The driver could do that after he had shown us the way. This he now did. We went through a door on the right of the square, down a short passage, and then into a small enclosed courtyard. There were no windows looking on to this, but a number of crude doors, on one of which the driver knocked. After a time a large coloured woman came out, amply dressed in European style, dimly discernible by the light of the hurricane lamp she carried to look responsible and also rather cheerful. A good start, I thought. The driver went back to guard Percy.

'You like girls?' said the woman.

Alastair nodded.

The woman went round knocking on some of the doors, and about five or six girls appeared in the courtyard. They were all very young, with short fuzzy hair, without shoes or stockings but respectably clothed in skirts and jumpers.

'You choose,' said the woman. 'All clean. Make nice present. For me, forty shillings, for them twenty, thirty shillings.'

'All clean?' said Alastair.

'Yes, clean. These girls not whores. Factory girls. Nice, clean.'

She held up her lamp. The girls looked shy and rather pleased. One held out a hand to Robin, who shrank back. A hurt look appeared on her face. She was so young and looked so pathetic, that Robin came slowly back towards her and took the hand she offered.

'You like?' she said.

'I . . . I'll stay with you here while the others . . . I . . .'

Meanwhile Alastair and I had both chosen girls. They looked

almost as young as Robin's, and smiled up with broad innocent grins.

The woman in charge then opened yet another door, and showed us a crude dormitory with several beds and a central table, on which was another hurricane lamp.

'Different rooms,' said Alastair, 'all different rooms.'

The woman shook her head.

'All here,' she said. 'Girls together, happy. Different rooms, unhappy, afraid.'

She swept us all towards the dormitory door. Robin hung back, but his girl pulled him gently on. The older woman put her arm round his waist and kissed his cheek.

'Nice, clean girl,' she said. 'You go with friends.'

Finally the six of us were all together in the dormitory with the door shut behind us.

'We'd better put that lamp out,' said Alastair, and went towards the table.

'No. Leave light, Darkness no good.'

My girl had darted between Alastair and the lamp.

'Leave light,' she repeated.

'How embarrassing,' said Alastair, and then giggled.

'We must make the best of it.'

I drew the girl I had chosen on to one of the corner beds. Alastair lay down, still fully dressed, on another bed, and his girl sat beside him and started to stroke his cheek. Robin was still standing near the door, whispering urgently to the little girl who had chosen him, resisting her attempts to make him sit down, but letting her run her hands up and down his coat.

After that I ignored them for a while. Pepromeneans are really only indifferent love-makers. They are too direct, too suspicious of anything remotely perverse. They come far too quickly to the point. But she was a nice girl for all that, with her tiny sharp breasts and the quick panting noises she made through her innocent, grinning mouth ... Later on, I turned my head to look at Robin. He was now sprawled across a bed with his eyes closed. His coat and trousers were in a heap on the floor, his shirt rucked up above the navel. I thought how tender his skin looked and noticed that only at the base of his stomach was there any sign of hair. I thought how that beautiful skin had been washed and tended by his nurse and his mother when there had been no hair at all. Bath time. 'But Robin, you must promise Nanny ... Robin, you must promise Mummy ...' And years later, 'Darling, you do promise ... ?' 'Yes, Mother, I promise.' And now that skin was being tended by a little black girl, who had taken off her sweater and was kneeling on the floor, her little breasts brushing Robin's knees as she leant over him, murmuring softly, passing her hands over the skin that might have belonged to another girl. Robin lay absolutely inert, until suddenly he gasped and quivered, raised his head to look incredulously at the girl and then lowered it and was still once more.

Now there's going to be guilt, I thought. Time to go. I looked at Alastair. He was still fully dressed. His girl seemed to have stopped bothering with him, and was sitting on the bed with one hand resting slackly on Alastair's knee. Alastair himself was looking intently at Robin and his face was as set as if he had been dead.

While we were on the way home a figure appeared in the head-lights weaving uncertainly down the road.

'Royd,' said Alastair who had hardly spoken since we left the girls. Percy was still asleep, Robin was sitting in a corner looking straight out of the window. Oddly enough there had been little fuss or bother.

'I'm quite glad I came,' was all Robin had said.

Alastair had just grunted. Any tensions in him were still un-relieved. I suspected they were now far greater than when we had set out. But he spotted Royd sharply enough, and tapped the driver's shoulder.

Royd was unquestionably drunk but still in control of his tongue.

'This is very kind, gentlemen,' he said, 'and I hope I see you after a pleasant evening. The Major seems to have done well, anyway.'

He looked round at the rest of us.

'It's clear where you've been,' he said, 'I'm ashamed of you, Mr Lynch. Taking Mr Hathaway too. But I'm afraid it's the same story with me, gentlemen. When I went out, I said. "Just a few drinks for you, Charlie boy, and home to bed. There's a move on tomorrow," I said, "and there's Mrs Royd, the sour old cow, sitting alone in Reading and knitting away like doom itself. Fair's fair," I said, "even if you would pay five pounds down for her to drop dead tomorrow." But all of a sudden there I was, and such a pig's break-fast you never set eyes on. They make you all go in one room in this country, and there was a whole gang from our own bloody Troop, Mr Lynch, crying drunk the lot of them, and your friend Harley clean out in the middle.'

'Did they all get out all right?'

'After I told them a piece or two of my mind. But a fair job we had with Harley. Cold drunk and stone naked and with a girl wound round him like ivy round a tree. Wouldn't leave him. But we prised her off and doused him down and a real pretty sight he was too, lying there like his mother made him. Hardly a hair on his body, the little bleeder, as soft as butter – and as pleased as a bird in spring when he came to and realised where he was.'

'But he did get out all right?'

'He did, Sir. "You little c——," I said, "It's a good job for you

65

I've no business here myself or I'd smash those white teeth of yours through the back of your bleeding neck. Mrs Palm's the girl for you at your age or a dimple in the barmaid's knee if you're lucky. And you have to get blind besides. You might have been murdered by some wog and flogged for curry meat. And there's Mr Lynch talks his chin loose with the Colonel on your behalf and *this* is how you pay him back." Then young Simes spoke up and said it was his fault and he'd made Harley come. They're getting very thick, those two, though they only set eyes on each other two days ago. But he's all right, young Simes, loud and cheeky, but knows a thing or two and speaks up for his mates ... The end of it was I packed the lot of them off in two taxis and had to pay the drivers myself. The little bastards were cleaned right out.'

It was evident to me, and I think to Alastair, that Sergeant Royd had either led the men to the brothel himself or else had got chance wind of their expedition and had gone after them to see fair play and a happy ending. In his odd way, he was irresponsible enough for the one course and yet responsible enough for the other. Still, the event seemed to have passed off harmlessly; and an excursion of this kind, the night before leaving for 'up-country', was not without excuse. Alastair, however, could not leave the subject alone.

'So you're sure they're all right? And what was that about Harley and the girl?'

'All over him she was, Sir, and not a stitch on either of them.'

And again that set look appeared on Alastair's face, and I remembered how he had watched Robin's fair skin in the light of the hurricane lamp.

In the morning, Alastair and I stood and watched the last of 'D' Company's tents being dismantled and piled for the trucks to take them up to Gikumo.

'A nice evening,' he remarked, 'though I'm afraid it was little good to me. I got far too engrossed in what Robin was up to.'

'So I noticed. Have you seen him this morning?'

'Yes. He seems all right. Which is lucky, because candidly I don't think we behaved very well.'

'*You* didn't. You positively dragooned him into going and then gloated over him like Juliet's nurse.'

'Well, it seems to have done him good and it was certainly a sight worth seeing ... You see that man there, the stocky one with the aggressive face?'

'Yes.'

'That's Simes, the one Sergeant Royd says persuaded Harley to go on the rampage last night.'

'You and Simes have much in common.'

'I don't know about that. But I think it's a bit much of Harley to go and get blind in a brothel two days after he promised me to behave himself.'

'He was off duty. No harm has come of it. It was only a farewell party.'

'I suppose you're right. But I don't think Simes will be good for Harley. He's a bolshy little brute, Simes, always kicking for trouble and putting people up to things. Loyal enough in a way. But resentful.'

'Resentful of you?'

'Anything or anybody that means authority ... Yes, Corporal, Killeen?'

I recognised the tall, slimy-looking corporal who had been in charge of the party that arrested Harley on the guard of honour.

'I have a complaint, Sir.'

'Then tell the Sergeant Major and form up to Major Berkeley.'

'It's a troop matter.'

'Well?'

'Very late last night, Sir, Sergeant Royd came swearing and cursing round the troop lines. He was drunk. He shouted and bawled and woke everyone up. He even tipped some of them out of bed. He said something about that would teach them to go putting their bare feet where he wouldn't put the end of his umbrella.'

'Well?'

'I thought you ought to know, Sir. That kind of thing's bad for discipline.'

'I dare say it is, Killeen. And tale-bearing is bad for solidarity and good will. If you want to urge this as an official complaint, go ahead and see the Company Commander. I shan't interfere. But meanwhile you can stop whining and snivelling round me and get on with your job. Now get out of my sight.'

Killeen flushed and walked away.

'Come back here,' shouted Alastair.

'Sir?'

'Now salute Captain Lamont.'

Killeen performed a sloppy and resentful half-salute.

'Do it properly, Killeen, or you'll be in a cell when we leave this morning.'

This time Killeen managed a tolerable salute.

'Now fall out. As a corporal, you should know how to salute. As a man, you should know better than to come to me with some sneaking tale about Sergeant Royd behind his back. Get away.'

'This is good *Daily Mirror* stuff,' I said, 'with Killeen as the wronged and virtuous soldier, and you as the sadistic officer who encourages the brutal sergeant to torment him.'

'Maybe. But he makes me sick. The truth is that he's after Royd's job. Royd has been broken a number of times for one thing and another, and Killeen's hoping it'll happen again and he'll get the extra stripe. I'd sooner shoot him in the back.'

Later on, as we rode out of camp and turned up the road to the north, I noticed that Harley and the man Alastair had pointed out as Simes were riding side by side. Simes was talking energetically, jutting his chin and shaking his head. Harley was listening, but at the same time he just looked straight ahead, with his lazy smile sprawled across his face.

CHAPTER FIVE

THE CAMP WE were to inhabit at Gikumo had been well sited by Duthwaite. The village itself consisted of a collection of native huts, a rough police post, the District Officer's bungalow and a general store. Just to the south of the village was a small valley, the Gikumo side of which sloped down to a stream at the bottom in a series of natural terraces. Duthwaite planned to erect two large huts on the topmost of these, one for the officers' and one for the sergeants' mess; on the second he would place a canteen and recreation hut for the men; and on the third and largest would be the company offices and stores and the men's lines, with the men's latrines, rubbish pits and whatever on yet a fourth and much smaller terrace about fifty yards above the stream. Offices, stores and sleeping accommodation would all be tented; so, for the present, would be the messes and the men's canteen, though, as I say, it was hoped to change these for huts as soon as possible. It was this latter question that led to disagreement between Duthwaite and Percy Berkeley, Percy maintaining that the Company must be properly settled in with huts and comforts before starting to patrol the district, Duthwaite urging that the Company was there to patrol and that the building of huts was only of secondary importance – though even he granted that they should be finished before the winter rains, which normally came in December. (It was late October when we arrived.) In the end a rational compromise was achieved. Only Michael Byrt's troop was sent off patrolling, while the remaining two, assisted by native labour raised by the District Officer, were put to work to make the camp neat and habitable. By the time they had finished, the camp was, of its kind, a thing of beauty. Overlooked by our hut and the sergeants' from the top terrace, it fell away, past the long low building of the men's canteen, to where the neat rows of the men's tents formed three sides of a grass square and the two large store and office tents made a fourth. Paths and painted posts appeared everywhere, nicely related to the small clumps of trees, both coniferous and deciduous, which grew all down the hill. For the first and last time in my life I even found shaving a pleasure, looking out from my tent in the early morning down the green and gentle slope to the little stream and beyond it to the delicate silver-trunked trees on the other side of the valley.

Anything less conventionally tropical would be difficult to imagine. But then the uplands of Pepromene are temperate in climate, particularly in the winter, which falls from November to May. The weather then is that of a superb English summer. The winter rains, though referred to as such, are in fact neither fierce nor long, and very often do not occur at all, the rainfall in that case being more or less equally distributed throughout the winter but more pronounced in November and December. The uplands summer was said to be hotter than was pleasant and rather arid, although even this, by Empire building standards, was hardly grievous. In any case the summer was far away; and every evening I returned with pleasure to our camp from my expeditions, noting with satisfaction the improvements and additions the men had made that day, giving thanks yet again for the truly green and pleasant land it was our fortune to inhabit.

Some days I used to accompany Michael Byrt on his patrols. But he was only surveying the Company's area, where as I had been instructed, as far as possible, to gain a broad idea of the whole Battalion's terrain and to liaise with every police officer and Colonial servant throughout. This might have been a tedious and difficult undertaking, had it not been for the assistance of Matthew Sach, the District Officer at Gikumo. Busy as he was, he spent whole days riding with me as a guide to visit other companies, and introduced me to every important man in the area – not only policemen and other district officers, but settlers, doctors and missionaries. But it was his company for which I was truly grateful. Matthew, by his account, had had an uneasy and eventful life, and was in no sense the type of man one expected to find as a district officer. His mother had been French and poor, his father Belgian and rich; he had been educated in Paris and at the London School of Economics; and after this had lived on in London, a well-liked if minor figure in the leftist literary circles of the early 'thirties. He used to gossip wistfully about Stephen Spender and Louis MacNiece and summer evenings in Soho – all of which he had left without a second thought to bear arms in the Spanish Civil War. Back in London in 1939, he had been refused facilities for British naturalisation and had only been able to get properly into the war when the Free French Forces appeared in England. Once soundly established as an officer of de Gaulle's, he had been able to find himself a number of interesting jobs in the private armies fashionable at the time : he had parachuted into Crete, dropped behind the German lines in North Africa, helped partisans in Italy. He was in fact a natural pirate; so that when he was allowed British nationality after the war, he speedily found the welfare atmosphere of the late 'forties oppressive and emigrated to Pepromene with what he had been able to salvage of his dead father's Belgian fortune. Here he set up as a trainer, lost all his money when his stable, which, characteristically, was uninsured, was struck by lightning, and finally gravitated to the Colonial Service in an irregular but secure appointment. As a former member of a number of eccentric and outlandish military bodies, he regarded our Battalion – a regular peace-time unit of a semi-smart Regiment – with suspicion; until he discovered our fondness for food and gambling, when he capitulated to us as a man, though he never did so as a public servant and an ex-soldier. Wry, cynical, tough and sympathetic, Matthew slowly showed me the area, the people and his own reading of the situation; until, wittily but with importunity, he had passed on all that ten years' experience of Pepromene had taught him.

In principle, he confirmed what General Peterson had said about Karioukeya and his 'brigade', but he had strong doubts about the methods Peterson was adopting.

'General Peterson anticipates a muddled and noisy attack by a lot of fuzzy-wuzzies,' he said one day as we rode home. 'In fact it will be very different. These raids, when they come, will come at night, silently and swiftly. By the time one of your nice little cavalry troops is on the spot, the whole thing will be over – everyone dead, Karioukeya vanished as though he had never existed. Peterson simply doesn't know the way these mountain tribesmen work . . . There is only one thing for it. You should establish strong parties at every farm in the area, so that someone is actually there in case of attack. You should then find guides who know the mountain forest – and a few of them do exist, whatever anybody says – and send a series of expeditions, in company strength at least, to parade through the mountain villages and on through the forests. Make Karioukeya see he's watched and that you're ready to slap him down the minute he moves. This thin cordon round the mountains is no good at all. It's composed of nothing but gaps for a start.'

I reminded him of the political objections to his scheme.

'Peterson's short of troops too,' I added.

'As to that, if he's short of men, it's clearer than ever that he must concentrate what he has got where it will create the most impression – in the mountains or at any rate the foot-hills. And as for this political business, I've heard about it of course, but I still say Peterson and the Governor General ought to go ahead and act off their own fuel. They can always exaggerate the reports of activity in the forest if they need an excuse . . . The whole thing's sheer blind folly and Socialist hocus-pocus. I'm a Labour man myself; I fought in Spain against Franco; I've spent much of my life writing and speaking, though admittedly with little distinction, against injustice of one kind and another. But I know – and so does any Socialist who has actually been to this country – that the mountain tribesmen are a set of blood-thirsty and retarded heathen who are not only not fit to govern Pepromene in the name of Native Independence but indeed have no right to do so, save possibly in their own mountain area. I know, and so does any Socialist who stops yapping and

71

thinks for a moment, that Karioukeya is a skilful and unscrupulous politician who is now organising what is in effect a Fascist outfit in order to try and impose a Fascist régime on the whole country. But no. The Socialists daren't admit this. For they know that in so far as their supporters know anything about Pepromene at all, they will conceive of the mountain tribesmen as a sort of coloured version of the Tolpuddle Martyrs, indeed as a coloured version of themselves. They will see them as sitting in mountain villages which resemble the provincial suburbs, each with his television set and the local pools to fill in, all of them being kind to their wives and kids and popping out for an occasional pint – and the only trouble with the whole set-up being the wicked Colonists, who are still, needless to say, exploiting these poor folk worse than the Victorian industrialists exploited the British working-class in 1850. So of course the mountain men must have their freedom, of course the wicked Redcoats, the heroes of Peterloo, must be forbidden to interfere. It's the old story. The Socialist leaders may be sane enough. But their rank and file really have no real interest outside domestic issues, and when something like this crops up, they simply see it with blind, sloppy ignorance in terms of virtuous, night-school visiting and exploited workers – their coloured brothers if you please.'

'Karioukeya is said to be a man of principle and integrity.'

'No doubt – when it comes to furthering the interests of his own people. But principle and integrity in this case mean taking the savage material at his disposal and using it in the only way he can as a merciless, fanatical, militarist force.'

'Well, I'm willing to lay long odds against anyone being sent to the mountains before blood is spilled by the other side,' I said, 'but the Colonel might well agree with you about keeping standing forces in all the farms. He never resents or ignores well-reasoned advice.'

'Yes, they say your Sanvoisin is a good man to work with. But what about our friend Percy Berkeley?'

'Percy will do as everyone tells him. He has Duthwaite, Lynch and Byrt to do that. They're all intelligent men. Hathaway's just a baby – but a nice baby and capable of being taught.'

'In no army other than the British would it be for a moment tolerated that a detached company should be commanded, on active service, by an incompetent drunk.'

'Now you're being unsubtle. Percy's fatness and drunkenness give us all a feeling of comfort and security. The men feel it – they feel Percy's burgundy glow radiating through the dark like a beacon of hope. And they know that he's tolerant of their shortcomings. Kind. Forgiving. They look to him as they might to the Baron in "Cinderella" – as a figure of fun, yes, but one who has appeared every Christmas since they can remember ... Percy represents an important side of human nature – the inefficient, debt-bilking, priapic and boozy side. People like to have this summed up and ready for them on the spot, to be trotted out for their reassurance when they've had an overdose of competence and self-sacrifice and heroism plugged at them. Hence those deplorable slapstick charades traditionally performed after Shakespearean tragedies ... We'd be unhappy without Percy.'

'If you say so ... But Duthwaite can carry him?'

'Oh, yes. We don't like him much, but he's a cool and efficient soldier.'

'Young Lynch?'

'Intelligent. Flexible.'

'And temperamental,' said Matthew. 'Impatient. You have to be patient in a country like this. There's so much of it to cover ... Of course the real trouble with your lot is that you're one cosy little family, happy to move about together anywhere on earth but only concerned with yourselves. So long as *your* Battalion does all right in Pepromene, you don't give a damn what happens to the country or the people. I don't mean that you're only interested in your own comforts – though there's a lot in that. I mean that for you Pepromene does not exist save in so far as Martock's Foot are compelled to serve here and you must therefore adapt yourselves a little if the honour and welfare of your Regiment are to be upheld.'

'Would you have it otherwise? We shall do our best. We can't take the world's woes on our shoulders.'

'I agree – up to a point. But I wish you'd try to realise more plainly what this business is all about – and how it will have to be conducted if trouble ever starts. In the end, whatever guards are provided and whatever defensive provisions made, *someone* will have to go into the mountains and *get* Karioukeya. Now all right, Peterson and the Labour Party won't let you go yet, in any case there hasn't been any trouble yet, you don't know anything about the mountains, you've simply been told to patrol the farmlands. But have you *tried* to find out about the mountain forest? Have you tried to devise any training that might help you when you get there? Have you given one moment's thought to the problems and techniques of fighting there? Have you hell! Percy thinks about his huts and his burgundy, Duthwaite arranges for efficient administration and tells Byrt where to take his patrols, Byrt goes conscientiously there and comes back with information I could have given him in five minutes, and Alastair Lynch just sits reading in his tent while Hathaway supervises the work round the camp. The whole set-up is based on the old Army maxim of everything being all right when the fun starts. "We're Martock's Foot and we shall know what to do." Well, you won't. You're nice people with nice manners, but you don't know the country, you don't want to learn about it, and you won't know what to do.'

'You yourself were recommending patience for others,' I said. 'You must wait.'

'And what are your N.C.O.s like?' said Matthew, ignoring my last remark.

'You can come and see for yourself tonight. The Sergeants' mess hut is completed to the C.S.M.'s satisfaction, and he is giving a little party to celebrate. All officers will be there, and he asked me to convey his cordial invitation to you. It will be a nice, cheerful party.'

'And not a word said about the forest, I suppose. I'll come, Andrew, with pleasure, and you can dine me first in your mess, if you like.'

'Gladly. If you promise not to talk about the forest.'

'Done.'

Matthew had been quite right. Whatever we had done since we arrived in Pepromene, we had shown little urgency and had given little thought to the probable shape of things to come. Myself, I didn't think then and I don't now that this was necessarily a bad thing. A unit which arrives in a strange country and is hysterically anxious to come to grips and draw deductions about it straight away merely succeeds, as often as not, in making a series of completely false estimates; and so comes to base its subsequent actions on totally irrelevant premises. Like an American tourist 'doing' Europe, such a unit rushes around cramming itself with ill-digested information and amassing great piles of guide-books; and by the end of the day, exhausted and querulous, it has seen everything and understood nothing at all. Much better to sit around outside Florian's, as it were, and give the atmosphere a chance to sink in. A man who determines to absorb Venice in three days invites ridicule. So does a military unit which, newly arrived somewhere or other, gears up an immediate programme and lectures and exercises in a futile effort to learn in a fortnight what would make itself automatically apparent after two months. And in this case, no one could say there was any real question of going immediately into action. We had been told to wait and to observe; and that is what we did. Nor was it very wise of Matthew to wish to break through our detachment and involve our emotions in the fortunes of Pepromene. He had lived there ten years and so was inevitably involved : for us to have tried to become involved in this fashion would have been a piece of emotional falsity on the one hand and probably a direct impediment, on the other, to what was an uninstructed but at least fresh vision on the country and the situation.

But however this may be, Matthew certainly stood by his promise and kept off the subject of Pepromene at dinner. For a time, he bickered mildly with Duthwaite, who was saying that the irregular private armies of the last war, with their glittering special missions, were an affront to conventional troops doing a steady and unpublicised job. No doubt, Matthew replied, people in normal and boring occupations always resented the flashy and privileged organisations singled-out to perform heroic stunts, especially since it was really just as dangerous to be an ordinary soldier in the front line as it was to be a colourful member of the Special Air Service dropping in romantic places with filmic assignments. But had Duthwaite forgotten that Martock's Foot was traditionally employed in a privileged role? And that military 'stunts', quite apart from their tactical value, had had tremendous morale effect on the civilian population? Unfair, possibly, but undeniable. From this subject we drifted vaguely on to the eccentrics and 'soldier-poets' who, like Bernard Ferguson, had belonged to such special units, and from there to poets plain and simple. Matthew, it seemed, had once for a short time shared a flat with Dylan Thomas.

'What was that like?' Alastair asked.

'Disquieting. Dylan never had a vestige of routine, but I did. Like Trollope, *si parva licet,* I used to work set hours and then forget it all till the next day. Of course my stuff wasn't poetry, it was political or critical essays, so I take no credit for my regularity. But the point was, after a week or two with Dylan, I hadn't got my regularity any more. He was enchanting and disrupting, and he enchanted and disrupted me, until my life became one long pantomime of dock-side bars and back-alley adventures, over all of which Dylan seemed to spread such magical significance that I couldn't imagine that any other life was worth living. Meanwhile, I got behind with my articles, editors complained, money got short; and finally my commercial Belgian blood came out, and I realised I should die in an asylum or a poor-house if I stayed with Dylan one moment longer. So I packed and pushed off one morning while he was still asleep. I hadn't the heart to say good-bye. And if I had, I'm sure he would have wooed me into staying against my will. I went to live some months in Wales. After listening to Dylan for two months, you see, I couldn't think of anywhere else to go.'

'What a sad little story. Did you ever see him again?'

'Once or twice in pubs or at parties. We were always on good terms. But then I went to Spain, and then the war . . .'

'Tell about Spain.'

'For a long time it was all rather irresponsible. People used to get drunk and organise a raiding party of a few friends just for the hell of it. After a time, though, they arranged us all in more or less conventional formations. I was never in on any of the really big shows . . . One remembers it all in wider terms, really – the big Tory-

SIMON RAVEN

Capitalist sell-out, the final disintegration of the good-form façade.'

'Rather a shallow judgement, surely,' said Duthwaite. 'You yourself admit being one of a number of irresponsible elements who turned up in Spain and organised drunken raids "just for the hell of it". And then, when your side loses, you talk about sell-outs.'

'Time to go,' said Percy, who rightly scented trouble here. He was taking all this in quite creditably, for it was his rule never to arrive drunk at the Sergeants' Mess, though once inside he permitted himself broader licence.

'We must all be nice to Moley about his new mess,' said Alastair.

We only had about a hundred yards to walk, and C.S.M. Mole was waiting to greet us at the door. Inside was Sergeant Royd, the other two troop sergeants, the local inspector of police, and one of the nearby settlers who was being generous to us all with his bathroom.

'Come in, gentlemen,' said the C.S.M. gloomily. 'Not what you're used to, I know, but you must take us as you find us. And very glad to see you, Sir,' he said to Matthew Sach.

'It was kind of you to ask me, Mr Mole.'

Alastair giggled.

'C.S.M.s don't get a "mister" in this Regiment, if you don't mind, Sir,' said Mole, 'and a good job, my name being what it is. Now if ever they make me an R.S.M. . . . but I don't suppose they will. Drinks on the table, gentlemen. Beer, whisky and gin. But there's a special bottle of burgundy for the Major, and only for the Major, gentlemen, please, and I've got some hock for you, Mr Alastair, because I know you like it.'

This was thoughtful of the C.S.M. Typically enough, the hock was well chosen, partly because Mole had served in Germany and partly because he would take any amount of trouble for Alastair. Percy's special burgundy, however, looked perfectly venomous and had obviously cost five shillings at the general store in Gikumo. It was difficult to see why Mole was being so protective about it. Indeed, this could only be explained as an inspired piece of malice at the Company Commander's expense : for after Mole's declaration, Percy must plainly grit his teeth and wade unassisted through the burgundy before asking for anything else.

At first the evening followed the normal pattern for such occasions. Michael Byrt and Robin Hathaway stood talking to their respective troop sergeants, while Alastair started drinking with Sergeant Royd. Percy and Duthwaite made themselves polite to the policeman and the settler. Matthew and I spoke to Mole.

'I expect you're glad to be settled in so nicely,' said Matthew.

'That we are, Sir. But I keep asking myself what's to happen next. The camp will be finished in a day or two. Now, I understand

76

about building camps and making paths and putting up notices and such. I've spent my life doing it. But when that's all done, what's to happen?'

'More intensive patrolling, for one thing,' I said. 'You'll be in control of a nicely running company base, and frequent patrols will be coming in and out and expecting hot water and large meals while they're here. You'll have enough to do but you won't be too pushed.'

'Ah, but how long will that go on for, Sir? You can't tell me that we're going to sit here for ever and wait for something to happen. There's those wogs in the mountains and surely we'll go after them?'

'That's just what we're not allowed to do. The only way we can guard against trouble is by patrolling so efficiently that we'll be on to anything as soon as it happens.'

'Patrolling ! ! !' said Mole with more heat than I should have thought possible. 'That's not how we settled things when I was a boy. We went after trouble in those days, found it and trod on it and stopped it there and then.'

'As it happens,' I said, 'there are many people who agree with you. Mr Sach for one.'

'I certainly do,' said Matthew. 'But it's not Major Berkeley's fault or even General Peterson's that you're not going into the mountains. It's political pressure from London.'

'That's the way it is, I suppose,' said Mole. '*After* we've all had our throats cut, they'll let us do something. Even then they'll try and make out we started it. "You started it, Mole." they'll say, "you arrogant, overbearing sergeant major you, you warmongering, imperialistic old c——". That's what they'll say. "So just you take care, Mole," they'll say, "those wogs are every bit as good as you, we're all equal nowadays, and if they want to cut your throat, you must give them a fair chance. And don't let me see you laying a finger on any of them, Mole, because they're all going to be voters very soon, even if they do put their votes up each others' bottoms." That's how it is, Sir.'

Mole pottered off and poured himself two thirds of a tumbler of whisky.

'Did I hear you being reactionary, C.S.M.?' said Michael Byrt.

'Reactionary nothing, Mr Michael. I'm a Labour man myself, from having so much to do with you upper-class lot. But that's not saying I think those heathen from the mountains will run this country any better than we do, or that I want to lie here rotting while they make plans to cut my throat.'

Everyone was now getting drawn into this discussion.

'Treat 'em rough, that's what I say, show 'em who's master,' said the police inspector, who had failed his examinations at Sheffield University and had come out on a three-year contract six months before.

The settler, an old, lined man in a suit of khaki drill, gave him an angry look.

'It's people of your sort who lose us everything,' he said. 'In a way you might be right. Either you rule a country or you don't. But it's no help to make great blundering remarks that set people's teeth on edge like saws. Hold your tongue till you've been here longer.'

'No quarrelling in the mess, Sir, please,' said Mole, helping himself to more whisky.

'I think we should remember,' said Duthwaite, 'that the political side of all this is no concern of the Army's. Strictly speaking, we are out of order in discussing it at all. All we can do is what we're told.'

'Which simplifies matters for you very nicely,' said Matthew Sach. 'What do you think, Percy?'

'I think I should like some brandy,' said Percy, finishing his special burgundy with an heroic gulp.

'No brandy, Sir, whisky.'

'Whisky then, if you please, C.S.M. I agree with Richard. We can do no more than we're told.'

'But what would you really like to do?' persisted Matthew.

'Sit in a casino until five a.m., and get up at one, and eat a heavenly lunch two thousand miles away from this perfectly bloody country.'

'And you?' said Matthew to Robin Hathaway.

'I should like to do my duty,' said Robin.

'Which is?'

'To fear God and honour the Queen,' said Robin in a determined voice.

'Meaning what here?'

'To do what I'm told, but with as much regard for other people as possible.'

'Good boy,' said Matthew. 'And what about you, Alastair?'

But there was no sign of Alastair. C.S.M. Mole looked distressed.

'It's not like him to go early without saying thank you,' he said, 'and there's that nice hock, not half drunk. I did hope he'd enjoy the party.'

'I expect he's only gone for a breath of air,' I said.

They all went on squabbling uneasily about socialists and colonies and military forces. But by now it had occurred to me that some time had passed since I had seen Alastair. If he had gone, it was a bad breach of protocol, as in theory no officer leaves a sergeants' mess party until the C.O., in this case Percy, has either left himself or else become incapably drunk. Not that Percy would mind, but the sergeants would. Alastair had last been, I thought, with Royd. I drew him away from the central debate.

'When did Mr Lynch go?'

'About ten minutes ago, Sir. He said he wouldn't be gone long, but wanted to check the sentries.'

This was all right – except that Alastair was not duty officer that night, a fact well known to Royd.

'But bless his heart, Sir, I know where he's gone. He wouldn't want everyone to know, but he trusts you and me.'

'What do you mean?'

Royd took a long pull at his gin and water. So long as he remained conscious he remained articulate.

'Well, Sir, it happens so often in countries like this. You get lonely, you get to liking the look of someone. Surely you've noticed?'

'You mean Harley?'

'That's it, Sir. Of course, you being away every day might not notice it so easily. But I thought there might be something afoot when Mr Lynch took all that trouble in Eirene. And so there is. Mr Lynch thinks the sun shines out of young Harley's navel. Not that there's anything wrong going on. But he's always getting him on one side to talk to. He has him come to his tent in the evenings. Hours they spend.'

'What on earth do they talk about?'

'Harley says that Mr Lynch asks him about his home and his family. And that Mr Lynch tells him things, you know, about foreign places and gambling and women and a lot of crap I dare say it is,' said Royd, 'but it's new to Harley, at that, and if it makes Mr Lynch happy, then I'm not going to poke my nose in for anyone to aim a kick at it.'

'What about the other men? Do they notice?'

'Can't not notice. But what's it to them? Mr Lynch has always treated them right, and does now. Corporal Killeen says a few dirty things on the side, but then he doesn't like Mr Lynch, so everyone knows he says it all from spite. Young Simes doesn't like it much either; says Harley's *his* 'oppo and why can't Mr Lynch find an officer to open his face to. But don't you worry. There's no harm done or will be, and I can take care of Killeen and Simes.'

'I'm sure you can.'

But as the evening wore on there was still no sign of Alastair. Duthwaite led Percy away at about one, the settler and the policeman and Matthew left soon after, and finally, at half-past two, it was plain that the rest of us must also go.

C.S.M. Mole, prone in an armchair, was very distressed indeed.

'Lovely hock, specially ordered from Eirene. And then he goes off and doesn't even say good night.'

'I'm sure he's tired or something,' said Robin. 'He'll come and tell you in the morning, C.S.M.'

'Well, thank you for that, Mr Robin. I'm sure it's not what I expected of him. And that nice hock will spoil if it's not finished.'

'Come along, old Moley,' said Sergeant Royd. 'Time for bed. Bed-time for soldiers. Don't you worry about Mr Lynch. Good night, gentlemen, and thank you for the honour. So come along, old Mole, old soldier, and we'll lay your old bones in bed.'

CHAPTER SIX

IT MAY BE that I should already have said something of Alastair's background and education; for after all he is the hero in all this – if not perhaps by modern notions of what constitutes a hero, then demonstrably by Aristotelian ones.

Alastair Lynch was the only child of a rich stock-broker and an Irish girl of excellent but impoverished family. His parents lived in Sussex 'stock-broking' country, got on together moderately well, and were pleased and surprised by Alastair's appearance which, as they say, was rather late in the day. In his childhood, then, he lacked neither for security nor love. As it happened, I had met his mother, who was certainly a woman of great charm and kindness and even in a book-society sort of way, of modest cultivation. His father, on the other hand, would seem to have been a morose kind of man, interested in very little save money and occasional rounds of golf on the more popular 'stock-broking' courses. Nothing very inspiring in all this; in fact the young Alastair must have woken up, in the pseudo-Tudor house, to spend days exactly like those of 20,000 other well-to-do little boys, loitering dully through the hours in a grey shirt and grey shorts, taken to his mother's drawing-room at five, removed at six, scrupulously bathed and made to say his prayers before hot milk and bed.

However, two things happened to assist Alastair out of the Sussex rut. In the first place, his father's persistence on the Stock Exchange was so rewarding that it would hardly have been decent for the family to remain in the pseudo-Tudor house any longer; and just before the war they moved to a large country house in Hertfordshire, which was still within easy commuting distance but indicated a definite social elevation – to the status of substantial gentry. Memories are short in that part of the world; and by the time the war was over, after all the comings and goings and deaths and impoverishments which had resulted in the neighbourhood, the Lynches were as firmly established, in a comparative fashion, as if they had been there since the Conquest. All of which enabled Alastair, who had meanwhile been sent to Harrow, to assume the airs and amusements of the 'young squire' – and without any of the concomitant annoyances; for there was no tedious estate to be administered (only a very imposing and amply staffed garden), and so far from being shut away in some deplorable country district, he was within an easy hour of central London. He could therefore put on a red coat and go hunting or a black tie and go to the theatre, both with equal ease and in neither case with the prospect of returning to accounting ledgers that told a tale of unpunctual tenants, dishonest agents, and idle, half-witted labourers.

This in itself might not have been much improvement on his Sussex condition, had it not been for the influence of his time at Harrow. Normally, this would just have confirmed the prejudices and assumptions implicit from birth in his mode of existence and carefully underlined by his smart Surrey prep school. But it so happened that Alastair's house at Harrow had been taken over for the war by one of those brilliant, worldly and rather suspect men, who occasionally turn up as schoolmasters in times of shortage and stress, but who would normally steer well clear of education in all its guises. This particular man was an old Harrovian who had spent a cheerful life of travel and dissipation, had been the friend, variously, of Lord Russell, Lord Berners and Ezra Pound, and had been quietly living in 'retirement' when the war broke out. Feeling he ought to assist the country which he had been at pains to stay away from most of his life, he offered his services and his degree to his old school, only to have them politely declined; for in those early days adequate stocks of the steady and mediocre young Christians so beloved of head-masters were still available. But when the steady and mediocre young Christians were all marched off to battle, and when even a few of the middle-aged Christians were discovered to have specialist qualifications for discomforting the King's enemies, the old sinner's offer was gratefully remembered. And since he was quite a rich old sinner, they gave him a house to look after, in which, when Alastair arrived there in 1942, he was fairly and squarely established with a large library and an excellent cellar.

Libraries and cellars are unpopular during wars. They betoken privilege, detachment, a lack of the team spirit. It is to the everlasting credit of Alastair's temporary housemaster that it was his library and his cellar above everything that he was anxious to share with his boys. At a time when schoolmasters everywhere were talking endlessly of character and effort and enthusiasm, were devising routines of unparalleled austerity, were making their boys traumatic and hysterical by ferocious recitals of the names of ex-alumni dead on the field of honour, this succulent and kindly man merely saw to it that those in his charge had decent literature to read and an occasional glass of decent wine to drink. An amiable and unusual attitude in a public school at any time, this was of quite disproportionate significance during the dreary and cant-ridden years of the war. As a result Alastair, who but for this happy chance might have emerged from school as one of the joyless little bullies so readily turned out at the time, in fact left Harrow in 1946 a tolerant, sceptical and often witty young man. Mistrustful of all enthusiasms, contemptuous of all causes, he was firmly and for ever convinced that in literature, conversation and wine were to be found at once the staples of civilised existence and, if one added travel, the only possible consolations for the bedraggled world in which he had grown up.

But there was a less happy result of all this. Like all gifted men of his kind, Alastair's housemaster had more time for graceful and intelligent boys than he did for lumpish and stupid ones. Fair to all, he was nevertheless over-generous to some, among whom were Alastair and several of his friends. Over these boys their housemaster had a particular influence; he took them on expeditions and had them to stay, during the holidays, at some of the pleasanter resorts which war-time England even then afforded. Seeing the time Alastair spent with this man and the very distinctive influence he was absorbing, Alastair's parents became jealous – and finally expressed their resentment in the viciously stupid fashion of rejecting the housemaster's suggestion that Alastair should go up to Oxford. It was doubtful whether his parents had, until then, given much thought to Alastair's future; but the moment advice came from another and increasingly detested quarter, they sprang into action with spiteful assurance. Alastair, they said, had always been going to follow his father into the city; to send him to Oxford would merely be to prolong an interval already liable to be conveniently lengthened by impending National Service. At Oxford he would simply develop idle habits and impractical notions for the future conduct of his life – and of these he had seemingly absorbed quite enough already. Let him get to the city and learn his business – as his father had before him. He must start standing on his own feet.

This inexcusable pronouncement was a shock to Alastair, who had hitherto been given anything, within reason, that he had asked for. If ever there was a place for the enjoyment of literature, conversation and wine – not to mention the liberal intervals allowed for travel – Oxford, he though, must be it. And as for this business of making money, his housemaster's teaching was that while money was to be treasured as an instrument of pleasure, the getting of it was an affront to any man of taste. Nor could it be said that it was at all necessary for him to get it. His father had made plenty, and could easily have afforded to retire the next day and present Alastair with enough to keep him in comfort for life. No doubt a young man must have an occupation of sorts – and indeed at that time an officious Labour Government was busy legislating to that effect; but to sweat away in a distasteful environment in order to add redundant gold to the existing mass of it was against all reason and every civilised canon of behaviour. Thus Alastair pondered with himself. But he had the restraint not to make a scene and the wit to see that his parents' attitude was in essence negative – that it was

more a question of stopping him doing what his housemaster suggested than of making him do something they themselves actually
favoured. But Oxford, it seemed, or, by extension, Cambridge, was
definitely out. It remained to find a happy compromise (another
frequent recommendation of his housemaster's).

One evening early in his National Service he came home for the
week-end, and announced that, if his parents wished, he could go to
Sandhurst and eventually be sure of a Regular Commission in Lord
Martock's Regiment. For Alastair had realised something which many
young men of his type would have entirely overlooked – that the
Regular Army, while superficially a harsh and over-disciplined institution, can in certain circumstances present a well-endowed young
man with a life that includes travel, a great deal of leisure, and the
company of pleasant and like-minded people of considerably more
intelligence than is generally allowed. The vital thing was to find the
right sort of regiment. The Foot Guards, he had heard, were rather
stuffy in peace-time; the rifle regiments, though extremely nice, much
too concerned with professional efficiency; most cavalry regiments
were tolerant and pleasure-loving, but with a tendency to flashiness;
the light infantry regiments were, frankly, middle-class; the fusiliers
even more middle-class. Finally, and again with the assistance of his
housemaster, he had settled for Martock's Foot. 'You'll be happy
with them,' the old man had said; 'they are unsnobbish, as the
Army goes, but unmistakably upper-class; unenthusiastic but with
a good military reputation; unconcerned with good-form morality
and totally unimpressed by the mystique of team games and beer.'
Another advantage, as Alastair well knew, was that Martock's Foot
was quite smart enough to appeal to the vaguely snobbish instincts
which had drawn his parents from Sussex to Hertfordshire and had
led them to enter him for Harrow. Again, surely the choice of a
secure and honourable career would indicate sufficient determination
to 'stand on his own feet' – even if that career would be intolerable
without a very generous allowance from his father? And so, in the
event, it proved. Unaware that Martock's Foot was the suggestion
of Alastair's hated schoolmaster, his parents gave calm but satisfied
consent : it was also settled that Alastair should receive £500 a year
from his father while he was at Sandhurst, £1,500 a year when he
was commissioned, and a large block of capital when he was thirty.
A few weeks later, he came happily enough to Camberley
and settled down to the rather disagreeable eighteen months' training that must unfortunately precede his chosen life of idleness with
honour.

The trouble with Sandhurst lies in the moral and disciplinary
side of the instruction. Military subjects are taught capably and
broadly, academic subjects with sympathy and even liberality; but
there is with all this a nagging insistence on the Arnoldian virtues

and a distinct tendency to employ Arnoldian methods. There is much talk of keenness and responsibility, much earnest endeavour to maintain a suitable 'tone' in one's company, and of course the prefect system, in the form of a cadet hierarchy of under officers and N.C.O.s, is one of the staples of the whole place. Literature, conversation and wine are thus at a discount. Alastair had been prepared for this, and he had also been prepared, up to a point, for a return to the conditions of existence in a public school; but he had hardly been prepared for the positive barrage of moral influence with which authority bombards its pupils at the R.M.A. To indulge in irony at the expense of the establishment's moral values was a dangerous and unpopular pastime; to accept them whole- or even half-heartedly was quite out of the question. Alastair was thus in the uneasy position of having to simulate enthusiasm and responsibility and similar virtues for days on end, with almost no one to whom he could turn for the release of a compensating bout of cynicism or satire. For most young men at Sandhurst are only too ready to accept the military-cum-moral values upheld there, since in the centre of these is the assumption that only very superior people are capable of absorbing them and that, by extension, each cadet belongs to a morally superior caste. This neo-feudal conception has a strong appeal for young men of uncertain intelligence and uncertain social backgrounds, and so there were few cadets willing to listen to Alastair while he analysed the Sandhurst *credo* into its absurd components and mocked it for the nasty, incongruous and ugly edifice of the spirit it was. Still, uneasy as he might be, he remained unconverted, though hardly unaffected, by the intensity of the moral atmosphere he had to live in. It might even have been a valuable educational experience for him, had it not turned a light-hearted eighteenth century scepticism into an almost paranoiac distrust of any kind of moral excellence.

For the rest, he got by well enough. Bad at drill but adaptable to games, with a good memory for military fact, a shrewd administrative intelligence and a distinct gift for languages, he passed his examinations with sufficient credit to disarm comment about the vaguely 'unsatisfactory' nature of his character. So his father was able to stand by with pride and his mother in tears as he marched up to the college steps for the last time into a commissioned life and £1,500 a year. This he did with relief. He was now a man and could put away the childish things of Sandhurst in the adult and congenial atmosphere of Martock's Foot.

It was at this stage that I first met him. Myself about two years older than Alastair, I was at that time in charge of the Mortar Troop; and since there was no troop available for Alastair to command during his first few months with us, he was sent to me to be of general assistance and to pick up what knowledge of the three-

inch mortar he could or would acquire. Two of his qualities became
immediately apparent. Firstly, he was excellent company for days at
a time; never intrusive, always ready for a little conversation, quick
to pick up and share private jokes about the situation or activities
in which we were involved. The only thing which made him disagreeable was the occasional necessity for making a bad or hurried
meal, when he would point out that one's meals were as surely
limited in number as one's days upon earth and that it was a positive
duty to enjoy them. The second thing I noticed about him at once
was his interest in, and very quick understanding of, the theoretical
side of mortaring, as opposed to a total disinclination to investigate
such minor and practical details as the way in which the weapon
worked or ought to be cleaned. He was, in short, given to generalisa-
tion – like most intelligent yet lazy people. Indeed, intelligence and
laziness were the two qualities for which he became famous throughout the Battalion. When he left me and my mortars, he went to a
subaltern's normal employment as commander of an ordinary sabre
troop – a task he was still performing two years later, at the time
of which I write, and would in the normal course of events continue
to perform for a further two years. Successive company commanders
recognised his undoubted competence and deplored or condoned, as
their natures might dictate, his infinite capacity for doing nothing
and his complete refusal to move a foot in any direction unless he
was firmly and personally convinced of the necessity. In fact, however, he was never guilty of a major *betise* and his attitude was
on the whole approved and appreciated in our Regiment. As Sanvoisin used to remark, Alastair's idleness might equally just be described as economy of action – a pleasing thing in an army where
so many officers rushed around and shouted their heads off merely in
order to deceive or impress their seniors. In the end it was arguable
that Alastair commanded and administered his troop in an efficient
and unobtrusive manner, giving the minimum of trouble or work
either to his men or himself. This the men were quick to recognise,
as they were to appreciate his undeniable friendliness and fairness
and his willingness to take great pains on their behalf, whether as
individuals or as a body, if he truly considered it necessary. Thus
one could really say that Alastair's two years with our Regiment
had made him a popular and respected figure both with the men
and with his superiors. Scandal there had been none, save for the
gambling debts the previous June, and this affair had really been
settled without much trouble. True, two or three of the more severe
officers, such as Sinclair or Duthwaite, looked upon Alastair as
'dubious' or 'equivocal'. But they were in a definite minority. His
contemporaries, like Michael Byrt, were at once proud and fond
of him. As for myself, I had known him intimately since our time
together with the mortars; and I shall only say that no enterprise,

whether of business or pleasure, ever had quite the same pith and joy in it for me as when Alastair was bearing a part.

Thus it was my strong affection for Alastair, combined with what I had always considered, since our mortar days, to be a certain responsibility for him, that made me wonder whether it was not my duty to find out what was afoot between him and Harley and, if necessary, actively to interfere. I knew that I should not be thanked. But better anything, I thought, than the kind of trouble Michael Byrt had hinted at. 'Very difficult,' Michael had said, 'even in a regiment like this.' Whatever the 'civilised' judgement might be, Michael was from an immediate and practical point of view entirely right. And so, early in the day after C.S.M. Mole's party, determined at any rate to find out where the truth of the matter lay, I sought out Alastair in his tent.

'No trips to the wilderness today?' Alastair said.

'Not today,' I said. 'Where did you get to last night? The C.S.M. was very put out.'

'Moley? I've seen him and squared all that. I told him I wasn't feeling well and just slipped away so as not to spoil his party.'

'He may believe that, but Royd doesn't. He spent a good half-hour dropping clangorous hints about your probable destination.'

'Lord, Lord . . . Who heard these clangorous hints?'

'Only me.'

'And were they scurrilous as well as clangorous?'

'No. Royd affected to believe that whatever you were up to was, as they say, platonic.'

'How tactful of him.'

'Was he right?' I asked.

'He *was*.'

'Was?'

'You have an inquisitive look, Andrew. Must I tell you about this? You can't really want to know.'

'I want to know very much.'

'Then you'll have to promise not to interfere.'

'How can I? Do you think we all relish the idea of you making a fool of yourself? Do you really think you can get away with something like this?'

'You don't know yet what I'm getting away with.'

'Tell me then. And I'll not interfere if you convince me you've got some sort of control over what's happening.'

'Good of you, Andrew. But then I don't know what degree of control will satisfy you.'

'I shall want to be convinced that no one is going to get hysterical. That there are going to be no tearful confessions leading to enquiries and courts martial.'

'Myself,' said Alastair, 'as you well know, I am not given to hysteria and tearful confessions. I don't think Malcolm is either.'

'Malcolm?'

'Malcolm Harley. A nice name don't you think? That's one of the things I first thought, when I started looking up his record while all that fuss was going on. Someone once told me that all the nicest names are trochaic. Andrew. Michael. Malcolm. The stress on the first syllable, he said, suited the English language. And if both names were trochaic, he said, then that was really a dream. Malcolm Harley. Trochee, trochee . . . Besides, Malcolm is such a suggestive name – the "l"s and "m"s make it soft and languorous, but the "c" redeems it from complete effeminacy – gives it a healthy, outdoor, English ring. And that has always been my weakness, Andrew. If there's one thing I can't resist, it's a combination of softness and masculinity. Like those boys at school who are all fair hair and enormous blue eyes but nevertheless lead the scrum or score dramatic centuries. I could never resist them at Harrow and I don't seem able to now.'

'You're meant to have grown up since then.'

'Not a very clever observation. Some people "grow up", as you put it much later than others. Some never grow up at all. Or perhaps growing-up has nothing whatever to do with it.

'For . . .   "Tell me, where is fancy bred?

                         Or in the heart, or in the head?"'

'Reply, Andrew, reply.'

' "It is engendered in the eyes," ' I said.

'Exactly. And can you talk of the eyes not "growing-up"? Or being retarded? Abnormal, some might say?'

'This was a different kind of fancy.'

'Have it your own way then. If it's fact you want, fact you shall have. The plain fact is that I liked the look of Harley from the moment I saw him in that boxing ring, and then, when he made that nonsense on the guard of honour, there was my chance to get him. Not that I had any particular designs. I just thought to myself, "There's a nice boy, and a plucky one : he'll suit us very well." You know what happened then, with Percy and the Colonel and so on.

'However, one thing which complicated matters a bit was that night out we had in Eirene. You may not have noticed this, but in some ways Robin is a little like Harley. Not to look at exactly, but Robin's got this same thing of being rather soft, of inviting protection, as it were, and yet at the same time being undeniably masculine and upright. I suppose it's a wonder that I've never fancied Robin in this way. But then he's got such an aura of innocence round him – even after that night out – that it somehow puts one off; it would be like seducing a ten year old cousin – semi-incestuous baby snatching. Still, when I saw Robin that night in the brothel, I was even more struck by the resemblance between him and Harley, and what I saw then was almost unbearably exciting – not because it was happening to Robin but because it might have been happening to Harley. This opened my eyes a bit. And then, when we met Royd on the way back, and he told us what he'd actually seen happening to Harley, I was almost beside myself. I wanted to go and find Harley there and then, but of course I couldn't, he was in a tent with God knows how many others and probably still drunk. Are you with me so far?'

'Very much so,' I said.

'Well then, when I next saw Harley, the day we came up here, it was rather a disillusionment. There was just a little west country boy, dirty with the ride, smiling nicely but obviously very ordinary and stupid, and taking in everything that loud-mouthed Simes was telling him. "How could you have been so silly," I said to myself; "even if he was all you imagined and more, what could there be in it for you? He'd probably run a mile the moment you put a hand on him – run a mile and yell blue murder." But after a short while, I changed again. Although there was no sign of the really desperate lust I'd felt on our night out, I found myself increasingly keen just to have Harley with me, to talk to him or have him sitting around in my tent. At one point, I thought of making him my batman; but I've had Jones for so long now that it would have been terribly unfair to get rid of him, and in any case it might have caused talk. But I managed to see a lot of Harley for all that. I used to pick him out to act as my orderly or runner for the day; I used to talk to him for hours in the evenings – I'd get him to meet me somewhere and we'd go for walks along the valley.'

'And didn't *that* cause talk?'

'Perhaps. But we've rigged up a fiction about Harley having some trouble at home which I'm trying to sort out for him.'

'But Harley himself? What does he think of it? You seeking him out every day and talking to him for hours and hours? And getting him to pretend he's got trouble at home?'

'I think he's rather flattered. And possibly he's interested in the sort of things I tell him. He's not very intelligent, but he absorbs things and seems to like listening. Besides, some of my stories aren't too bad at that.'

'But for hours and hours?'

'Sometimes we don't talk very much. We just sit – very pleasant and comfortable. And sometimes Malcolm tells me things. About the village he lived in and the girls there; and what the men think of all of us . . . It's all rather childish, I know.'

'It's worse than that,' I said, 'it's catastrophic. It's a full-blown Theocritean Idyll – set to music for a full orchestra by Verdi. Indiscretions nicely scored for the attention of the big drum and the man with the cymbal.'

'It's not as bad as you make out. Most of this happens at night. Malcolm doesn't talk much to anyone, though he does a lot of listening, and there's always this cover story. But I'm not finished yet. Do you want to hear the rest?'

'I can't wait.'

'Well, last night I'd asked him to meet me rather late. I only meant to spend a few minutes with him and then get back to Moley's party. So there he was waiting by the stream and we walked off down the valley about a quarter of a mile and sat down in the grass. Then I said I'd got to get back fairly soon or you'd all wonder where I was. He looked a bit put out at this. He said I'd promised to tell him some story about the time you and Michael and I went to Cannes and got asked out to that yacht for an orgy. But I said it was a long story and I'd do it better justice another night. I was really quite agitated, because I knew that Moley would soon notice I'd gone if nobody else did and how sensitive he is about that kind of thing. So in the end I started to get up. But then Malcolm put his hand out to help me and by pure accident touched my leg just above the knee. And when that happened, it was just like that night when Royd was describing what had happened in the brothel. All this time, though I'd wanted more and more to have Harley with me, I'd never wanted him really urgently in the physical sense. Subconscious check, I suppose, and thinking about the trouble that might come. But when he touched my leg like that, it really set me off. I just sat down again, put my hands on his shoulders and looked straight into his eyes.'

'And then?'

'At first he was a bit taken aback. "I'm not a woman," he said – in rather an ugly voice. But there was no stopping me now. "You once said you'd do anything for me," I said, "and now you can do this." "But why?" he said. "Why do you want to?" "Because I'm in love with you," I said. This seemed to settle things. He lay there rather stiffly at first. But after a bit he seemed to get the measure of things. And everything Royd had said about his body was true. How can I put it? He seemed to have a natural gift, once he had lost his shyness, for giving pleasure, and taking pleasure in giving pleasure. Then, later, we lay absolutely still on the grass; until suddenly he roused himself, gave me a slight push, and started to get dressed. "We shouldn't have done that," he said, "it's all wrong". So I started to try and explain that I didn't think it was all that wrong, and anyway it had given me a lot of pleasure. "And this was why you always wanted to see me?" he said; "why you got me off that charge and went to all that trouble?" "No, no, no," I said, and tried to do some more explaining about the sexual side only being part of it all, not very important most of the time, and that my feelings for him were just the same now as they had been before, stronger in fact, and that what had happened only made me want to talk to him and be with him in the ordinary way a whole lot more.'

'You seem to have got into a proper muddle.'

'After a time, he began to understand what I was getting at. In any case, I don't think he's a guilty boy by nature. "So you'll still want to see me?" he said: "and this ... you'll want to do this again?" "If you don't mind too much." "No," he said, "I don't mind, not if it pleases you." And then he told me that something of the kind had happened before, just before he joined the Army, with a farmer in his village. He hadn't liked it much because the man was rough and unkind, and in any case Malcolm was only doing it because he was offered money. But he realised that I was genuinely fond of him, that it would be very different with me.'

'For Christ's sake,' I said, 'are you going to carry on this liaison for weeks and months right under everyone's nose?'

'No harm's come of it so far.'

'No harm to speak of has come of it so far because it's only just started. But Royd has a fair idea what's in the wind. And he told me that your Corporal Killeen is getting his nasty tongue wrapped round this thing. And that Harley's got a friend called Simes who doesn't like it. It'll be all over the place in no time.'

'Then it'll be my funeral. Not yours. You keep out of this, Andrew. You said you'd say nothing if you thought it was under control. I say it is under control. And what's more, I will have this. It's the most exciting thing I've ever had. I will have it, do you hear? I may be like a silly schoolboy, or some damned old queen doting over his fancy piece in a London club for all I care. I still won't give it up. As you say, it's only just started. I've just begun to get it right. And I won't, *won't* stop now.'

'And your friends? You won't mind what they will feel about it? Or perhaps you'll have no time left for us.'

'Don't be silly, Andrew. There's time for everything up here. Nothing to do all day, except for a few patrols; until the trouble starts – if it starts. And of course I mind what you all feel. You'll have to try and be sympathetic for a little while, that's all.'

But I felt very bitter when I left him.

I thought a lot about what Alastair had told me. For a long time I thought, as you may think, that I had been unsympathetic to Alastair, heavy, unhelpful and humourless. For ridicule might well have been a better weapon than protest. And in any case, where was the need for either? I wasn't an ageing schoolmaster or a suburban housewife; I was an adult and educated man, who prided himself on his tolerance and knowledge of the world. Who was I

91

to start objecting to such behaviour? Liberal was what we claimed
to be in Martock's Foot, I thought, liberal, detached, and ironic –
with an irony that was directed equally against the upholders and
the transgressors of the moral law, should either class behave with
too much absurdity. Even then, we had a sound tradition of minding
our own business. We might occasionally comment but never
interfere. And here was I behaving like a beer-swilling, back-
slapping, bird-brained, narrow little field officer from some God-
forsaken midland country regiment.

For it could not properly be said that Alastair's behaviour was
absurd and therefore a target for our traditional irony. Ill-judged,
yes; rash, dangerous, corrupting, selfish – but hardly absurd. If
people fall in love, they fall in love; and they only become absurd
if they want too much and spend too much time and money trying
unsuccessfully to get it. Alastair had time on his hands, had spent
no money, had got something tangible for his pains and seemed to
think he liked it. This was hardly absurd. And then all that nonsense
I had talked about upsetting his friends; what sort of friends were
they who flew into tantrums the moment one of their circle started
a love affair? It was a friend's office to be helpful and sympathetic,
to act as ally, towel-bearer, or even as pimp, but not to go sounding
off the moral law like a hedge priest ... But then again, I thought,
it wasn't exactly the moral that I was sounding off. I had really
been concerned to point out, as Michael Byrt had pointed out to
me, that for an officer to conduct an affair of this kind within his
own unit and not with another officer but with a private soldier,
was simply to invite trouble and disaster in the book. Whatever
the moral state of the contest might be was beside the point; the
point was that Alastair was heading for court martial and dismissal,
and that I, as his friend, did not want to see him drummed out of
the Army and out of my life.

But what was to be done? Just what was I to do, I thought,
as I walked by the little stream at the bottom of our camp. In a
few days I should have to go back to Eirene. I had almost finished
my job up at Gikumo. Should I tell Percy Berkeley before I went?
He wouldn't begin to understand what I was talking about. Duthwaite? He would understand all right, but would scarcely be very
sympathetic towards Alastair and would likely enough be actively
hostile. Matthew Sach? What was it to do with him? And in any
event I had more or less undertaken not to interfere. But there was
one possible way. Colonel Nicholas would both listen and understand. If I told him, not what I knew, but enough to make him see
danger, then I had little doubt he would just quietly arrange for
Harley to be brought back to Eirene and reinstated in the Corps of
Drums. They could say a lot of trumpeters had fallen sick, that
Harley's posting to 'D' Company had in any case been only tem-

porary – they could say what they liked, but Colonel Sanvoisin would think of something convincing, Giles Bancombe would accept the Colonel's judgement, and Alastair would hardly be able to object. Nor, if the thing was worked with the Colonel's customary finesse, would Alastair necessarily suspect my interference.

And so I decided to let the matter take its own way until in the normal course of events, I was called back to Eirene. Then I would tell Sanvoisin – just enough to rouse him and yet not enough to convict myself of undue delay or Alastair of dire imprudence. Meanwhile, Alastair could have such happiness as he could get during the next few days and hear no more from me. This settled, I turned to walk back through the evening towards our camp. When I was about fifty yards from the path which led up from the stream to the lowest of the terraces, I came on two men who were washing clothes in the water. They were Simes and Harley. As usual, Harley was just listening, with his quiet smile spread contentedly across his face. Simes was talking vigorously, slapping his clothes about with great energy, twisting and nodding and shrugging.

'So what you want to listen to all that for I can't think,' Simes concluded his harangue.

'It's quite interesting,' said Harley.

'Well if you've got time for your own mates tonight, we're having a bit of a beer-up in the canteen. I took some back credits last pay-day and—'

They saw me coming and both rose to salute.

'Evening, Sir,' said Simes, 'lovely evening.'

'Very nice. I hope the rains keep off.'

'There'll be some soon,' said Harley, 'at least if it's the same here as at home.'

'How would you know?' said Simes.

'I was brought up in the country. You can often tell.'

'Will it be soon?' I asked.

'Day or two, Sir. Not much then, I dare say. But some. In a day or two.'

'I hope those wogs keep off,' said Simes, 'never mind the rain. Or would you be knowing about them too?' he said to Harley.

'Not about them. But Mr Lynch says it may be months or years before they come.'

'I hope he's right,' I said.

'What would you say then, Sir?'

'I think that perhaps Mr Lynch is a little optimistic.'

'You think there'll be trouble then?' said Simes.

'Yes.'

'Trouble?' said Harley.

'Trouble. Good night to you both.'

'Good night, Sir.'

'Now what do you think about that, young Harley?' I heard Simes saying as I left them.

What do you think about anything, young Harley, I thought. What do you think about Mr Lynch? Or the brimstone over Sodom? Or the wogs that think God meant them to be as independent as you and Simes? If you could think at all, young Harley, I thought, you would probably agree with your lover; Cassandra, he says, was a public nuisance and deservedly unpopular. He's fond of saying that. Or quoting from Shakespeare. Let me have men about me that are fat. Men that sleep of nights. Men that go to plays like Anthony and not like Peterson or Duthwaite, who are too mean or too poor to go to anything. But Mr Lynch has made an exception in your case, young Harley. You may be sleek but you're not fat. And it doesn't look as if you are going to be encouraged to sleep of nights. I only hope you don't get pouches under those beautiful, stupid, country blue eyes.

Then I went slowly up the hill to our mess.

PART TWO
JOURNEY TO THE HILLS

CHAPTER SEVEN

Two DAYS LATER, Colonel Sanvoisin sent up a note with the rations to say that Sinclair and himself would visit 'D' Company the following day to see the completed camp, and that he would be grateful if Percy would give them luncheon. This note was a pleasing civility, as we had wireless communications between Gikumo and Eirene and used to report to Battalion H.Q. twice a day over the air to receive instructions. Most C.O.s would just have sent a brief and casual wireless message – 'Expect Sunray and Sunray Minor at 1000 hours tomorrow. Provide lunch'. But it was Sanvoisin's custom to make even a routine duty visit appear as much like a purely social occasion as possible. By so doing, he hoped to find people at their ease when he arrived, ready to answer sensible questions in a sensible manner, not tensed up and red-eyed after a night spent making themselves and their camp artificially and uselessly spotless. Even so, Duthwaite had his own ideas about the appearances which should be maintained for a visiting C.O., and went off with a purposeful look. C.S.M. Mole, I thought, was going to have a busy day. Percy occupied himself with the details of the luncheon.

'I think we might have a curry lunch,' he announced. Colonel Nicholas used to enjoy them in India, and the man at the general store here makes quite a good curry paste. Or so Matthew Sach says. Yes, a curry lunch with *lots* of gin first.'

When Sanvoisin and Sinclair arrived the next day, they first inspected the camp, which they found very pleasing save for Sinclair's contention that the latrines should have been dug deeper.

'Dysentery,' he said. 'If the latrines are thirty feet deep, then the flies don't get down to bring out the germs. But these can't be more than fifteen.'

Percy quoted Matthew Sach's opinion that fifteen feet were sufficient in the relatively cool climate of Gikumo.

'He ought to know, James,' said Percy. 'He's lived in the uplands ten years.'

'Uplands or no uplands,' said Sinclair, 'we're in the tropics. Army medical regulations say that in the tropics earth latrines will be at least thirty feet deep. These regulations do not recommend or authorise Colonial servants as experts in the matter.'

But Sanvoisin was plainly uninterested, and it was too nice a day for even Sinclair to be cross-tempered for long. After a time, he went off with Duthwaite to look at the stores and the men's canteen, while I took Sanvoisin to a little 'intelligence tent' I had to discuss the results of my explorations. Percy hurried away to supervise the preparation of his curry lunch. A great mid-morning peace enveloped the camp. This was the hour at which cricket matches began in England or travellers settled in the Piazza San Marco to wait for the midday gun.

At first, when I had heard of the impending visit, I had thought of telling Sanvoisin straight away what I meant to let him know about Alastair. But then I had decided against this. I had, after all, settled with myself to allow Alastair such time as there would be before the normal course of events should bring me back to Eirene. This could not be long; and nothing had happened in the last two or three days that made it imperative for me to advance the date of my revelation. Quite apart from my unwillingness to disturb what Alastair conceived as his happiness, I was not at all looking forward to telling Sanvoisin what I meant to tell him; it would be a difficult as well as a dishonest interview, for the matter was delicate and Sanvoisin was only to hear a very abridged version of the truth. Time enough for that, I thought, when I get back to Eirene and can collect my wits in peace at a suitable distance away from the whole affair. And so, with relief, I put Alastair out of my mind that morning and settled down to explain my opinions of the Battalion frontage.

At the end of what I had to say, I told Sanvoisin of the views advanced by Matthew Sach.

'He is a thoughtful and experienced man, Colonel. He is also witty and charming. You would like him.'

'Shall I meet him at luncheon?'

'Unfortunately not. He was invited when we heard you were coming, but he has to spend the day up on the escarpments seeing some of his agents.'

'And he thinks that we ought to keep standing guards at all farms?'

'He does. He also feels very strongly that large detachments should be sent into the mountains.'

'I've had much talk with Peterson about that. As you know, he really feels the same. As you also know, generals do not become field marshals by disregarding the Government's wishes. In any case, if we *do* place guards at all the farms, we simply shall not have the men to send into the hills.'

'So you think Matthew is right about the farms?'

'Very likely,' said Sanvoisin, 'though you should remember that there are a lot of them, and that if we adopt his advice, we shan't even be able to continue our present system of patrols at all adequately. We should thus be more static than ever ... What I'm going to do is this. I shall think it all over very seriously during the next week – and if you can get your man Sach to come down to Eirene and talk to me, so much the better. After another five days, I want you yourself to come down, and we'll go over what I have decided together – so that you can check me if I've got my geography wrong. I'm then going to have all company commanders back to Eirene for the day, hold a slap-up conference and briefing in the light of what we all now know about the country, and give them a massive dinner to cheer them up. They can return the next morning. They've all settled in now – though not all so comfortably as you have here – and it's high time to get a fresh overall plan of action going.'

'But surely, Colonel, this "overall plan of action" is unlikely to be very different from what is happening now? It's possible that you may decide to keep a lot of men on static patrols at the farms rather than mobile throughout the area; but otherwise ...'

'There is one more element in this, Andrew. As I say, Peterson is still adamant about not sending large bodies of troops into the mountains. But every three months or so it is the custom to send mounted patrols of the Pepromene police on short tours through the foot-hills – to remind the mountain people that there is such a thing as a Government in Eirene, and that it does possess a police force, however unpoliceman-like. Now, Peterson and the Governor General have more or less agreed that there would be little harm in substituting military patrols for these police ones every now and again. No one can say it's aggressive action; merely a convenient way of performing a routine and traditional duty. The patrols would have to be very small and, like the police, confine themselves strictly to touring the foothills and bivouacking for a few nights at certain important villages – where the patrol commander will have to carry out certain prescribed courtesies towards the Headman and the village elders. But this would be something; it would give people an idea of the mountain country and we might pick up odd bits of information.'

'It would certainly be something. How soon will they finally reach an agreement?'

'Any time. Certainly before my grand conference next week ... And now we must go and eat Percy's curry lunch.'

This was a great success. Percy had made pints of some long gin drink, and reminded us that as water was the only civilised drink with curry we must drink as much gin as possible before eating. The lunch itself was an exquisite affair. Rice fried and plain; curried prawns, curried beef, curried chicken, curried vegetables; three kinds of chutney, nuts, raisins, shredded onions and tomatoes, red peppers, green chillis, bananas, nutmeg, apples, chapatis, poppadoms and stuffed parathas. Even Sinclair was impressed by the kindness and ingenuity that had gone to raise all these ingredients in such an out of the way place. The only thing I suspected was the prawns. These had come from some tins procured in the general store; and while the smell of the curry obscured any tell-tale odour they might have had, they looked curiously undesirable, disagreeably pallid against the rich red juice in which they lay.

'I think,' said Alastair, 'that we would all be wise to avoid the prawns.'

'Nonsense,' said Percy. 'That's what curry and indeed all sauces are for – to disguise the fact that things are going off, *if* they're going off. Hence the magnificent sauces of the *haute cuisine* – all designed to camouflage the fish, which in an age of no refrigeration stank to heaven even at Versailles. And curry is the best of the lot, in a way, because it's also a disinfectant. It opens up the bowels and swooshes out anything which might damage the stomach. I shall eat *lots* of prawns.'

As indeed he did; but the rest of us were cautious.

So lunch proceeded in a haze of good humour and curry sweat. Sanvoisin had something to say of the Governor General's reception; for as this had occurred on the eve of our departure for Gikumo, none of us had seen him since.

'It was quite ghoulish,' he remarked. 'To start with, the refreshments : I expected to be offered champagne, which I should then have politely declined and asked, like the man in the advertisement, for White Horse Whisky. But no. There was South African "hock" of infinite acidity, or South African "Red Burgundy" which made you feel as though your mouth was full of gravel. And the food! Pompous silver salvers of indescribable design with enormous but at the same time wizened pieces of toast, and for each acre of toast a blob of imitation caviar or a tiny shrimp, even more malignant than these suspicious prawns of Percy's.'

'Nothing suspicious about them,' Percy said : 'they're scrumptious.'

'But it was the company which finished me off,' Sanvoisin continued. 'The Governor General, as you may know, is an Oxford Buchmanite – not at all scrumptious; serious, condescending, smarmy, looking as if he pitied you with all his soul for your unregenerate condition and would indeed invite you to "confide" your sins to him there and then – were it not for his fear that these would kill his wife. *She* is a female Oxford Buchmanite, who looks as if she were normally confined to a hen run and only let out, once in a way, to help with the entertaining; she has that flustered, pecking, egg-laying look. But then of course I only had to spend a moment or two with them, so off I went to look for someone amusing. There was a district commissioner whom I remembered from my time at Trinity, a great oarsman and a thoroughly dull dog, but surely, I thought, a suitable guide for the occasion. "Come on, Jeremy," I said, "find me somebody interesting to talk to." He didn't look very confident, but finally found someone whom he said was to do with oil and was called Lyle.

' "Colonel Sanvoisin commands Martock's Foot," my Cambridge chum explained.

' "Oh, a *soldier*," said this man Lyle.

'And do you know, not another word would he say. I spoke of everything, I even mentioned oil, and indeed at that he bowed his head as if I had paid him a personal compliment, but still not another word. So then Jeremy introduced me to one of the local wives. So indelicate.'

'Not mindful of her marriage vows?' said Alastair.

'A positive Clytemnestra. Before I knew what was happening she'd rammed her pudgy knee between my thighs and almost into my crutch.

' "I always wish my husband had stayed in the Army after the war," she said.

' "What does he do now?" I asked.

' "Drinks,' she said, "and ignores me completely."

'I really stood fair to be suffocated by the cloud of lust she was emitting. But at the moment Peterson appeared – tight trousers, spurs, the lot – and I saw he was heading straight for me, no doubt to rebuke me on account of my dinner jacket. So I made a little plan.

' "I was – er – damaged in the war, Madame," I said, "but I can assure you that General Peterson over there is known throughout the Army for his ... gallantry. He has a boring wife, and was only telling me the other day that he hopes to find consolation in this hospitable country. I'm afraid he is a lonely man."

'At this she leapt forward like a lion at feeding time, grabbed Peterson – whose appalling wife was dragging along behind him – and with a great shout of, "General, they say you're lonely", carried him off, spurs and all, straight through the doors into the garden. His feet hardly touched the ground. His wife's mouth fell open and stayed open, like the entrance to the Tunnel of Love, for about ten minutes.

' "An eccentric woman, that, Lady Peterson," I said, "but I don't expect she'll eat your husband. Mangle him a bit, perhaps, but not eat him." This was silly of me because she has a good deal less humour than Peterson has. However, I then did my best to be charming, talked to her about Ascot last summer and the Royal Garden Party and how it was no longer compulsory to wear a dinner jacket at the "Four Hundred"; but her mouth was still wide open, and she clearly thought of me as a frivolous character who probably had something to do with the abduction of her husband, so eventually I slipped guiltily away. Just as I went out into the hall, I saw Peterson come back in alone from the garden. He looked ashen – though whether with rage or fear or desire or *tristitia*, it was impossible to say. I wish I could find out what happened in the garden. I fear we shall never know. But at least I got away unrebuked for my black tie.'

By this time lunch had finished and we were drinking coffee. Suddenly I noticed that it was much darker. Sinclair had noticed this too.

'Rain on the way, Colonel,' he said. 'We'd better be off. That track to Nike will turn to mud in no time.'

We all went to the gate of the camp where Sanvoisin's Land Rover was waiting. Percy was looking most peculiar. He was sweating as though he were still eating curry and his face was aquarium green. He was walking very unsteadily. This was not as obvious as it might have been, for by now mad purple clouds were over the whole sky and we were walking in a deep twilight. Sanvoisin either did not notice or affected not to notice Percy's condition.

'Good-bye,' he said, 'and many thanks. I'll see you in about a week at my conference, Percy. And remember, whatever happened to Peterson in the garden, he is undeniably still alive and may well pay you a visit without warning. So be prepared . . . And if he does come, don't poison him with tinned prawns.'

Sanvoisin and Sinclair drove off. We all saluted and the sentry on the gate presented arms. For a while we stood watching the Land Rover grinding away down the track. But it was now almost pitch-dark. One spot of rain. Two spots. Percy's cheeks bulged and receded.

'I don't feel at all well,' he muttered, and vomited copiously, clasping his stomach, retching and moaning.

A spatter of rain, a forked flash like the veins of a leaf and an explosion of noise like God in agony. Streams of vomit from Percy. Rain pouring solidly from the sky – and then Matthew, wrapped in an enormous mackintosh cape, his face distorted, appearing from nowhere and leaping off his horse.

'It's started,' he yelled, 'it's started.'

Percy was doubled up with pain and effort, and all round him were piles of white vomit flecked with red.

'Don't you understand?' Matthew screamed through the rain. 'It's started. They're coming down from the mountains. Karioukeya is coming out to war.'

From that moment Duthwaite had taken charge. Four of the guard had carried Percy to his tent. Matthew had sought shelter in the mess. The rest of us had been told to go and change – 'No point in having pneumonia about as well as a case of over-eating' – and report down to Duthwaite in the mess as soon as possible – except for Robin, who was to go to Percy's tent and keep an eye on him. When Alastair, Michael and I came down to the mess again, Duthwaite and Matthew were already examining a small map. Matthew was by now considerably calmer; and as soon as he began to explain what was happening, it was clear that though the situation was materially changed, it had not yet assumed the dramatic significance implied by his words at the gate.

The map showed the escarpment at the bottom left-hand corner and beyond it, to the north-east, the large area of scrub or veldt that lay between the escarpment and the Mountains of Dis. At the top right hand, about a third of the map was occupied by the foothills and then the beginning of the mountains proper.

'You will notice,' said Matthew, 'that between the foot-hills and the mountains are marked two villages, Glukeia and Likanga. There is a rough track between them. There is also a rough track which runs north-east from Glukeia and enters the mountains proper through a narrow valley. About fifteen miles from Glukeia this track peters out in a mountain re-entrant. But just before this it passes within a mile of the village of Tokoroa – which is set on the very lowest slopes of the massive mountain at the extreme top right hand of the map.

'As you know, I have today been up on the escarpment talking to some of my agents. They are all absolutely agreed that for the last twenty-four hours one "battalion" of Karioukeya's "brigade" has been working its way down from the centre of the mountains, accompanied by Karioukeya himself, and that last night this "battalion" arrived and encamped just to the north of Tokoroa, in the re-entrant where the track fades away. I suppose it will only be a matter of hours before the Army gets similar information through its own intelligence channels.'

He seemed, however, none too sure of this.

'Colonel Sanvoisin has just left, you say?' he said to Duthwaite. 'What time can you next get in touch with Eirene by wireless?'

'Eighteen hundred hours,' said Duthwaite, 'six o'clock.'

'Which gives you two and a half hours to debate the situation before reporting it,' said Matthew, 'but I should be grateful if you would let me make a point or two first from local knowledge . . . Firstly then, Karioukeya's men have hitherto been tucked away in the far reaches of the mountains, anything up to 150 miles from here. The "battalion" which has now arrived at Tokora is only forty miles away – that is to say within easy striking distance of the farmlands. Again, the probability is that this "battalion" is very heavily armed, having been provided with some of the weapons normally used by the rest of the "brigade", which as far as we know is still in the remote mountains. Add to this the fact that Karioukeya himself is with this "battalion", and you will agree that it all looks rather high-powered.'

We all nodded rather stupidly. Matthew continued.

'A little geography for your benefit. Tokoroa, Likanga and Glukeia make three corners of an almost equilateral triangle. But in the centre of this triangle, and stretching out across the side formed by the line between Likanga and Tokoroa, is a large and very steep mountain called Sideros. On the other side, the even larger mountain to the east of Tokoroa and Glukeia, which is called Chalchos, is nearly as steep. Thus for all practical purposes, and despite the skill and hardiness of the mountain men, if the "battalion" wants to get out through the foothills and on to the veldt, it must *either* come down the valley from Tokoroa to Glukeia, *or* go due west to Tokoroa, to the north of Mount Sideros, and down through the foothills by way of Likanga. You might think, then, that the only two exits available to Karioukeya are reasonably easy to guard. However, you must remember that the lower slopes of both Sideros and Chalchos are very heavily wooded. Steep though these mountains are, the lowest slopes of Chalchos at least would offer a possible route. As you can see from the map, instead of going straight down the track to Glukeia, he could simply pursue a parallel route, *under heavy cover*, along the Chalchos side of the valley and come down into the foothills some miles east of Glukeia – by which time he would be only twenty-five miles from where we are now.'

'But whatever else,' I said, 'he'll never be able to bring a substantial force across the open veldt without being spotted.'

'Not at night? There is a lot of the veldt, you know. And perhaps with heavy rain to help him?'

'How long will the rain last?'

'Not long at this strength. But I think myself that it will drag on at intervals for some days. When the winter rains are spread out, as they look like being this year, the first instalment is not generally very heavy but often persists for ten days or more.'

'How right Percy was to get the huts finished,' remarked Alastair. Then Robin came in.

'I'm worried about Percy,' he said. 'He went on being sick for a long time. He's stopped now, because I don't suppose there's anything left to bring up, but he keeps retching and straining and bringing out little bits of . . . well, little bits of his stomach, if you ask me.'

Once again Duthwaite was prompt and precise.

'Get hold of the medical orderly,' he told Robin, 'and tell him to give Percy a standard injection of morphia. He'll know how to do that. Then send one of the batmen for Dr Llewyllyn at the mission. Tell him to saddle up carefully and look sharp about getting there.'

'This looks like more than gin and over-eating,' said Michael as Robin went out.

'The prawns,' said Alastair.

'He'll be all right,' said Duthwaite curtly. 'We'll get him fixed up comfortably somewhere when this rain stops. Meanwhile we'd better concentrate on this.' He rapped the map with the back of his hand.

For a clear minute no one spoke, and the rain dripped steadily through a leak in the roof as though it were some kind of water clock.

'If I understand you,' said Michael to Matthew Sach, 'you think the best course, not easy but the easiest, is to block the two exits from the mountains in the areas of Likanga and Glukeia.'

'I haven't said so yet, but I think the *best* course is to march two battalions straight up to Tokoroa and settle the matter,' said Mathew.

'It'll take days to get two battalions together in this rain,' said Alastair, 'even if they allow such "aggressive" procedure merely on the strength of what your informants say.'

'But meanwhile we *could* bottle him up at Tokoroa,' I said, '*if* we could find, say a company to guard each exit.'

'That's what I'm going to suggest on the wireless this evening,' said Duthwaite, 'that this company takes Glukeia and our nearest neighbour to the north takes Likanga. But a lot depends on what military intelligence has had to say to the General and how urgent he judges the situation to be. With London policy what it is, and everyone remembering the row there was about Kenya, he'll be far from anxious to commit himself.'

'Policy, policy,' said Matthew. 'There's 500 men armed to the teeth and only forty miles away. And all anyone can think about is policy.'

'It's nothing to do with any of us,' I said, 'as you very well know ... But there's more ground for hope than you think.' And I went on to tell them about the scheme, outlined to me by Sanvoisin that morning, for substituting small military patrols for the normal police patrols in the foothills.

'Small military patrols will be a fine help,' said Matthew.

'But if they've already got that far, perhaps now they may see their way to something more formidable.'

'We'll see,' said Duthwaite.

And indeed we did see. At six o'clock, Duthwaite got on to Eirene by wireless and asked to speak to Sanvoisin personally. He then told him briefly what had happened, and emphasised that in his opinion at least two companies would be needed to contain Karioukeya's 'battalion' until such times as an attack in force, for which at least two battalions would be required, could be mounted. He also explained that Percy was *hors de combat*. Sanvoisin replied that he would have to get the General's permission before he could send a single man into the foothills. He would go and see the General immediately, he said. Meanwhile, he would arrange for the signals' office at Battalion H.Q. to remain permanently open in case Duthwaite received further information, and Duthwaite, for his part, was to see that the 'D' Company set was kept open ready to receive Sanvoisin's further instructions, which he would transmit personally as soon as he had seen the General.

While we were waiting for this to happen, Dr Llewyllyn arrived to examine Percy. It seemed that Percy had acute food poisoning but would certainly be all right. 'He hasn't got a dying face,' Llewyllyn said. The best thing would be to move him out of his tent to the spare room in Matthew's bungalow. As soon as the weather and the track were suitable, Llewyllyn would send up a large and comfortable car to carry Percy in state to the Mission.

'He'll need attention. But at the moment I can hardly get my Land Rover up the track at all – leave alone with Falstaff's twin brother inside it.'

Sanvoisin finally came through at about nine in the evening. We waited in the mess to hear the outcome of his conversation with Duthwaite. Matthew had stayed to dinner and was drinking liberal glasses of brandy. So was Alastair. Michael and Robin were quietly reading. When Duthwaite came up from the wireless set, he looked calm, but rather strained.

'I'm sorry to say,' he said, 'that military intelligence does not really confirm Matthew's information. The Colonel pointed out at G.H.Q. that the District Officer's net was likely to be a good deal more reliable, but apparently the General was unwilling to accept this. According to military sources, there are only vague reports of "a small band" being in the vicinity of Tokoroa, and this, they say, is probably nothing more than a hunting party from one of the inner mountain districts.'

'They all hunt their own country,' said Matthew. 'No hunting party from an inner mountain district or anywhere else would come down to Tokoroa. Their laws and customs are far too strict.'

'As it happens, I entirely agree with you,' said Duthwaite. 'I'm on your side, Matthew. But this matter rests with the General. That's the information he has, and he's sticking by it.

'Nevertheless, as a result of our representations and the Colonel's, General Peterson has agreed on two things. Firstly, he has agreed that two companies of this Battalion, though they must not leave their present positions, should be placed under warning to be ready to mount an immediate attack on or near Tokoroa. Secondly—'

'*Two companies* for the actual attack?' said Matthew. 'And not yet to move?'

'I've already said I'm on your side, Matthew. Now kindly allow me to address my officers without interruption. Yes. Where you and I would send in two battalions straight away, G.H.Q. is only prepared to authorise the *static* preparation of two companies. And where we wanted to employ two companies, as guards on the exits from the mountains, the General is only prepared to concede that we send two troops – one to the area round Glukeia, the other to Likanga. He has emphasised that he is only doing this because they can appear there as though in lieu of police patrols. (You will remember what Andrew told us this afternoon about that.) Their job will be to bivouac at points I will show you in a moment, to liaise in friendly fashion with the villagers, and to keep their eyes open. If they spot anything big, then they will communicate with me here by means of the short range wireless sets they will take. I shall then be able to get on to the Colonel in Eirene, where the wireless will now be on twenty-four hour watch, and he will ask the General's permission to send in the two alerted companies.

'Now the two troops I am going to send are Alastair's and Robin's. Robin will go to Likanga and camp at the foot of the hill just to the west. You, Alastair, will go about five miles beyond Glukeia, though you must still pay daily visits to the Headman, and camp on the bottom slope of Mount Chalchos at the point where the valley is thinnest. You will thus be overlooking Karioukeya's route out through the valley proper and also sitting somewhere near the covered route which Matthew thinks he might adopt. You should put out of your head any idea of delaying him if he starts to move; but you are in a good position, with a little luck, to spot him if he does move and give us the word here. Any questions about the general side of all this?'

'Yes,' said Alastair. 'It should be easily possible from where I shall be for me to take a couple of men up to Tokoroa and confirm the truth of Matthew's report. That might speed things up?'

'I'm afraid the C.O. was emphatic about that. In no case, the General said, were either of you to move forward of your positions. Such movement, even if it only involved two or three men, might well be considered as "aggressive" activity and certainly runs counter to your nominal role – which is that of substitute for a routine police patrol. Tokoroa is way outside the police beat, which only extends to the foothills. As it is, I'm putting you further forward than you should be.'

Matthew shrugged his shoulders and poured himself more brandy.

'These camps of ours,' said Robin, 'would it be wise to consider them as possible defensive positions?'

'That is difficult. You must not fortify your camps openly, or this again will be construed as evidence of "aggressive intent". In any case, should things really start moving, it is your duty to report over the wireless and beat it back here quickly. You are not to attempt futile delaying actions – you have not the men. But I should not disguise from you both,' said Duthwaite evenly, 'that there must be quite a possibility of Karioukeya making a direct attack on you or Alastair, either to give his men an appetiser or in the hope that he can prevent you reporting further on his movements. In that case, if he is as competent as they say, you may not find it very easy to get away. So my advice to you both is to site your positions carefully with a view to all round defence, and then to dig the appropriate trenches at night and keep them covered by day . . . You will thus be prepared without giving offence,' he added grimly.

Michael opened his mouth to speak.

'Just one more thing,' said Duthwaite quickly. 'I realise that you may find these instructions confusing and frustrating. You have my sympathy. But please do as I ask. Remember, above all, that you are there to observe – not to make reconnaissances or to fight, but to observe. Yes, Michael?'

'I was merely thinking that as I am senior to Robin it might be my place to take one of these gay little expeditions.'

'It is because of your experience that I am keeping you here. The future might hold something even, as you would say, gayer . . .

'And now, the administrative details . . .'

And so it was settled. Somewhere away in the rainy night, two companies were warned to consider themselves permanently at an hour's notice to proceed to Tokoroa – should the word ever be given. Michael and his Troop were to stay at Gikumo, guard and administer the Company camp, and await what might come. Matthew was to help as much as possible with information and advice – though he plainly considered the whole situation farcical. And Robin and Alastair were to leave next day at dawn with small-scale tentage, short-range wireless sets and a week's rations, to watch over the routes that might bring Karioukeya from the Mountains of Dis.

CHAPTER EIGHT

DURING THE NEXT few days, everything calmed down again. Robin and Alastair reported over their wirelesses that they had settled in quite comfortably despite continuous but no longer very heavy rain. They had seen no signs of activity, and had both been well received by the respective Headmen of Likanga and Glukeia, who had in each case assured them that they knew nothing of Karioukeya beyond the common rumour that he was still established with his 'brigade' a hundred miles away in the central mountains . . . On one of the brighter days, the track dried sufficiently for Dr Llewyllyn to send a car up for Percy, who was now down at the Mission five miles from Nike and would be sent from there to Eirene when he was fit to move that far. I myself was told to stay at Gikumo until further notice, as any information, whether from Robin, Alastair or Matthew Sach, would be more immediately available there than elsewhere. Colonel Nicholas cancelled his conference : we were now committed to a definite if static course of action, and there seemed no point in making new plans just yet. Robin and Alastair continued to report a quiet life incommoded only by incessant rain – far worse, it seemed, than what we were having at Gikumo, though that was dispiriting enough. Matthew came daily to confer with Duthwaite, who was now Company Commander in name as well as in practice, and with myself. I missed my long rides with him but thanked heaven I had completed my explorations before the rains had come. It was a damp, dreary and disconsolate time, which Duthwaite spent in routine administrative work and Michael and I in endless hands of piquet.

On the fifth day after Robin and Alastair had left, Matthew appeared in the afternoon for the usual daily discussion.

'No less than four of my most reliable men have been in Gikumo this morning,' he told us. 'They all confirm, yet again, that at least 500 of Karioukeya's men are encamped near Tokoroa, that Karioukeya is with them, and that every man is armed. Mercifully they seem to have nothing in the way of mortars, but as far as rifles and brens go, they are armed exactly as your own Battalion . . . But I don't suppose *my* information will carry any weight at G.H.Q.'

'The Colonel was on to me this morning,' said Duthwaite. 'As far as military intelligence is concerned, the situation is the same as it was five days ago. Though they are prepared to concede that there may be several hunting parties about and not just one. Our orders are to stay put and continue as at present.'

'The trouble is,' said Matthew, 'that your intelligence people don't know how to pick good agents. How should they? They don't know about this country and they're not bursting to take advice. It's quite clear to me that their men are either just inefficient, or, more probably, in Karioukeya's pay as well as the British Army's. They'll go on plugging this hunting party tale till the last possible moment.'

'Robin and Alastair have reported nothing very dramatic,' I said.

'Of course not. You don't suppose Karioukeya is going to stage a march past with band for their benefit. Alastair's the nearest to Tokoroa, and he's a good ten miles away. Added to which he has strict instructions not to move an inch except to go and play the *bara sahib* in Glukeia. There's a lot of room in the mountains. Of course they've seen nothing.'

'Anyhow, I'll go and report what you say to Battalion H.Q.,' said Duthwaite, 'but I shall be surprised if it makes any difference.'

He went off to the wireless.

'You know,' said Matthew, 'leaving aside any question of whether this whole business is being conducted properly or not, I'm worried about Robin and Alastair.'

'Alastair's adult and Robin must learn.'

'Quite. And at the moment they're undergoing nothing except discomfort, which will be exceedingly good for Alastair. But do you remember what Duthwaite said about the possibility of Karioukeya attacking them?'

'Yes. But surely that would be merely futile. If Karioukeya attacks one of their troops, the alarm will be given, sooner or later the whole Division will be at his throat, and all for an attack on thirty-odd men. Surely, if Karioukeya is prepared for open hostilities, the best way of sending the balloon up is by a full-scale and really significant action – five or six simultaneous raids on the farmlands, perhaps. Not just a piddling affair against a troop in bivouac.'

'If Karioukeya attacks undefended farms, he will forfeit a lot of sympathy in certain quarters. But supposing he were to provoke an action with Alastair? Here is a troop of fully-armed soldiers in mountain territory : what are they doing there?'

'Substituting for the police.'

'Tell that to the United Nations. No. Suppose he attacked Alastair and wiped him out. Think of what he could say. "We were alarmed," he could say, *urbi et orbi*, "by the appearance of an armed military patrol. Usually these are police patrols, usually they bivouac in Glukeia – not five miles up the valley. So I headed a deputation to wait upon the patrol commander and ask him his intentions. But when we got near the camp, the patrol commander lost his head and fired on us. My men love peace, but they are mountain men and also love their liberty. I could not restrain them, and now they have destroyed the patrol. For this I am sorry. But what was this armed patrol doing in the unspoiled mountains of my peace-loving tribes?" And then up goes the usual screech: "Armed aggression provokes tribes. Government blunders again." And then where are you? Alastair and his Troop all dead. Karioukeya triumphant and vindicated, teetotallers and humanitarians and anti-colonialists pouring into Pepromene to interfere . . . The works. The old story.'

'But you yourself favour a policy towards Karioukeya that would create ten times as much fuss.'

'Possibly. But at least the whole thing would have been cleared up. Karioukeya's men wiped out or dispersed. Karioukeya himself dead – we'd need to be jolly sure of that. And then it's for us to say our piece. "Armed aggression provokes peace-loving colonists. Unwilling but successful security action." The great thing is to be the only person to survive to do the talking.'

Duthwaite came back and flung his sodden mackintosh into a corner.

'The C.O. says he'll see the General,' he said, 'but he doesn't think it will help.'

'Cint major,' said Michael, 'a terze to a queen, and a quattorze of aces.'

We played the tricks and I lost all but two.

Michael added up the points.

'That's forty-seven pounds you owe me for the week,' he said.

I wrote him out a cheque. The cheque book was damp and the ink spread.

'If they don't pass it,' I said, 'there'll be plenty of time for my cheque book to dry out and for you to have another one before we get back to England.'

'Don't worry,' said Michael. 'I haven't been so rich for years. That's one thing about living in places like this . . . Poor Alastair, now, has no one to play piquet with. Unless he teaches Royd . . . Still, he's got his chum Harley to talk to.'

'Yes. I expect they'll be seeing a lot of each other in Glukeia.'

Duthwaite came in and shook the water off his cap.

'No change,' he said. 'The General says that his sources are quite firm about their "hunting parties". We've to carry on as at present.'

'Thank God Percy saw to it there was plenty of burgundy here,' Michael said.

Matthew came in.

'Come and have dinner with me tonight. You all need a change of food and air.'

'Thank you very much,' said Michael, 'if we can get to your bungalow without being swallowed in a bog.'

C.S.M. Mole came in.

'Rations, Sir,' he said to Duthwaite, 'for Mr Alastair and Mr Robin. They took a week's ration with them. Tomorrow they'll have been gone just that.'

'Pack them up another week's rations,' said Duthwaite. 'Get two dry shirts for each man from the stores, two pairs of socks, one towel and pair of breeches. Spare wireless batteries. All their letters. Chocolate, soap, razor blades, cigarettes.'

'How are we to account to the Q.M. for issuing all that extra clothing from the stores?'

'Exigencies of active service,' said Duthwaite.

C.S.M. Mole came in again.

'Shall I send them up some beer from the canteen?'

'No,' said Duthwaite.

'Who,' said Michael, 'is going to take the ration party up?'

'The C.S.M.,' said Duthwaite. 'It'll give him something to do.'

'It'll give him lumbago. And I could do with something to do myself.'

'I want you here, Michael. The round trip is going to take over twenty-four hours. He'll have to leave tomorrow morning, get to Alastair some time in the afternoon, push on and spend tomorrow night with Robin, and get back here the afternoon of the day after. Anything could happen while that's going on.'

'As you say, Richard. I just hope Moley won't get lumbago.'

C.S.M. Mole came in yet again. This time Duthwaite was out, so he addressed himself to us.

'Everything's ready, gentlemen, if you'll kindly tell Captain Duthwaite. The clothes are a bit damp, but dryer than what they'll have up there, I dare say. And I still think they ought to have a little beer, not but what it'll be a relief not to be bothered with it.'

'I bet he takes some drink up for Royd and Alastair, if nothing more,' said Michael when Mole had gone.

Matthew to dinner again. Situation unchanged. Carry on, you're doing a good job. Everything damp. Percy's burgundy bottles sweating, the corks wet on top, but the wine still mercifully sound. Mole to leave in the morning, hope he doesn't get lumbago, good luck, C.S.M., give Mr Alastair and Mr Robin our ... best wishes? ... love? ... blessings? ... prayers? Give them this at any rate, a bottle of burgundy each. Mr Alastair prefers hock, I know, but he'll need

110

something to keep him warm in the mountains. The Mountains of Dis.

C.S.M. Mole returned punctually, early in the afternoon of the day after he had left. He seemed unharmed by his expedition and though soaked to the skin was quite cheerful. We had him into the Mess to give him some whisky and hear his report.

'Well, they seem all right, gentlemen,' he told us. 'Everything was delivered as you said, Captain Duthwaite, Sir, and I've brought a lot of letters and dirty laundry back with me. I've also brought Corporal Killeen from Mr Alastair's Troop. Says he's got dysentery. Soiling himself with fright, if you ask me, but Mr Alastair was pleased enough to see him go at that.'

'And they've still seen nothing?'

'Nothing at all. Except the villagers. Friendly they are, it seems, and giving them little presents of eggs and chickens and such. Every comfort, you might say, if it wasn't for the rain.'

'What are their positions like?'

'Sound enough, Sir, I should say. Mr Robin's got good fields of fire all round. Mr Alastair's aren't so bright because of the trees. But he's cleared the area for fifty yards all round, or nearly. And they've both dug trenches. It seems all right to me ... Killen will be wanting an interview with you in the morning, Sir.'

'I thought he had dysentery,' said Duthwaite.

'Not so bad that he couldn't ride back here. But we'll send him down with one of the ration trucks to Eirene. They're still getting up the track all right?'

'Just,' I said.

'Well, that's what we'll do with Killen, Sir. Send him down. But he wants to see you first.'

'Nine o'clock in the morning,' said Duthwaite.

At about eleven the next morning, I saw Mole lean out of the stores tent and beckon to me. He took me into a little inner cubicle he had contrived from crates and ammunition boxes, presented me with an enormous cup of tea, and started to talk.

'I'm not one for wanting trouble, Captain Andrew, and neither are you, so we'd better get our heads together. And this is the shape of it.

'When Killeen was marched into Captain Duthwaite this morning, he said that what he had to say was private and confidential. So out I went and turned the clerks out of the outer office, and it was a clear twenty minutes before I was called for to march Killeen out again. Captain Duthwaite looked as cool as ever, but Killeen, he looked mighty pleased with himself. Sort of sneering he was, and mighty pleased.

' "Well now, you with the dysentery," I said. "You get into the ration truck when it goes back to Eirene this evening. But before you go off to sit squirting on the bog all day long," I said, "I want to know what it is that's so confidential that *I* can't hear about it. Because secrets are a bad thing for any company and we don't have them in this." "It stands to reason, Sar' Major," he said, "if it was confidential when I was marched in, it's confidential now I'm out again. But if you really want to know, Sar' Major, I'll tell you this much. I was brought up proper myself, for all my father had no money and not much education, and if I know what's right and what's wrong, then so ought those with advantages. And that's all I'm saying." So then I wished him to the devil, Captain Andrew, and did a little thinking. And do you know what I thought?'

'I've a fair idea,' I said, 'but you tell me.'

'We all know that Mr Alastair's very taken with young Harley. Well, that's as it may be when you've seen as much as I have and I'm saying nothing about right or wrong or golden harps or souls a-burning. But they're all very close together up there in the hills, and what's not noticed so much down here sticks out a sight plainer up there where there's a whole troop living in each other's breeches all day long. And there's another thing. I had a word with Charley Royd up there and he was saying the same as me and more. "Moley," he said, "it's one thing people just having a fancy. But there's Mr Lynch can't hardly bear to have young Harley out of his sight – day or night, Moley," he said. "He's made him bring his trumpet up here and he calls him the Troop Trumpeter – if you ever heard of such a thing – so that he can be in Troop Headquarters. Well now, Moley," said Charley Royd – and you mark this, Captain Andrew – "if we've got to have a troop trumpeter, then there are worse things in the world than that, and it's quite homely having him blow 'Lights Out' and one thing and another. But that's not saying we need our troop trumpeter marching into the Troop Commander's tent in the middle of the night – and not a man in the Troop but can hear it as plain as a twenty-one gun salute in Portsmouth harbour." In fact, Sir, from what Charley says it's not what you might call discreet. Young Simes was going on something shocking, Charley told me, though nobody else seems to mind much – but you can't tell me it's a good thing even then. And then there's this Killeen. He doesn't like Charley and he doesn't like Mr Alastair, and the nub of it is I think that's what he's been seeing Captain Duthwaite about. Making trouble if you ask me. And if I'm right, I mean trouble. Captain Duthwaite's a strict man, and even if he weren't . . . So what do you think, Sir?'

'I entirely agree with you, C.S.M.'

And then I told him what I had planned to do, how I had intended to enlist Sanvoisin's aid when I returned to Eirene – though without giving too much away – and leave the rest to him.

'And not a bad plan at all, Captain Andrew. But now you're staying here. And what's more, it seems as if Captain Duthwaite may be in the know. What'll he do?'

'I don't know,' I said. 'He can't do anything much except refer the whole matter to Lord Nicholas. If he only says as much as I was going to, there's not much harm done. Harley will be moved in the same way as he would have been if I had spoken, and that will be that. But what worries me is that Captain Duthwaite may feel it his duty to tell the Colonel a whole lot more. As you say, he's a strict man. I wonder just how much he heard from Killeen?'

'You can depend on Killeen having done his bit without missing much out.'

'I suppose so . . . There's no point in worrying, C.S.M. I'll do my best to find out what Captain Duthwaite knows and what he intends to do. Meanwhile, we must just hope for the best.'

But as the long, rainy days went on, I was far from cheerful. Every morning, when I awoke, I determined to write to Sanvoisin or even to fake a reason for visiting him in Eirene. In this way, at least something definite would be decided. But writing seemed so shoddy, so feeble an expedient; and again, whenever I considered the genuine importance of what was going on in the hills, I realised how ridiculous it would be for me to turn up in Eirene with some half-baked story about Alastair having formed an attachment that was growing dangerously romantic. Alastair, who was stuck up there in the rain doing a painful and even perilous job . . . Duthwaite's silence was another inhibiting factor. If only he would plainly declare what he knew and what he meant to do, then perhaps my own course would become clear. But not a word did he say. The evening Mole had spoken to me, I had asked Duthwaite as casually as I could what Killen had been to see him about.

'It was a confidential matter,' he said.

And not another word.

Michael, when consulted, advised silence and patience. 'Neither of which can do any harm,' as he remarked. So we played more piquet. Duthwaite did more administering. Matthew came and drank more brandy. C.S.M. Mole hovered about, for ever eyeing me with anxious and knowing looks. Often I joined Matthew in a long night's drinking and retired to my camp bed in the early hours of the morning, sick at the stomach and sick at the heart, restless, fretful and afraid.

We were walking in the Fellows' garden at King's, just as I used to sometimes when I was up there during the war. Alastair and Matthew were with me, and so was C.S.M. Mole. But Mole looked

113

very important, dressed in cassock and bands, with a silk sash and a vast black gown.

They must have made him Provost, I thought. Whatever possessed them to do that? I knew the last election was going to be rather peculiar, but C.S.M. Mole . . .

'We'll go and see the Judas tree, gentlemen,' said Mole. 'It ought to be in blossom now.'

'Yes, the Judas tree,' said Alastair looking at me. 'That will be very appropriate.'

The Judas tree was in full red blossom, and Harley was lying underneath it, naked and showing signs of his pleasure; for two little black girls were bending over him, assiduously kissing his legs.

Alastair sprang forward.

'Don't you lay a finger on them, Mr Alastair,' said Mole; 'those wogs are every bit as good as you are nowadays.'

'We're all equal,' said Matthew : 'hadn't you heard?'

'And here's something to prove it,' said Mole, pointing to the new building behind the garden. 'New building with specially cheap rooms for poor students.'

'Do you live there, Moley?'

'No, I don't, Mr Alastair. I live in the Provost's Lodge, not what you've been used to at all, so don't you go calling me Moley any more. It's bad discipline.'

'All right, Provost Moley. But can we go back to the Judas tree?'

'No, we can't, Mr Alastair. You've seen the last of that.'

'But I'm a guest. Surely . . .'

'Guest or not, there's a surprise coming your way, Mr Alastair.'

'You wouldn't learn, you see,' said Matthew.

We walked on towards the croquet lawn. I looked for the tower of the University Library, but saw instead the twin peaks of Mount Eirene.

'The Fellows gave it me when I was elected Provost,' Mole explained. 'It was either that or a case of cheap burgundy they said.'

'You chose very wisely.'

'But there's some hock for Mr Alastair in the summer house. I only hope they'll give him time to drink it. It spoils very quickly.'

But now the whole garden was full of scarlet-coated figures.

'Typical of Martock's Foot to put on full-dress uniform,' said Matthew.

'This is a very special occasion, Sir,' said Mole.

And indeed it was; for there was a gallows where the summer house should have been and a platform underneath it, and on the platform stood Lieutenant Colonel the Lord Nicholas Sanvoisin, also in scarlet and with a superb ivory-hilted sword.

'Please tell the men to keep off the flowers, my Lord,' said Mole.

'I'm a Trinity man myself, Provost Mole,' said Sanvoisin, 'and

I don't give a *foutre* for your flowers. But it's time for business. Is Mr Lynch here?'

Alastair stepped forward and stood in front of the platform.

'Lieutenant Alastair Lynch,' said Sanvoisin, 'we have gathered together here to pass sentence on you for bringing disgrace on our Regiment. You have seduced and corrupted the boy Malcolm Harley, and even just now, on your way to this assembly, you tried to take from him the natural instruments of his delight. Have you anything to say?'

Alastair passed a thick white bundle of money up on to the platform.

'Fivers?' said Sanvoisin. 'Just as well, as a dead man's cheque is invalid. But though this money will be useful, I am not to be bribed where the honour and welfare of the Regiment are concerned. Your defence must be more eloquent.'

'You would have sent Harley to prison,' cried Alastair, 'but I spoke to save him. Is this not eloquent?'

'You only saved him for the purpose of your own lusts.'

The great scarlet crowd murmured in approbation.

'Will anyone present speak for this degraded wretch?' called Sanvoisin.

Mole stepped forward.

'My Lord, as Provost of this College, a royal foundation and therefore privileged, I forbid you to continue your business on College ground. Mr Alastair has sanctuary here.'

'No good, Provost Mole. I hold the Queen's Warrant to proceed.'

And once again the crowd murmured its assent.

Matthew Sach stepped forward.

'I speak for liberty. You are only sacrificing Lynch because hysterical Labour politicians are asking questions in the House.'

'Not so, Mr Sach. The Army is above politics.'

I stepped forward, but no words would come.

'Then I myself must speak for him,' said Sanvoisin, 'and I speak thus. When I was young we would have provided brothels. These might have distracted Alastair Lynch and would certainly have exhausted Malcolm Harley beyond the point where he could be any man's catamite. But since men like Peterson have reached high positions, and since the general public have had the impertinence to concern themselves with Army affairs, no brothels have been available. Hence such deplorable scandals as this.

'I also say, since this is traditionally a tolerant Regiment, "Judge not that ye be not judged." However, you will recall that this is a maxim which applies only to the upper class, and we may therefore proceed against others if we wish. Bring forward the boy Harley for judgement. There is a different sort of punishment reserved for Alastair Lynch.'

Harley was led forward, still naked. The two little black girls clung to him, but Sergeant Royd was there to prise them off.

'How dare you presume, Drummer Harley, to have sexual relations with an officer? Answer me that.'

'It's like you said, Sir. There were no brothels and Mr Lynch isn't bad looking. And then he was always kind to me and I wanted to be kind to him.'

'You're now going to find out that being kind is no excuse for being socially presumptuous.'

'I meant no harm, Sir. Please let me show them that.'

'You're certainly going to show them something.'

As Harley stepped up on to the platform, the crowd became wild with pleasure and lust. Duthwaite and Sinclair tried to quiet them, but there were great yells of 'Come on, Godiva' and 'Where's your knickers' and 'Sweet eighteen from the Depot.'

A masked man in scarlet came and fastened the noose round Harley's neck. It seemed to me that it was Killeen behind the mask.

'The little bleeder's got all excited again,' said Sergeant Royd, 'and after all that talking Mr Lynch did in front of the Colonel.'

There was complete silence as Sanvoisin stepped down from the platform. Alastair seemed to have disappeared. Sanvoisin nodded and a trap-door opened in the platform and Harley hung there dying while the hangman bowed gracefully to the crowd with his left hand on the hilt of his sabre. They were yelling and cheering again now and each time Harley jerked they cheered more wildly, until the hangman began to take off his mask so that all might know who had hung the boy so skillfully. As his hand went up to unfasten the mask, the clamour of the crowd grew and grew both in stridency and admiration, until he whipped it from his face and stood there revealed as Alastair.

And then one morning, just as Mole was about to set out on yet another trip with rations for Alastair and Robin, the sun came out again. We all walked together, Michael, Matthew, Duthwaite and I, down towards the stream.

'This will be the last of the rain in Gikumo for a week or two,' said Matthew, 'though they may have more rain in the hills.'

It was a warm, grateful evening, with the steam rising, in the strengthening sun, from the wet grass which had grown rank and ugly in the weeks of rain.

'Our stream is getting quite puffed up,' said Michael. 'Do you want to be a river, little stream? There is a story about a frog—'

'Captain Duthwaite,' came a yell from the terrace above, 'Captain Duthwaite, Sir, quick. It's Mr Alastair on the short range set. He's been attacked.'

116

CHAPTER NINE

'HULLO ONE,' SAID Duthwaite, 'Sunray speaking. Over.'

'Hullo one. Sunray here,' came Alastair's distorted and crackling voice. 'Have been attacked by enemy in estimated strength figures one company. Strong light machine-gun fire from several quarters. Over.'

'Hello one. Report ammunition state. Report supplies of food and water. Also numbers so far wounded. Over.'

'One. Figures two men slight flesh wounds. Food and water sufficient for figures two four, twenty-four, hours at normal rates of consumption. Can be made to last indefinitely. Checking ammunition now. Wait. Out.'

'See whether he knows if the main enemy force have gone on past him to the foothills,' I said.

'One,' came Alastair again. 'Ammunition state. Figures one zero, ten, mortar bombs. Figures one five, fifteen, hand-grenades. Figures 1,000 nine-millimetre for use in sub-machine-guns. Figures 20,000 normal rounds for use in rifles and light-machine-guns. Estimate this adequate for figures one zero, ten, hours at present rate of firing. Over.'

'One,' said Duthwaite. 'Hang on. Hang on. S.O.S. going out to greater Sunray. Expect relief within figures eight hours latest. Have you seen rest of enemy force? Over.'

'One. No sign of enemy in open valley. Impossible to tell how enemy deployed or whither proceeding under cover on slopes Mount Chalchos. Myself estimate—'

There was a venomous crack and then silence.

'Hullo one, hullo one,' said Duthwaite. 'How do you hear me? Hullo one, hullo one. Over.'

Silence.

'That's all we shall hear from him,' said Duthwaite coolly. He turned to the signals corporal. 'Get on to Eirene on the large set. Ask for the Colonel. Priority.'

'Heavy rate of firing,' said Michael. '2,000 rounds an hour. He must be in a muddle.'

'Not surprising if he's surrounded,' said Matthew. 'How long will it take to get the two companies under warning there?'

'It was originally calculated as six hours,' I told him, 'but all this mud about the place isn't going to help.'

While waiting for the Colonel to come through, Duthwaite got on to Robin. He had seen nothing. Duthwaite told him to stay where he was, but to be prepared for an immediate move and also to keep a careful watch against attack.

'They'll leave him,' said Matthew. 'They don't like attacking in daylight over open ground. They'd never have attacked Alastair by day if it hadn't been for all that cover on Chalchos.'

The Colonel came through from Eirene. Duthwaite told him what had happened. The Colonel said he would get immediate permission from G.H.Q. for the waiting companies to move. He would alert them now and by the time they were ready to start he would have had the green light from G.H.Q.

'This'll make Peterson's boys sweat,' said Matthew: 'even now they'll probably try to think of some excuse for doing nothing.'

But he was wrong. The General gave immediate permission for the two companies to move. Then, however, a further difficulty arose. Colonel Sanvoisin, having been on to the two waiting companies, came through to us again to say that their one route up on to the escarpment, which was in any case much higher in their area, had been washed away the previous night in the last of the rains. This meant that they would have to come right down south and use our route up. Their journey up to Alastair's position was thus doubled in length and would take twelve or even fourteen hours instead of six. Duthwaite conferred a little longer with Sanvoisin on the wireless and then turned to us.

'Matthew,' he said, 'can you persuade the Inspector to lend me ten or twelve of his policemen?'

'Probably.'

'Hullo five,' said Duthwaite into the microphone. 'Co-operation granted here. Your instructions fully understood. Wilco. Wilco. Out.

'Now this,' he said to us, 'is what we are going to do. We cannot leave Alastair without relief for more than ten hours at the outside. The waiting companies will take at least twelve hours to reach him. Robin hasn't got enough men to go in and help him. So we are going to mount a relief party from here, which will be reinforced by Robin when we get to the foothills. Michael, you and half your Troop will stay and guard the camp here. The rest of your Troop, plus six men from Company H.Q., plus a minimum of ten native policemen will accompany me. Robin will be instructed to join us a mile or two south of Glukeia, and we shall thus have a force of about sixty men to take in to Alastair's assistance. I'm afraid it will take two hours to jack this thing up, so we shall leave at 1400 hours – two o'clock. We should reach Alastair by eight o'clock tonight – all being well. We can hardly expect the relief companies there until midnight earliest. Any questions?'

'Can I come with you?' I said.

'If you wish, Andrew ... Would you like to come, Matthew?'

'Very much. But in fact I thought of taking two of my people and going on quickly to keep an eye on young Robin. As I say, they won't attack him in the open by day. But if he's waiting round for you in the dark near Glukeia . . . All right?'

'I should be most grateful. But please get those policemen for me before you leave. Michael, detail the members of your Troop who are to come with me. Andrew, you can make your own arrangements. Corporal, get on the short range set to Mr Hathaway. And now, Sergeant Major Mole . . .'

And so it was that Duthwaite and I came to be riding to the Mountains of Dis.

The last thing I wanted to do that afternoon, as we rode over the scrub-land towards the hills, was to listen to Duthwaite. His conversation, I thought, would consist either of a precise and careful appraisal of the military situation, of which I knew more than enough already, or else of a string of tiring platitudes about some general subject which he considered suitable and necessary to pass the afternoon. However, he was commanding the party; so that courtesy and military custom alike dictated that I should join him when he beckoned to me from his place at the head of the column.

He looked round to make sure that only native policemen were within hearing, and then began.

'You asked me the other day what Corporal Killeen came to see me about,' he said. 'Perhaps you had some idea already?'

'Perhaps.'

'Well in any case I'm going to tell you now. I've thought a lot about this, Andrew. It's a bad business and it concerns you indirectly and I'm going to tell you. You may be able to help.'

'Well?'

'Killeen came to me to make a report about Alastair Lynch. For a long time, he said, Alastair's been very thick with that young Drummer Harley he would have in this Company.'

'They say Harley's got trouble at home. Alastair's trying to sort it out. He can be very good over that kind of thing.'

'Yes, Killeen mentioned that. He also said that according to Simes, who's one of Harley's friends, Harley's got no trouble at all; that the whole thing was just an excuse . . . But in any case, it's got far beyond that now. It makes no difference what trouble Harley has or hasn't got at home or anywhere else.'

'Oh?'

'No difference at all,' said Duthwaite. 'You see Killeen says – and he's prepared to swear to it – that he's actually seen Alastair and Harley in bed together.'

'When?'

'Up at Glukeia. It seems that Killeen was in charge of the picket one night. He thought he heard something in the forest and went to Alastair's tent to rouse him. He had a torch of course, and he flashed it into Alastair's tent and there they were. Alastair didn't turn a hair, apparently. Just got up, satisfied himself there was nothing to worry about, and went back to his tent – and Harley.'

'Killeen's an unreliable and vicious man,' I said. 'He doesn't like Alastair and he wants Sergeant Royd's job for himself. Alastair has made it disagreeably plain that he's on Royd's side. Killeen's the sort that would swear to anything.'

'I agree with you. I wish Killeen were dead,' said Duthwaite with an unexpected turn of viciousness in his voice, 'but I'm afraid it goes still further. I as good as accused Killeen of deliberate and untruthful malice. I told him he could get many years' imprisonment. He said that he wasn't a fool, that he knew that perfectly well, and that he could corroborate his story. As far as he knew, he said, no one else had actually seen Alastair and Harley together as intimately as he had, but their relationship was common knowledge throughout the Troop. Everyone had heard Harley going to Alastair's tent at night. Some of them had seen him going. Harley, when taxed with this, made no real attempt to deny it. He had said they "just talked", but no one "just talks" all the time between two and five in the morning. Harley's friend Simes, Killeen said, was furious about it, and spoke of Alastair as turning Harley into a "bloody little brownie". Not *absolute* corroboration, perhaps, but I should like to find the jury – or the court martial – which would reject Killeen's statement after hearing the other stuff from the rest of them. *If*, of course, they were to tell what Killeen says they'd tell. But as he says, he's not a fool ...'

'They're all very attached to Alastair. They'd keep quiet if told to.'

'Would they? It doesn't sound to me as if Simes would keep quiet. And I'm not sure that they ought to keep quiet. You've got to remember that these west country boys very rightly treat an oath as a serious matter. If they were sworn in on the Bible and then properly instructed by the president of a court that it was an absolute moral and religious duty to tell the truth, however painful ... But first of all, I've got to know the truth behind all this. What do you yourself know about Alastair and Harley?'

'From what I know, everything Killen says is only too likely to be true.'

And then I told him what I knew. There could be no further advantage in concealment. If anything, the other way about. So I told him about the boxing match, where it had all started, and about Alastair's efforts to enlist Killeen's help after the fiasco on the guard of honour; I reminded him how Alastair had spoken for Harley in front of the Colonel; I told him of the night-out in Eirene, of what Royd had said in the Sergeants' Mess, and of what

Mole had reported when he returned from his ration trip to Glukeia; and finally I told him what Alastair himself had told me before he left for Glukeia, about the growing intimacy, the night by the stream, and Alastair's determination not to let Harley go.

'I see,' said Duthwaite. 'Not a pleasant story. You shouldn't have kept this to yourself, Andrew.'

'Alastair is my friend, Richard. But I was going to try and clear it all up through Colonel Nicholas.'

I told him what I had intended.

'Because of course,' said Duthwaite bitterly, 'you don't trust me.'

'In most ways I trust you implicitly. But I did not expect you to take a very tolerant view of all this.'

'Morally speaking, I don't. I think Alastair's conduct has been wicked and despicable. But did it never occur to you that I have been in this Regiment, as an "other rank" or an officer, far longer than any of you, that I love it and prize it above everything, above my wife and my children and myself, and certainly above any moral opinions I may possess? Could you not conceive that rather than have something like this break into an open scandal, there is nothing, absolutely nothing, I would not have done? Were you so blinded, Andrew, by your affection for Alastair and your contempt for me, that you did not realise that I, if only because I *have* served for so long in the ranks, am quite as qualified as the C.O. to devise some sudden shift, some almost unnoticed piece of cross-posting of the kind needed here? And besides, do you think I wish Alastair harm? He is my comrade if not really my friend. When all is said, he is a promising officer and an able man. The Army needs good officers, this Regiment needs them, and for that reason if for no other I should have tried to see there was no trouble. But where do we stand now? You've kept quiet all this time but Killeen hasn't, and Killeen is safe in Eirene. It's probably only a matter of days before he leaves hospital and goes to tell the Colonel all this. And meanwhile, here we are, going up to relieve Alastair's Troop and *knowing* that every man in it is more or less convinced that Mr Alastair Lynch, the Troop Commander sleeps with Drummer Harley – "the one Mr Lynch was so keen to get into the Company, Sir". Maybe they don't mind and maybe they do. The fact remains: they all *know*. So just what do you think we're to do about it now?'

'I'm sorry, Richard. It was very difficult. And if I'd realised that you . . .'

'Never mind that now,' said Duthwaite gently; 'we're all to blame in one way or another. But Alastair most. Yes, Alastair most. Why in God's name did he have to go on with this thing in a tiny little troop encampment? In Eirene, all right: plenty of room. Even in Gikumo. But up in a Troop bivouac? He must be insane.'

' "The blind god blinds his victims." '

121

' "*Quem deus vult perdere,*" if you ask me. Oh yes, Andrew, I read books too. Not, like Alastair, during parade hours, but in the evening when you're all out, gambling or drinking or seducing private soldiers.'

'I think that's enough, Richard.'

'Yes. My turn to apologise. But you see, I just do not know what ought to be done. For a whole week, since Killeen came to see me, I just have not known which way to turn. As I say, if you'd spoken up before this was common knowledge, I'd have dealt with it straight away and be damned to the morality. But here was a *corporal*, telling me this to my face, telling me that every one of Alastair's thirty men knew all about it; telling me, in fact, that we were already half-way up the road to the open scandal I dreaded. Do you wonder I was at a loss? Mind you, I knew what it would be safest and simplest for me to do – for my own good. What the book said. The book said that if things had reached this stage then I went straight up to Glukeia and arrested Alastair, sent him down to Eirene under escort, forwarded a full report of what I knew, and left the whole thing to the C.O. – to start enquiries or what he pleased. Passed the buck right on. Well done, Duthwaite. Responsible action promptly taken. But well done? Started a blazing scandal, wrecked a good man's career, humiliated a comrade – and all for a mealy-mouthed, self-satisfied runt of a corporal and a messy little drummer-boy with beer running out of his ears. Was this well done, Duthwaite? So you see, Andrew, I was the same as you. I hesitated. Delayed. And now I can't do what the book says, even if I ever wanted to, because by keeping my mouth shut for a week I've condoned Alastair's conduct. My silence has made me an accessory. And I'm glad. Very glad. It won't be me that brings shame on this Regiment, whatever shame I may bring upon myself.'

'But what *are* you going to do? I suppose you still don't know.'

'Oh yes, I do. Now. I don't know what I ought to do, and only God knows that, but I know what I'm going to do. I'm going to get hold of Alastair Lynch and shout and scream at him till I can't bear it another moment. He won't forget it, I promise you. And I'm going to shunt that little bugger Harley right out of this Company and out of this Battalion if I can. I told you I'm good at that sort of thing. A little job for Master Harley at the Ordnance Depot – or on the menial staff of the Detention Camp they've got out here, to give him a good idea where he's heading. Out of sight, out of mind. I shall just pray that Alastair's men forget the whole thing and don't gossip too much. And then I'm going to tell Alastair, calmly this time, that I've cleared this mess up, not for him, but for the Regiment; and that if anything like it ever happens again, I shall know beyond all doubt that he's not fit to wear the honourable uniform he looks so handsome in and I shall then drag him on his knees to the Colonel with my own hands and denounce him there and then without leaving one bloody thing out – even if they cashier me too. So that's what I'm going to do, Andrew. Pick up the shit and swallow it myself.'

'Richard ... But what about Killeen? You say he may talk at any time.'

'Before we left Gikumo this afternoon I wrote a personal letter to Killeen, which will go down to Eirene on the ration truck this evening. It says that if he keeps quiet, then I give him my word that he will be made up to the rank of sergeant within four weeks of today. He'll have to leave this Company, I've said, but I'll see him made up to sergeant, and I'll also see him in a fair way to become a colour sergeant before another eighteen months are out.'

'And if he rejects your offer?'

'He won't reject it. Killeen wants stripes and a comfortable life. But if he does start anything, or if he has already, then I personally will swear that the whole idea of a bribe started with Killeen and that he tried to blackmail me when he came to see me in Gikumo.'

'Did he?'

'No, though there was just the merest hint. But that's what I shall swear. I shall say my letter was the consequence – it's so phrased that it might be. In which case Killeen would go down the line for longer than anybody he informs on.'

'Not a big consolation.'

'It would get the swine out of the way. But don't you worry, Andrew. Killeen will accept my offer. I told you I'd spent a long time in the ranks and I'm right about this kind of thing. He probably expects an offer of this sort. I told you he hinted, and he's intelligent enough to have a little patience. It will have been well rewarded.'

Robin and Matthew were waiting, with Robin's Troop, at the rendezvous two miles south of Glukeia. It was seven o'clock when we reached there and pitch dark. The moon would not rise for another hour, Matthew said. But in any case there was no longer any hurry. Two men had been sent down by Alastair and had stopped Robin on his way through Glukeia to the rendezvous. It seemed that at five o'clock in the afternoon the attack on Alastair's position had just ceased. At first there had been dead silence. Then Alastair had tried to draw fire by showing a dummy. No response. Finally, Alastair and a small party had gone out into the forest. No sign of anything, except for some black corpses, some spent rounds and a lot of cigarette ends where the enemy had been. He had patrolled wider and wider. Still nothing. The men added that the Troop was still standing-by in case of further attack, but Alastair had sent the two of them down to reassure the relieving companies, which they had expected earlier, and to guide them in to the position in the darkness. The password was 'Sweetness', the answer 'Light'.

It was settled that one of the men whom Alastair had sent down should remain in Glukeia, with some of our party for company, and guide the relieving companies up when they finally appeared. The second man Alastair had sent could take the rest of us to him straight away. This man seemed dazed and puzzled and could scarcely be brought to answer the questions we put to him on the way. Yes, it had been a grim business. Very noisy. Firing almost solidly from eleven in the morning until five in the evening. Rushes by the enemy. A wonder they had never got inside the circle of trenches. He fell silent again till prompted by Duthwaite. Yes, Mr Lynch was all right, he supposed. Supposed? Well, he was all right. So was Sergeant Royd. Six men wounded, two very bad. How many dead? Well, four were dead, and five if you counted . . . Well, he'd rather not say.

'What do you mean, boy?' said Duthwaite sharply.

But the soldier turned his head away and started sobbing into the night, choking and heaving and sniffing like a child.

'Leave him,' said Matthew. 'We'll find out soon enough.'

Then the moon came up. We were riding diagonally up a gentle slope, trees and thick bush all around us, but seemingly on some kind of track. At first there was no sound at all, save for the sobs of the guide. But after a while, as if cheered by the moon, one of the men behind us started whistling very gently. I thought Duthwaite would stop him; and indeed he half-turned his head as though to do so, but then apparently thought better of it. I suppose he felt the men would need to arrive in good heart. So the soldier went on whistling, and presently others joined him. It was an old song that soldiers sing, common in one form or another to all the armies of all ages, sad yet ironically gay, resigned yet cheerful, but with the melancholy of it emphasised, on this occasion, by the low shrill tone of whistling. Reedy, I thought. Pan at noon-day.

> So show me the way to go home.
> I'm tired and I want to go to bed.

They were still only whistling, but every soldier knows the words. No, it wasn't Pan at noon. It was tired men at the end of a long day. And what did that boy mean? Four were dead, and five if you counted . . . Counted what? . . . Counted whom?

> So show me the way to go home
> I'm tired and I want to go to bed.
> I had a little drink about an hour ago,
> And it went right to my head.

And Mr Lynch was all right, he supposed. Supposed? Rather not say? What do you mean, boy? Only sobs for an answer.

> So where so 'ere I roam
> On land or sea or foam . . .

Well, that boy hadn't roamed far. He didn't know what he meant. But know it or not, he didn't like it. But Mr Lynch was all right. And Sergeant Royd. All right. All right.

> So where so 'ere I roam,
> On land or sea or foam,
> You will always find me singing this song,
> Show me the way to go home.

And so the guide sobbed and the men whistled and the moon shone and we came to Alastair's camp.

'Halt. Who goes there?'

'Friend.'

'Give the password, friend.'

'Sweetness.'

'Light. Advance, friend, and be recognised.'

So Duthwaite and I advanced to be recognised by the sentry, and were also recognised by Harley's friend Simes, who rushed up gibbering and shrieking and screamed out with all the force in his body :

'Murdered. Murdered. Murdered.'

CHAPTER TEN

A FEW MOMENTS after we arrived, Sergeant Royd appeared. Simes, shocked into sense by the absolute silence with which Duthwaite received this outburst, slunk away to one of the little tents.

'What's the position here, Sergeant?'

'Half the Troop on watch, Sir. Half resting.'

'Mr Lynch?'

'In his tent. He'll take over from me later on.'

'Which tent?'

'Over there. But if you could leave him for a little, Sir? He's done in.'

'I'm sorry. I must talk to him now.'

Duthwaite and I dismounted, and Royd led us over to Alastair's tent. He plucked at the flap and called out softly: 'Mr Lynch, Sir, Mr Lynch. Here's Captain Duthwaite wants to see you.'

But there was no sound from the inside of the tent. Duthwaite put his head through the entrance, and then withdrew it quickly. He motioned to me to look in myself. Inside Alastair's tent there was a sour smell of vomit. By the light of the storm lamp I could see a bottle of brandy, two thirds empty, and an empty tumbler. Alastair lay flat on his back and evidently unconscious on a low camp bed. Even then I found myself wondering how there had possibly been room both for Harley and himself in the bed. There was a pile of vomit on the ground near Alastair's head and more of it lying across the pillow and encrusted in his hair.

'How long has he been like this?' asked Duthwaite.

'Since after the attack stopped, Sir. When they stopped firing, about five that must have been, Mr Lynch took a party out to check the area. Then, when he came back, he said to me, "I think they've gone, Royd, though God knows why. Half-and-half watch." He said: "Would you like the first shift or shall I take it?" We decided that I'd be on from six to midnight and then he'd take over. So he gave a few instructions and went to his tent. After a bit, I went to tell him that I'd got the Troop fed and that half were bedded down and the other half on watch. He'd already started on that bottle then. "Have a drink, Royd," he said. "Not now, Sir, thank you," I said, "but would you like me to bring you some grub?" "No," he said, "no, thank you." "But you must eat something, Sir. You've had nothing all day." "You can leave me now, Sergeant," he said: "wake me at midnight." I looked in again about half an hour ago, and there he was like he is now. But he's all done in, Sir.

And then there's something else too ... young Harley ...'

'One thing at a time, Royd. I'm told six men are wounded.'

'That's right. Four with flesh wounds, but two really bad I wouldn't wonder. We've given them morphia, and there's more if they come to.'

'I'll have a look at them in a moment. The relieving companies will have spare horses, and we should be able to rig something up and get them away first thing tomorrow. Now, the dead.'

'Five, Sir. Young, Evans, Burke, Teague and Harley.'

'Where are they?'

Royd led us to a large tree some twenty yards from the camp perimeter. Underneath it, there were twenty bodies laid out in four rows of five, all with groundsheets covering them from the head to the knee.

'Ours in the front row, Sir. Enemy dead behind.'

'I see ... Now can you kindly tell me why Simes made that disgraceful exhibition when we arrived?'

'I think he blames Mr Lynch for Harley being dead, Sir. Harley was running away, in a manner of speaking. Mr Lynch ... well, Mr Lynch shot him.'

'You saw this?'

'I did, Sir.'

'But running away? Where could he run to? You were surrounded, surely.'

'More or less, Sir. It's a complicated business. He wasn't quite running away, and yet again—'

'We'll go into all that later,' said Duthwaite curtly. 'Now please go and detail a party to bury the enemy dead. Captain Lamont will search them in your presence for documents and so forth. Then bury them. Good and deep and within the hour. The men I've brought will bed down as best they can inside the perimeter of your camp. We've got food, so they can eat now. After that, arrange for them to bear a part in the watch. And ask Mr Sach to join us here.'

When Matthew came up to us, Duthwaite said:

'There's something very bad happened. Alastair shot one of the men while he was running away.'

'I should have thought there was good precedent for that,' said Matthew.

'It used to be accepted without question. But not since the war. There's always a full-scale inquiry, often a court martial. The accused officer is normally cleared, but hard things are said in the Press and it makes a nasty smell all round. And in this case there's something odd going on. I can tell from Royd's manner.'

'Let's wait till we've heard the full story,' I said.

'You're right,' said Duthwaite. 'Bring Royd and join me as soon as you've seen those bodies underground.'

'What are we going to do with our own dead?' I asked.

Duthwaite looked across at Matthew.

'Twenty-four hours in this country,' said Matthew, 'hills or no hills, winter or no winter. Particularly when there's been rain.'

'We'll bury them up here then,' Duthwaite said. 'It'll be hard enough getting the wounded down. The bodies can always be collected later if necessary. There's no reason why they shouldn't be buried where they fell. Unless,' he said to Matthew, 'the tribesmen might violate their graves?'

'No,' said Matthew. 'These people are chivalrous in their barbaric way. The graves of dead warriors will be as safe here as at Thermopylæ.'

The fifteen native bodies had nothing of interest on them. Three large pits were dug without difficulty in the rain-loosened soil. Five bodies were placed in each, the souls of the dead were briefly recommended to their creator, and then the fatigue party shovelled the earth back.

'What about our own?' said Royd.

'Tomorrow. Have a party dig five separate graves early in the morning. Over there,' and I pointed to a small hollow about fifty yards from the camp.

'And now,' I said 'Captain Duthwaite wants to see you. He wants to hear everything that's happened.'

'Everything?'

'Everything. He already knows about Mr Lynch and Harley – not what happened today, any more than I do, but all the rest of it. Killeen told him what's been happening up here, so I filled in the remainder. He's going to cover up for Mr Lynch if he can, but I suppose today's business may make a difference. Anyway, if one thing's essential, it's that we should know the complete truth – everything that's happened since you got here. So get ready to do some talking.'

Duthwaite was talking quietly to one of the sentries. When he saw Royd and myself, he led us off to a grass bank some fifteen yards from the tents.

'All right,' he said to Royd, 'I want to hear the lot. And keep your voice down.'

So Royd began his story. Everything, it seemed, had gone well for two or three days after the camp had first been established. Alastair had gone daily to Glukeia with a small escort to pay compliments to the village headman : the Troop had been digging trenches and making the camp as comfortable as possible.

'Nice boy-scout holiday but for the weather,' said Royd. 'Rain such as you've never seen. Not hard, mind you, but on and on and on. Still, we got the trenches dug, and fixed up some drains to draw the water off down the hill, and young Simes and several more got hold of some branches and made rough floors for the tents. So one way and another it wasn't too bad, and soon we got used to being wet all day and not minding, just like a lot of bleeding seals.'

Harley's elevation to the role of 'Troop Trumpeter' had caused a certain amount of discreet mirth, but only Killeen, 'with his snarky hints', and Simes, who resented Harley's constant absences with Alastair in Glukeia, had taken much notice. However, it came to be an open secret that Harley went to Alastair's tent almost every night; and by the time they had been there a week and C.S.M. Mole appeared with the next issue of rations, Royd was getting worried.

'So finally I had a word with Mr Lynch, Sir. I said I knew how he felt and all the rest, but didn't he think that in a camp as small as this there wasn't quite room for goings-on as would shake the Ritz Hotel? "There's no harm done, Royd," he said : "and anyway we'll be out of this place in a day or two." He wouldn't see it, Sir. Just wouldn't see it. Like a blind man. And then the Sergeant Major came up with another week's rations. "That means at least another week up here," I said : "now turn it up, sir, for Christ's sake." "It's no good, Royd," he said, "I can't turn it up and that's the size of it." Well, at any rate Corporal ——ing Killeen went off back with the Sergeant Major, and that was one good thing. But we still had young Simes here, and he was playing up like Hamlet with his bloody mother; and one day I saw him go off to talk to Mr Lynch in his tent, and what they said to one another I *don't* know; but Simes came back looking like he'd poisoned the whole Royal Family at their high tea. "I told the bastard," he said, "I told him what I thought of his fancy talk and his fancy ways." "You mind your place, Simes," I told him : "Mr Lynch has been with this Troop two years and not a man in it the worse for that. There's plenty of trouble in this Army," I said, "and he sees to it that as little as possible comes our way. So don't you go looking for any on your own account. And if he is a bit daft about young Harley, it's not you the devil will roast and eat, but him." "I'm thinking of Harley," said Simes. "If he goes on like this, he'll end up swaying round Piccadilly Circus like some half-dollar nancy boy." "Not him," I said : "you live as long as I have and you'll know it takes more than a squeeze or two on a dark night to turn a man queer. Harley's not the first to sleep with an officer and he won't be the last."

'Still, Sir, you can see it was an edgy business, even if it was only Simes that shouted the odds in the ring. He might be the only one to shout, but sooner or later, I thought, he'll find some takers. As for Harley himself, you'd have thought bread would turn to manna in his mouth. He just sat about smiling as though nothing had happened at all. Smiling and smiling and cleaning his bloody trumpet as if it were the Grail; and if anyone asked him what he

129

got up to in Mr Lynch's tent, he just said, "Talking. Talking about this and that" – an expression of Mr Lynch's, I dare say. So there we all were; me worried enough to bring on the shingles and hoping like Jesus Christ you'd call us back to Gikumo; Mr Lynch, sharp and clever as always, but infatuated with Harley as if he was an emperor's daughter; Harley grinning all day like a bloody cat; and Simes stirring up the shit with a steam shovel.'

And then, that morning, just as Alastair was setting out, rather later than usual, to Glukeia, a burst of fire swept through the camp and they all dived for the trenches.

'Good thing he hadn't gone before it started,' said Royd, 'but in any case there was a proper mess at first. Half the men had left their rifles in their tents, there was six men in one trench and none in the next, and as far as I could make out they were firing at us all ways at once. If they'd come in there and then, that would have been our lot.

'One thing, though, they didn't seem able to fire very straight. That Karioukeya may be a good general, but his weapon instructors haven't got very far. And then again, they weren't firing all that thick. Constant fire but not heavy. Still short of ammunition, I dare say. Anyhow, we slowly straightened ourselves out. Mr Lynch concentrated our fire on certain points where the wogs seemed to be hidden and gradually everyone was able to crawl to his tent and get his weapon and get properly sorted out in the different trenches. The only trouble was the horses. The horse-lines are about fifty yards from the camp and on the slope there up above. The poor brutes played hell when they heard the firing, and we couldn't see up there properly to shoot at anyone who might start getting at them. As it turned out, they left them alone – planning to take them away for themselves, I wouldn't wonder. Or perhaps they didn't like the screen of fire we kept going to either side of the stabling area. Mr Lynch saw to that very prompt.

'Any road, by the time we got through to you on the wireless, we were fairly well settled. Not a single wog could we see, but we knew where they were firing from and we gave them steady fire back to keep their heads down. Horse lines screened off as far as we could. Only two men wounded. Nothing to do but keep it up till the relieving companies arrived. Then the wireless set got knocked off of course, but two million wireless sets wouldn't have got those companies here any quicker.'

And so it had gone on. A steady, tedious business of staying put in the trenches and returning the enemy fire. Whoever among Karioukeya's officers had planned this raid had shown little imagination in his conception and was showing little ingenuity now. Nor did the enemy's aim improve. Then two things happened. The corporal who was opening up the ammunition boxes and preparing the rounds in clips for distribution reported that eight boxes out of twenty had been totally spoiled by damp. This meant that they had enough ammunition for only six hours at the present rate of firing, and not for ten hours, as Alastair had supposed. And secondly, just after they had made this disheartening discovery, the enemy started a rush attack over the open ground. This the Troop had cleared to a depth of between fifty and seventy yards all round, save only for that segment of the camp which faced up the slope towards the horse lines. The ground there had been scheduled for clearance that very day, Royd said; but as it was, there was thick cover there, and why the enemy didn't use it was a mystery to him. But in any case they hadn't; they came pouring over the clear ground on the three open sides of the camp, and a bad moment it had been.

'Like a Legion of black souls screaming out of hell,' Royd told us 'but not one of them knew how to fire properly in the advance. They had bayonets fixed though, and a wicked sight it was. I've never been on the receiving end of a bayonet charge before and I didn't fancy my chances, I can tell you. "There's a pension coming your way, you old hag," I said to Mrs Royd inside myself, "and much good may it do you." But Mr Lynch kept his head. "Grenades," he shouted, "grenades all round and close in." And this did the trick. Only one grenade had been issued to each two men, but they were evenly split up right round the line. The men kept their heads, too, and lobbed the grenades over very easy when the wogs were forty yards out; so that the grenades fell in a ring all round the camp and about ten yards away and went off just as the wogs ran over them. "Everything you've got with the brens," called Mr Lynch, and they certainly turned it on. But the grenades settled the wogs. I thought they were trained to use them themselves, but from the shrieking and moaning that went up even from them that wasn't hurt you'd have thought they'd never seen one go off before. So back they went into their holes with a few bursts of bren up their bottoms and didn't try that again – and a good job, because there wasn't any more grenades, not unless Jesus Christ was going to drop them down from heaven.'

And indeed the ammunition problem was now critical. Eight boxes out of twenty of the normal .303 had been found to be useless: a great deal had been used, quite apart from the grenades, during the enemy's rush attack. Assistance of some kind they now must have, and by five o'clock at latest. They could not even hope for the relieving companies to arrive before six and they ought not to depend on them arriving before eight. It was now almost two in the afternoon. The ammunition might last another three hours, until five, or it might not. If there were more rush attacks, it certainly wouldn't.

131

'Someone must get through to Mr Hathaway,' Alastair had said, and cursed the broken wireless.

Quickly he and Royd thought up their plan. A concentration of all their fire, including the two inch mortar, on the known enemy positions might create enough distraction for a small party to get away up the slope at the back, through the cover there, past the horse lines, and so, with heaven's aid, round past the enemy and down to Glukeia. The concentrated use of ammunition for the five minutes necessary for the men to get clear would be a heavy gamble : it must be taken. If one or more of the party got clear, then it would take them forty minutes to Glukeia, where they could commandeer horses from the headman. (They could never take their own from the horse lines and saddle them up quickly enough, and even if they succeeded in this, they would make far too prominent a target when mounted.) But once at Glukeia, with the headman's horses, they could get to Robin in a further forty minutes if they killed the horses doing it. And then, if Robin was prompt, he might be able to come to the Troop's aid as early as half past four. He could make a diversion if nothing else. It might even be that the arrival of another troop, which the messengers must instruct to bring every available grenade, would scare the enemy off altogether.

'A party of four,' Alastair had said. 'Corporal Barnett in charge. Evans and Teague are good men. One more?'

'Simes?' said Royd.

'Fair enough.'

But at this stage Harley, who as a member of Troop H.Q. was in the same trench as Alastair and Royd, had joined the conversation.

'Let me go,' he said, 'that'll show them.'

'No,' said Alastair.

'Let me go, Sir. Not Simes. He's my mate. Don't send him. Please, Sir. Send me instead. I want to show them I'm not just a little pouf like they call me. For God's sake don't send Simes.'

'Simes is a tough man,' Alastair had said patiently. 'He and the rest of them are cut out for this . . . Have them all come over here, Sergeant Royd. I'll brief them. You go round and get everyone set to start rapid and continuous fire at two o'clock exactly. Divide the fire power up equally against the four enemy positions I showed you. Tell the mortar man to switch from one to another. It's now ten to two. That gives us ten minutes.'

Royd called to Corporal Barnett and the others who were to constitute the party. They came crawling over and huddled into Alastair's trench. Royd crawled off to organise the fire power. Calmly and carefully Alastair started to explain what was required of Corporal Barnett's party. How they were to make straight up the slope the moment the fire concentration started, go on past the horse lines and then turn off as quickly as they could and head through the forest for Glukeia.

'You must let me go,' said Harley interrupting.

'For Christ's sake shut up,' said Alastair, 'and let me get on briefing these chaps.'

Harley cowered into a corner, red and trembling. Royd returned from his round.

'Five minutes to go, Sir,' he said.

'Don't forget,' said Alastair, 'it's vital that one of you gets through. There's to be no stopping to help any one that gets hurt. Push on. Once you're past the horse lines, Corporal Barnett, see they spread out as much as possible and it's every man for himself to Glukeia. If the headman makes trouble over lending horses, shoot him. You all know what to tell Mr Hathaway?'

They all nodded.

'And then, Sir,' went on Sergeant Royd to Duthwaite and me, 'Mr Lynch looks at his watch and says, "Four minutes to go. Just sit here quietly till I give the word." But then young Harley starts up again. 'I must go, I must go,' he says: "they all think I'm just a little nancy boy and it's *your* fault. Let me go. I'll go instead of Simes." Mr Lynch says nothing to this, but he looks at Harley as if he was going to wallop him one and much worse. In fact, Sir, it's not the sort of look I want to see again in a hurry: white with anger he was and sort of gleaming. But then Simes cuts in to keep the peace. "Shut your face," says Simes to Harley; "no one thinks you're a little nancy boy. But they will if you sit there whining." "You think so. You said so." "Only in fun," said Simes, "and no one else has said flog all." "They all think it though," says Harley; "I can see it in their faces. I *will* go," he says, "I'll show you all." And with that he was up and over the side of the trench. "Come back here," shouts Mr Lynch. But Harley runs flat across the camp towards the slope, yelling and screaming. "I'll show you," he yells, "I'll show you." "Come back," shouts Mr Lynch. And then Simes begins to get out of the trench to go after Harley. But Mr Lynch pulls him back, seizes my rifle, and before anyone knows what's happening he's aimed and fired at Harley, drops him as he runs, gets him right through the back. "Now you know what happens when people disobey orders in action," he says. It looks as if Simes or one of the others is going to say something to that, when all of a sudden our brens start firing like the clappers of hell and "Off you go", says Mr Lynch, "and good luck".

'So off they went, the poor sods, right past where Harley was lying, out of the camp and up towards the horse lines. But for all the noise and muck the brens were turning loose, some wog must have been keeping an eye that way, because there's a burst of fire on the right and down comes Evans and Teague. Then Simes

133

and Barnett take cover behind a bank but there's bullets kicking up all around them. "Blast," says Mr Lynch, "they'll never get through now. But how are we going to get them back out of there?" And indeed, gentlemen, there was a question for you. But young Ferguson on the mortar spots where the fire's coming from and lobs a bomb out of his mortar clean on to the black bastards, so that Simes and Barnett can get up and start running again. "Back," yells Mr Lynch. "Come back." And a good job they hear him and come back, because just as they get to the camp again a whole squad of blacks comes charging along on to the slope between us and the horse lines and go to ground in the bushes. They'd have had Simes and Barnett for sure. As it is, we hold them there with fire, and everything's more or less as it was before, only Harley, Teague and Evans are dead and we've used about half an hour's ammunition in five minutes.

' "Normal rates of fire," Mr Lynch shouts, and everyone settles down again. Only they don't really settle because they've most of them seen what happened to Harley. "What did you do that for?" I asked him. "Poor little perisher. Why did you have to shoot him?" "For two reasons," said Mr Lynch, and now he's as cool and sharp as a winter's morning, "for two reasons, Sergeant Royd. Because he was disobedient when under enemy fire, and because if he'd got out of camp he'd have drawn attention to the route Barnett's party was going to take. As it is," he says, "it was probably Harley running that way which alerted them and let them spot the get-away so quickly." So I left it at that, gentlemen. It'll all come out in the wash, I thought. And Mr Lynch, cool as he might be, was looking right peculiar.'

'Two questions before you go on,' said Duthwaite.

'Sir?'

'Is there any possibility at all that Harley was killed by an enemy bullet and not by Mr Lynch?'

'Mr Lynch's was the only shot fired for about twenty seconds both before and after Harley came down, Sir.'

'You're sure?'

'I am that.'

'Secondly then, how do you explain this empty bottle of whisky I found in Mr Lynch's trench just now?'

Royd's face fell.

'I wasn't thinking to explain it, Sir. I meant to chuck it away.'

'Then since you're the victim of your own incompetence, I want to hear the truth about the whisky. And I mean the truth.'

'I've told you the truth about everything else, Sir. But it was just ... well, there wasn't meant to be any drink up here, so I didn't want to mention it... The Sergeant Major brought it up for me when he came. "Keep the damp out, Charley boy," he said:

"you're too old, you poor old ——er, not to leak a bit in rain like this." "Poor old ——er yourself," I said, "and thank you very much." Well, I must have left the bottle about or something. It was only half drunk, and when I looked for it this morning, I couldn't see it. "It'll turn up, Charley Royd," I said to myself, and thought no more about it – not until after young Harley was shot and I see it rolling in the bottom of the trench – empty. Not a drop had I had, no more had Mr Lynch, and I'd forgotten I had it till I see it rolling about there and all polished off. And then I thought, "So that's what's made you so contrary all of a sudden, you poor little sod you, you've been pouring my whisky on to an empty stomach." Which explains a lot, Sir. Because after all, Harley did act very odd, interrupting Mr Lynch and all, and no one in his right mind would volunteer for a game like that get-away without being a bit over-excited first – leave alone make a start on his Jack Jones. So I pointed out the bottle to Mr Lynch; and he said, "Yes, I know. He was drinking it all the morning when he thought I wasn't looking. He was so frightened, you see. I hadn't the heart to stop him." "Frightened?" I said : "young Harley? He's a plucky one that – or was." "Oh, he'd have tried hard enough," said Mr Lynch "he'd have hidden it and been as brave as he could. That's why he was so plucky – because he had so much fear to hide. But he was also weak. And when he spotted that whisky of yours, he thought it would help."

'So I was just getting to wondering whether he'd whipped it before or after the attack started, and thinking how it would have been sweeter in a live belly than a dead one, when suddenly young Simes pipes up from the other side of the camp. "You murdered him," he shouts, "you'll answer for this, Mr Alastair Lynch." Hadn't opened his mouth in half an hour, not since he got back from trying to get away with the rest. Stunned, I suppose. But he wasn't stunned any more. Hysterical he was. "Bloody murderer," he calls out, "bloody murdering swine." "I'll shoot you too if you don't shut your mouth," says Mr Lynch : "when we get out of this, you'll have your chance to tell what you know. But until we're finished with this, you'll keep quiet and watch your front." But even then Simes starts up again, and so Corporal Barnett hits him over the head with a rifle butt, which settles his conversation for a bit.'

And so it had dragged on through the afternoon, ammunition getting lower and lower, hearts sinking with the sun, eyes peering bloodshot into the bush, hands trembling and hope fading.

'But Mr Lynch, for all he was looking so peculiar, he kept us going,' said Royd. 'Kept the firing rate as low as he could without letting on we were getting short. Crawled over to the other trenches to look at the wounded and chat with the rest. And for all they knew he'd shot Harley, they still looked to him and he knew it,

135

and he deserved they should, gentlemen, for good lads as they are it was him put the extra heart in them to carry on. So he chatted away and told his stories and helped the wounded, and then later on he got them all to singing. Hymns they sung, "For All the Saints" and such; ballads, marching songs; any old thing. "Watch your front, all of you," he said, "and sing your ——ing guts out."

'And sing they did, the poor worn out bastards; sung and fired till it did my heart good to hear them. "O God our help in ages past" they sung and "Polly put the kettle on" and "All the nice girls love a soldier" and "Angeline was sweet sixteen", the dirty-minded ——ers, and "Onward Christian Soldiers". And at the end of that I said, "There hasn't been a shot fired our way for ten minutes, Sir." "No more there has," he said. Well you know the rest, gentlemen : how Mr Lynch tried to draw fire and then took a party out and went further and further and found nothing . . .'

So Alastair had come back, and told Royd the enemy was gone, and made arrangements for guides to be despatched and for watch to be kept. And then a young soldier had called out to Alastair.

'We must say a prayer, Mr Lynch, and you must lead us all.'

Then there had been silence, the silence of assent.

So Alastair searched in his sceptical mind for the one passage of the Scriptures he had by heart :

' "But the souls of the righteous are in the hand of God, and there shall no torment touch them . . ." '

And one by one the soldiers had knelt down.

' ". . . and their departure is taken for misery, and their going from us to be utter destruction : but they are in peace. For though they be punished in the sight of man . . ." '

Corporal Barnett had knelt, and Fergusson the mortar man, and even Sergeant Royd.

' ". . . yet is their hope full of immortality. And having been a little chastised, they shall be greatly rewarded; for God proved them and found them worthy for Himself." '

But Simes had not knelt; so that only he and Alastair remained standing when Alastair began again :

' "Our Father, which art in heaven . . ." '

And all the men repeated the ancient formula after him.

The relieving companies arrived long after midnight, long after Sergeant Royd had finished his story. They would arrange to take over the posts in the hills, so that 'D' Company could retire to lick its wounds in peace. So the next day we buried Malcolm Harley and the rest in the forest that grows on Mount Chalchos, and then we left Glukeia for that time.

PART THREE

THE TRIAL

CHAPTER ELEVEN

'I HAVE HERE,' said General Peterson, 'an order signed by Field
Marshal the Lord Mountford of Larkhill, V.C., G.C.B., D.S.O.,
Commander-in-Chief Far East Central, which convenes a general
court martial to sit this day in the city of Eirene to try the accused
person named in the margin, that is to say 383318 Lieutenant
Alastair Lynch, of the 121st Mounted Infantry (Lord Martock's
Regiment), on a charge hereinafter specified.

The Court is to be constituted as follows : I myself, General
Sir Stewart Winlove Peterson, K.B.E., C.B., General Officer Com-
manding in Pepromene, am named as President; the other members
to be Major-General Randal Osborne, C.V.O., late of Her Majesty's
Foot Guards; Brigadier George Michael Godfrey, D.S.O., of The
Royal Engineers; Brigadier Keith Andrew Milner, O.B.E., of The
Royal Army Ordnance Corps; and Colonel the Honourable Napier
Grail, M.C., late of the 25th Dragoon Guards, all these officers save
myself being at present on the staff of Field Marshal Lord
Mountford.

'A Judge Advocate has also been appointed to advise the Court.
This learned gentleman is Geoffrey Goddard Keyes, LL.D., M.A.,
sometime Fellow of Trinity Hall in the University of Cambridge,
and at present the Judge Advocate General's department.

'Mr Lynch, you will be so good as to signify any objection you
may have to myself, as President, or to any other member of this
Court Martial. Failing which, we may proceed to swear the Court...'

The day of Alastair's trial was as wet and depressing as many days
that had preceded it, though at least the occasional scarlet coats
that were to be seen around the camp had a cheering effect. For
as Sanvoisin had insisted, an officer of Martock's Foot was court-
martialled in full dress or not at all; and this necessitated the
appearance in scarlet of anyone in our Regiment who was attending
the trial, whether in some official capacity or merely as a spectator.
Alastair himself was permitted to wear his busby with his full dress
but had to proceed to the Court without either spurs or sword. He
had, however, exercised his privilege as an officer of our Regiment
by marching into the Court Room without an escort; and now he
stood alone in front of the line of tables behind which the Court

and the Judge Advocate were standing, his busby supported on the crook of his right arm, while the oath was administered to all the members of the Court, to the Judge Advocate, and finally to the short-hand writer. The tent which served as a Court Room had been patched up as soundly as possible and did not leak unduly; but the damp had risen through the boards which made up the crude floor, the chairs were sweating, and when I put my hand on the blanket which covered the Defending Officers' table, it was like feeling a blanket which covered a corpse.

At the far end of the tent, a bedraggled Union Jack had been fastened to the wall. In front of this, on a ·slightly raised dais, would sit the Court, and in front of them on the dais was a line of precarious barrack-room tables with folding metal legs, these being covered with green Army blankets and already littered with papers, pencils, water carafes and brief cases. Down from the dais, to the Court's right, was the Prosecutor's table, and facing this, from the other side of the tent, a table behind which were Sanvoisin, Michael and myself, with an empty chair placed ready for Alastair. About five yards beyond us a rope was stretched across the tent, behind which sat the members of the Press and the public. In all, some fifteen Press-men were present, at least five of whom had been specially flown from London. (One of these had kicked up a terrific fuss when Sergeant Godawake, the Court Orderly, had forbidden him to bring his camera into Court, though how he could have conceived such a thing would be allowed remained a mystery.) For the rest, by common agreement, the only officers among the spectators were James Sinclair and Giles Bancombe; but there was a great splash of scarlet where Sergeant Major Mole and about two-thirds of Alastair's Troop were sitting; for these latter had insisted on coming, to show Mr Lynch, as they said, that they were on his side, and eventually they had been given leave from Gikumo to attend. Just on the Court's side of the rope was a tent flap which acted as a doorway for the comings and goings of the Court Orderly and those present for official purposes. Through this doorway Sergeant Godawake now marched out the witnesses; for these, in accordance with custom, had been present while the Court was sworn, but must now wait in a separate tent nearby until called for. When Godawake had done this, Duthwaite and our Medical Officer, the only witnesses of commissioned rank, saluted the Court and marched out by themselves. The decks were cleared for action : the Trial by Court Martial of Lieutenant Alastair Lynch could now begin.

This was happening some four weeks after the events at Glukeia and our departure from the mountains. The whole of 'D' Company had immediately pulled back to its stronghold at Gikumo to find a pale but recovered Percy Berkeley ready to rule once more. After a few days, two troops from the relieving companies had been left occupying the positions previously occupied by Alastair and Robin, and the rest of the two companies had returned to their proper locations below the escarpment. There had been no further sign of Karioukeya; and the information was that he and the battalion which had been at Tokoroa had returned to join the main force in the central mountains. This recent excursion, it was thought, had been by way of experiment – and not very successful experiment; so that now he would probably stay put for a while, concentrating on further and much-needed training and waiting for supplies of ammunition, an acute shortage of which was held to account for the suddenness with which the attack on Alastair's position had been abandoned. The *status quo,* from a military point of view, had been resumed.

Other affairs had been more dramatic. Alastair had been sent down to Eirene, under nominal arrest, to wait there while the circumstances of Harley's death were investigated. He then attended while a summary of evidence was drawn up by James Sinclair. By this time, I myself was back at Eirene, my business in Gikumo being now finally concluded. When the summary of evidence was complete, it had been despatched by air to General Peterson's distant superior, the Field Marshal and Commander-in-Chief of the Far East Central Forces; his instructions had been received a few days later and immediately communicated to us by Peterson.

'The position is this,' Sanvoisin had told us later. 'Normally, important civil offences are tried, if committed in the United Kingdom or one of the Colonies, by civil courts; and of course Alastair's shooting Harley, though both of them were Army personnel, is really a civil matter. But in this case two factors are held to make it desirable that Alastair should appear in front of a court martial rather than the high court in Eirene. The state of emergency that now exists in this country; and, secondly, the repeated ruling of high court judges in the U.K. that even civil offences, if the people and circumstances involved are *exclusively* military, are best dealt with by military procedure. And in this case, the circumstances are so specialised, as you might say, that there isn't much doubt left which is the better course. So notwithstanding the displeasure that elements of the Press and the Labour Party are bound to show when they hear that a really important case is being tried by court martial, the Field Marshal has told Peterson to get the local judiciary to agree that the Army had best deal with Alastair, and from what Peterson tells me, the authorities here were only too glad to be rid of the matter.

'So there it is. The Court is to be convened by the Field Marshal so that Peterson may be free to sit as President. There'll be a judge advocate, of course, to advise Peterson, and the prosecution will be conducted by some senior and legally qualified officer from the Army Legal Department. And as for the actual charges to be preferred, we shall know all about them in a day or two . . .'

'The Court being duly sworn,' said General Peterson, 'the accused shall now be arraigned. All present remain standing and replace head-dress.

'You, Sir,' he said directly to Alastair, 'are you No. 383318 Lieutenant Alastair Lynch, of the 121st Mounted Infantry (Lord Martock's Regiment), and at present serving with the 1st Battalion of that Regiment in the Colony of Pepromene?'

'I am, Sir.'

'Then, Sir, you are hereby charged before this Court Martial with committing a civil offence contrary to section 70 of the Army Act, 1955, that is to say Murder : in that you, on November the 26th, 1956, at a camp near the village of Glukeia, did murder by shooting Mounted Infantryman (Drummer) Malcolm Harley, a soldier of Her Majesty's Forces.

'But how say you, Alastair Lynch? Are you guilty, or not guilty, of the felony whereof you stand charged?'

'I am not guilty, Sir.'

'Then your plea shall so be entered.

'But it is now my duty, Mr Lynch, to ask you if you wish to apply for an adjournment on the ground that any of the rules of procedure before trial have not been compiled with, or on the ground that you have not had sufficient opportunity for preparing your defence.'

'I wish to make no such application.'

'You are aware, Mr Lynch,' said the Judge Advocate, 'that the Officer instructed for the Prosecution, Lieutenant-Colonel Lovesy, is an experienced member of the Army Legal Department, and not only experienced but legally qualified?'

'I am, Sir.'

'Then you are still sure you wish to entrust your defence to Colonel Sanvoisin and these other officers? I in no way impugn the abilities of these gentlemen, but they will be the first to admit that their experience in such matters is slender.'

'I have every confidence, Sir, in the gentlemen whom I have charged with my defence.'

'What do you say, Sir?' asked the Judge Advocate of Sanvoisin.

'I have made every effort to persuade Mr Lynch to engage learned counsel on his behalf. However, he insists that as this is a court martial he is entitled to nominate his brother officers to defend him. Since this is most certainly true, and since it is clearly what Mr Lynch wishes, then I am fully prepared to undertake his defence.'

'Very well,' said the Judge Advocate; 'but let this exchange be entered in the proceedings of the Court.'

'You may sit down, Sir,' said Peterson to Alastair.

As Alastair walked away from the dais to join us at our table, he was greeted by a salvo of amiable grins from the members of his Troop. These he acknowledged with a slight movement of his hand, and then sat down next to me.

'Very well, Colonel Lovesy,' Peterson said, 'you may now open the case for the Prosecution.'

And Lovesy rose to begin.

When we first heard that Alastair was to be tried by court martial, we had all hoped that the whole thing would be a mere formality. The charge, we had thought, would be manslaughter, the facts of Harley's death would be briefly stated before the Court by the Prosecutor, Sanvoisin would then rise to urge that, since Harley's death was clearly a military necessity, there was no case to answer, and Alastair would be immediately and honourably acquitted. Even so, we had been doubtful of Alastair's wisdom in declining to engage professional counsel; but he had turned the matter into a joke by saying that he could not possibly afford such a thing after his gambling losses to Sanvoisin on the boat. This I knew to be nonsense. However, since there was plainly a genuine wish, underlying the joke, that Sanvoisin and no one else should speak for him on this occasion, and since he then asked that Michael and myself should sit in with Sanvoisin 'to improve my morale', it was settled that he should be allowed his own way. After all, we thought, the whole thing won't last more than half an hour; and if the three of us can't handle a simple formality of this kind, then we need our heads looking into.

Then came the first hint of serious trouble. Alastair was to be charged, not with manslaughter, but murder.

'Of course it could be,' Sanvoisin had told us, 'that they are preferring the more serious charge in order to clear his name more effectively. The Court will assume the greater importance attached to the greater offence; it will attract all the more publicity – nothing hole and corner – and will finally clear the whole matter up, once and for all, with the greatest possibly authority and without any compromise whatever. A charge of manslaughter, you see, might have been held by some of the snarkier elements at home to be a deliberate ploy to protect Alastair against the worst.'

'But why should there be any question of murder?' Michael had asked. 'To prove murder you have to prove guilty intent – malice aforethought. Now in this case you may have grounds for a charge of manslaughter : people *might* say that Harley's death was unnecessary, that there had been muddles, mistakes, confusion or even panic on Alastair's part. But none of this adds up to malice aforethought. What possible reason for malice could Alastair have had?'

'If my theory's right,' said Sanvoisin, 'and they're merely trying to clear him more effectively, none of that would matter. The murder charge would simply mean that the Secretary of State for War would have the fullest possible answer if some hysterical M.P., instigated perhaps by Harley's mother, demanded to know what had been done about the deliberate shooting of Drummer Harley. "Lieutenant Lynch," the Government could say, "was tried by a court martial. This was convened by a field marshal and presided over by a full general. The charge was murder – which left the Court free to bring in an alternative verdict of manslaughter if it wished. The House will be glad to know that Mr Lynch was honourably acquitted on all counts." You see what I mean? Policy. This charge of murder could be pure policy … The only thing is,' said Sanvoisin, 'I'm very much afraid it's nothing of the kind.'

'What do you mean?'

'If you read the summary of evidence,' said Sanvoisin, 'you'll find there's a great deal in it about this business of Alastair's relationship with Harley. I understand Harley had a friend called Simes, and that Simes was an important witness about the actual shooting. He did not neglect the opportunity of telling the investigators everything he knew about Harley and Alastair. They followed it up – and so did James Sinclair in his summary. They got hold of Killeen and they questioned Richard Duthwaite. Richard seems, from what he tells me, to have had some scheme for hushing it all up. But with Harley actually dead and this enquiry going forward, there was plainly no more hushing-up to be done. This was all news to me, and I think someone might have told me before, but that doesn't matter now. What does matter is that Simes, Richard, Sergeant Royd and several others have all, willingly or unwillingly, given conclusive testimony about this very unsavoury affair.'

'But there is no reason,' I said, 'to connect Alastair's infatuation for Harley with Harley's death. If it proves anything, it proves that Alastair must have been more than ever unwilling to have shot him.'

'Does it?' said Sanvoisin. 'Well let me tell you something you may not know. You heard Royd's story : how Simes finally went to Alastair and cursed him up and down for corrupting Harley? And how Alastair sent him away telling him to mind his own business?'

'Yes.'

'Well, after that something apparently happened that Royd didn't know about and so didn't tell you up at Glukeia. Something which alters the entire balance of the case. According to Simes – and this is what he has told the investigators and also James Sinclair – when he left Alastair he was still very angry and so he went along to say some disagreeable things to Harley. He told Harley that Alastair admitted sleeping with him, that the whole thing was disgusting, that Alastair was a vile seducer and he, Harley, wasn't much better; that he was a revolting little nancy boy and the good Lord knows what else. Naturally, Harley was rather put out by this, though it wasn't the first time Simes had spoken of the matter, so he just looked rather hurt and went away. This happened four days before they were attacked.'

'Nothing much in that . . .'

'But then, Simes says, when it was only two days before the attack, Harley sought him out and started to talk about Alastair again. Simes is prepared to swear that what Harley said was this : that he had been thinking over what Simes had said, that he knew Simes was right, that he'd made up his mind not to have anything more to do with Alastair, physically at any rate, and was going to tell Alastair this the next time he saw him. In short, Simes says, Harley was giving Mr Lynch the bird. Now Alastair himself denies that Harley ever passed this good resolution on to him; and adds that the pair of them slept together the very last night before the attack. Again, the whole thing stinks to heaven of hearsay and might very well be disallowed as evidence. But if, in whole or part, it *was* admitted, and if it *was* believed, it could be very damaging indeed. The implication being that Alastair was angry with Harley for suddenly withdrawing his sexual compliance – as Simes would say, "for giving him the bird".'

'It seems jolly thin to me,' said Michael.

'Then look at it this way. A skilful and determined prosecutor gets up in Court and produces a lot of unshakeable evidence, given by people well disposed to Alastair, and all of it going to show that Alastair was conducting a passionate and sexual affair with one of the youngest soldiers in his Troop. Think what sort of an impression that is going to create. The prosecutor then puts Simes on the stand – honest, rugged, decent, God-fearing Simes. Simes then gives a lot of evidence which has already been confirmed by previous witnesses – the early stages of the infatuation and so forth – and then produces his show piece. In a round about way, devised by the ingenious prosecutor to get round the Rules of Hearsay, honest Simes reveals that as a result of his own well-intentioned if blunt remonstrances his friend Harley was getting all ready to refuse and frustrate the perverted and unbalanced Mr Lynch. Do the members of the Court believe this? They lap it up. And what does it mean to them – particularly if they are morally prejudiced and therefore suggestible?'

'It might mean a motive of jealousy, I suppose.'

'So you see what I'm getting at?'

'Granted much over-simplification and question-begging,' I said, 'yes.'

'Of course I've over-simplified. I'm merely trying to indicate, in

143

SIMON RAVEN

a crude form, the sort of thing a skilful prosecutor might try to put across a morally prejudiced court. Peterson is a fair man and won't let himself be prejudiced. But I know nothing about the rest of them, and for all I've heard they may be bigots of the first order. I might add that Alastair still declines to brief professional counsel, though I've warned him this may be much more complicated than we first thought.'

'I see the prosecutor is a certain Colonel Lovesy,' I said, 'of the Army Legal Department. What do we know of him?'

'He's said to be both keen and cunning,' Sanvoisin had told us, 'and if he's going to have a try along the lines I've indicated, we shall have a very good chance of watching him at work.'

And so now, in the Court Room, we were watching Colonel Lovesy at work. He was a large, sleek man. Unlike the Judge Advocate, who was angular and preying, he gave a first impression of being almost serenely indifferent to the matter in hand. But he had a mean mouth, close set eyes, a piggy nose and, rather incongruously, a slight lisp.

He began very quietly, by stating the facts he proposed to prove as to the actual killing. The Medical Officer of the Battalion, he said, would confirm that he had exhumed and examined the body of the deceased man, Drummer Harley. He would say that Harley had been killed by a .303 bullet which had entered his heart from behind. Other witnesses would state that the accused had fired a shot in such a way as to kill Harley in the manner described, that Harley had dropped immediately this shot was fired, and that the shot fired by the accused was the only shot to be fired, whether by friend or foe, for as long as twenty seconds both before and after Harley had dropped. In any case, he understood that the Defence was prepared to concede that the actual killing was brought about by the Accused's action, and that no attempt was to be made to prove that anyone else had fired the shot which killed Harley.

Sanvoisin rose to confirm this.

'It is now my duty,' proceeded Colonel Lovesy, 'to say something to you of the law regarding murder. You must clearly understand, of course, that anything I myself, or the most able gentlemen opposite, shall say to you about the law or its interpretation is subject to the approval and confirmation of the learned Judge Advocate, whose duty it is to guide you in such matters. Having thus qualified what I am about to say, let me put the principles to you as follows :

'The killing of one man by another is either justifiable, excusable or culpable. If it is culpable, then it is either murder or manslaughter.

'For manslaughter to be proved, the killing must be established by the prosecution to be neither justifiable or excusable, and to have been committed by someone with the necessary criminal capacity.

144

That is to say, the Accused must be shown to be responsible for the error of commission or omission which led to the killing in question. This error need not in itself be criminal, though frequently, as in the case of careless driving, it may be so. Equally, of course, this error need not be more than fortuitously connected with the death causes. A careless driver has no deliberate intention of killing anybody; but as a result of his carelessness, somebody is fortuitously killed. In short an avoidable and unnecessary and potentially dangerous act has been committed by someone who knew it to be an act of this kind; this act has led to somebody else's death; and so the person who originally committed the act is held responsible for the death — but only to the degree of being guilty of manslaughter.

'Now, for murder to be proved, the Prosecution must not only establish that the killing was neither justifiable nor excusable, and that it was an act of the Accused's for which he was responsible that led to the killing; the Prosecution must also show that the act in question was deliberately designed to cause the unlawful death of the Deceased. It must demonstrate the presence in the Accused person of "malice aforethought", of the deliberate and guilty intention of doing the victim to death.'

Lovesy then went on to elaborate this a little. Such malice, he said, the celebrated 'malice aforethought' round which so many murder trials had turned, was said to be 'express' when the accused, at the material time, had a guilty intention such as constituted malice; and he must stress that evidence of such an intention was usually circumstantial. Nor should the Court be misled by the epithet 'aforethought'; this did not mean that the intention must be long premeditated to become a 'guilty intention'; it merely meant that the intention must first be formed and then carried out — a process which could occur in an instant of time.

In order, therefore, to prove Alastair Lynch guilty of murder, there was an onus on the Prosecution, said Lovesy, to prove the following points:

(a) That Alastair's act had caused Harley's death. (This was no longer in dispute.)
(b) That the killing was unlawful and neither justifiable nor excusable.
(c) That Alastair was responsible for this act, i.e. was not an imbecile or otherwise affected in a way that would disqualify him from 'having the necessary criminal capacity'.
(d) That Alastair had acted with malice aforethought, having carried out a deliberate and guilty intention.

As a final observation about the law, he added, he must remind them that when a charge of murder was preferred, the Court was entitled to bring in an alternative verdict of manslaughter if, in its opinion, murder was not proven and manslaughter was.

'I must now outline to you,' Colonel Lovesy continued, 'the evidence which the Prosecution proposes to bring and which the Court may be pleased to consider relevant to the Accused's motives in shooting Drummer Harley.'

'One moment, if you please, Colonel Lovesy,' said General Peterson. 'I am sure the learned Judge Advocate will concur with me when I give you the following warning : as President of this Court, I have been allowed to study the Summary of Evidence, and I am, therefore, roughly acquainted with the line of investigation you propose to pursue. You are most sternly adjured that this investigation must relate strictly to the motives of the Accused in the matter now under discussion; and that if any use is made of the evidence to cast general discredit upon Mr Lynch without at the same time eliciting something of relevance to this case, then the Court will stop the trial and return an immediate verdict of "not guilty".'

The Judge Advocate concurred without qualification. Lovesy seemed none too pleased by the admonition. He gave a momentary but malicious look towards the Court and then said spikily :

'The Court will perhaps concede that my experience—'

Peterson waved this aside.

'The Court merely bids you be relevant,' he said. 'Please continue.'

'As the Court pleases,' said Colonel Lovesy. 'Apart, then, from medical evidence as to the cause of Harley's death, the Prosecution will call witnesses as follows . . .'

Lovesy then proceeded to give substance to Sanvoisin's predictions. He was going to call Killeen, he said, to state that he had seen the Accused in bed with the deceased man, Drummer Harley, some ten days before Harley's death; Barnett and Fergusson to say that they had seen Harley, on different occasions, going late at night to the Accused's tent : and then he was going to call Simes. Simes would attest that he was a close friend of Harley's, that he knew of Harley's friendship with Lynch, and that he had discovered, at Glukeia, that the relationship was criminal. He would tell the Court how he had remonstrated both with Harley and Lynch on this account four days before Harley's death; and how Harley had come to him, only two days before his death, to speak further of the matter. Simes would stress that this interview, an exact report of which was forbidden by the Rules of Hearsay, had been calmly and sensibly conducted. and had given him great pleasure and relief on Harley's account.

Colonel Lovesy was then going to pass to evidence about the actual attack on November the 26th. Simes, continuing his testimony, would relate how Harley had begged to join a get-away party which was to seek help; how Harley had insisted that he must go instead of Simes and in order to prove to his comrades that he was not the soft and effeminate creature they thought his association with Lynch had made him. All this would be confirmed by Corporal Barnett and Sergeant Royd – who would support Simes in saying that the Accused became violently angry at Harley's request. Finally, all three witnesses would give the same account of how Lynch shot Harley when Harley, disobeying Lynch's wishes, leapt from the trench and attempted to go for help on his own. Lynch had said, after the shooting, 'Now you know what happens to people who disobey orders in action'; and Simes at least would say that this remark had been made in a cruel fashion.

'Having established all this,' Lovesy concluded, 'the Prosecution will later proceed, in its closing address, to develop certain arguments based on these facts and indicating a guilty intention in the accused person, Lieutenant Lynch, unlawfully to kill Drummer Harley. Meanwhile, the Prosecution submits, with the greatest deference, that nothing it proposes to prove can be held irrelevant to the case at issue.'

General Peterson then conferred briefly with the Judge Advocate.

'The Court is of opinion,' Peterson said, 'that provided evidence is brought strictly on the lines indicated by the able Officer for the Prosecution, then such evidence may fairly and relevantly be admitted before the Court. The Court will now adjourn until half past two o'clock.'

147

CHAPTER TWELVE

So THERE IT was, I thought. No formality. They were going for Alastair in earnest.

Still, it would be untrue to say that we had really been expecting anything else. Since Sanvoisin had first told Michael and myself of Simes' claim that Harley had determined to reject Alastair, I had realised that here was the one link needed by the Prosecution to connect what most people would regard as Alastair's vicious and perverted conduct with the actual circumstances of Harley's death. Of course Peterson was right. 'Such evidence,' he said, 'may fairly and relevantly be admitted before the Court.' How else? A man sleeps with another man and then he kills him. Their relationship is inevitably relevant. But at least, I thought, one good thing would come of the Prosecution's determination to make an all-out attack on Alastair. The facts of his connection with Harley were now going to be so pawed and mauled and quarrelled over in open Court, so fully and appetizingly reported to the world in general, that no judge on earth would ever accept them as the subject of separate and subsequent proceedings against Alastair on the ground of indecent conduct. Since Harley was dead, it was unlikely that such proceedings would ever have been instituted; and now it was impossible. If Alastair came through the present trial in one piece, then, though he would certainly have to resign, in one piece he would stay.

This was a consolation; but it did not alleviate the gravity of Alastair's predicament. The Prosecution was alleging that Alastair had behaved towards Harley in an infamous and unnatural fashion; and it was obviously going to make out that the relationship which had resulted had finally gone sour even by the standards which obtain in such intercourse, and that Alastair, in a fit of spite and jealousy, had seized an opportunity of revenging himself on his catamite for daring to obey a decent impulse and reject his seducer. From all of which, it followed plainly that the Defence, apart from emphasising the many admirable aspects of Alastair's behaviour during the attack itself and the sound military reasons that had existed for killing Harley, would be best employed in proving conclusively that Alastair and Harley had remained on the most affectionate possible terms right up to the day of Harley's death. Alastair himself maintained that this was the case and claimed that Harley had slept with him on the very last night before he was killed. The only trouble was that beyond Alastair's own word there was no proof of this. For all the people who had seen and heard Harley going

148

to Alastair's tent on one occasion or another, not one single man could be found who knew this to have occurred on that vitally important night. Nor was this very surprising : Harley's visits had no doubt had a certain novelty scandal value when the Troop first reached Glukeia, but by the time a fortnight had passed the topic was probably a stale one and everyone had long since ceased to care or to notice where Harley spent the hours of darkness. It had become, no doubt, a matter of routine – accepted without thought, just another boring commonplace of a disagreeable assignment.

The fact was, then, that the Prosecution, what with Harley's words and behaviour to Alastair during the attack and the implications of Harley's discussion with Simes, had something of a case for asserting that the lovers had fallen out, against which the Defence could only produce Alastair, whose interest and vanity were alike deeply involved, to assert that everything had remained sweet and unchanged until the very last. Michael and I had tried everything we knew in our efforts to find evidence that would support Alastair's claim. But at last, totally defeated, we had fallen back on our only witness – Alastair himself; and two nights before the trial we had gone to his tent to hear once more the story we now knew almost by heart – his own version of what had happened the night before the attack.

But at first we had discussed the whole affair in a more general light.

'You'll be glad to know,' said Michael (who had that afternoon returned from final and futile investigations in Gikumo), 'that your Troop is very much behind you. But what none of them can understand is why you carried on with Harley as you did up at Glukeia. In some obscure way they seem to connect all that with the subsequent disaster – and of course in some senses they're not far wrong. But why did you, Alastair? Out of sheer human interest, I want to know what can possibly have induced someone of your intelligence to carry on an affair like that so very blatantly and in such superlatively unsuitable surroundings.'

'Everyone seems to wonder that,' said Alastair. 'It was rather odd, I suppose. But then there was a feeling I had in that forest that nothing which happened there really counted as having happened at all. The rules, I thought, must surely be suspended in mountains as remote as these. After all, I don't suppose a hundred white men in all had been there until we came. And then again, I'd known Royd and the rest for so long that they seemed, so to speak, to be in the family : they might perhaps complain but they'd never do anything . . . Oh yes, I knew Killeen and Simes wanted watching. But even with them, I thought, there could never be any question of taking the matter beyond the Troop itself. Even now, I don't think Simes would have done it if poor Malcolm hadn't been killed :

for one thing, he'd have been too frightened of getting Malcolm into trouble as well as me.

'And then you must remember that we were really very dangerously placed – as was later made plain enough. In the circumstances one needed what comfort one could get. And by this time Malcolm meant more than comfort. In the hills at any rate he meant everything there was. Even if I hadn't loved him as much as I did, even if he had been only a plaything, he would still have been a substitute for everything I hadn't got there – books and wine and you two and Robin and Percy... But since I did love him, and since I thought we might both get killed at any time... Can you understand this, either of you?'

'Perhaps,' I said, 'and anyway it's done now. Now we've got the consequences to deal with. If they really go for you at this trial, they're going to try to prove that you and Harley had a row just before the end. They're going to say that Harley's conversation with Simes indicates that Harley broke with you; that his behaviour in your trench confirms this; that your anger when he persisted in wanting to go confirms it still more; and that finally you lost control and shot him. Now, Michael has just come back from Gikumo – and he's had no luck at all. The only evidence that you were still on good terms with Harley is going to be yours. So once more, and for the last time, let's go over it again and make certain you've got it all straight. Firstly then, they're going to say that considering how often Harley was spotted arriving in your tent, it's very odd no one noticed him on that last night. So what is your answer to that?'

'I shall say that he was making a definite effort to be quieter since he'd had that row with Simes; and that in any case it isn't true that he was seen coming *all* that often. He came to me nearly every night, I shall say, but he probably wasn't spotted more than three or four times.'

'All right. Then they're going to press you. Both the prosecution and Colonel Nicholas. So do you *swear* you were still on good terms with Harley?'

'Yes, I swear it.'

'And do you swear that he came to you on that last night as willingly as ever? That he behaved in the same affectionate manner as he always did?'

'Yes.'

'All right. Well then, one side or the other will possibly ask you for details. So let's have the story again.'

And for the fiftieth time Alastair started on the story of his last night with Malcolm Harley.

'He came at nearly three, long after I had given him up for the night. "Sorry I'm late," he said, "I was thinking." "Thinking?" "Thinking about this forest and how I wish the rain would stop."

"And that was all?" "And how I hope no one will attack us here, because I'm not sure I could stand it."

' "You'll be with me," ' Alastair had told him.

' "But I've never been in action before." '

' "Neither have I." '

' "Well, that makes two of us, I suppose." '

' "Yes, two of us. Two of us here and now." '

'And later on,' Alastair had told Michael and myself, this time and so many times in those days before the trial, 'later on we went to sleep. It was damned uncomfortable in that little bed, but I never minded with Malcolm. Then it grew light, so I woke him up. "Time to go," I said. "All right," he said, and put on his clothes, sitting all hunched up on the floor of my tent. "Good-bye," he said, "and thank you very much." And then he was gone and that was the last I really saw of him except later in the trench, when he started drinking straight away and made no sense at all.'

Normally Alastair's account finished here. But on this, the last time before the trial that he told us his story, he had merely paused for a moment, and then continued :

'Sometimes I think the real Harley disappeared somewhere when the fighting started, and that what I killed wasn't Malcolm at all, just his body with another and alien soul inside it. So that *his* soul is still wandering about in the forest, trying to find his body again and wondering where we've all gone to and looking at the graves up there, hoping that none of them was for him but despairing more and more as the days go on.

'And perhaps, I think, his soul will eventually find its way to Gikumo, still looking for his body, and, not finding it, will drift on down to Eirene and realise that there's one place his body must be – here with me in this tent. So sometimes I dream that his soul really comes here in its search, twitching open the flap of the tent like a breath of wind and gliding towards the bed. And when it finds only me and not the body it yearns for, it gives a great moan of despair and sorrow and flies off into the night for ever.'

In this way, before ever he was tried, had Alastair rebutted for our benefit the charges that Colonel Lovesy was now urging against him. As for his three defending officers, Sanvoisin, Michael and I believed every word he said : he was our comrade and our dear friend and he had fought the good fight – if not without introducing regrettable complications; and now, hearing Lovesy's lisping and insinuating tones, we hated the able Officer for the Prosecution as though he had been a common hangman.

For after the adjournment for luncheon, Lovesy started to call his witnesses. The first of these was our Medical Officer, Surgeon-Captain Nicolle.

The Surgeon-Captain's evidence was little more than a formality. Yes, he said, he had attended while Harley's body was exhumed five days after burial : Harley had been killed by a .303 bullet which had entered his back and then his heart. But for all that this fact was simply routine evidence, for all that I had known for days everything Nicolle was going to say, I suddenly felt sick and depressed at the idea of Harley's body being dragged up to the light again, realising for the first time the condition it must have been in after five days uncoffined in the damp earth. I thought of the grim little party in the forest : the soldiers with spades, digging at first quickly and later with great care, until eventually someone's spade hit something soft and yet resistant ...

'Yes,' said Nicolle, 'death would have been instantaneous.'

'Call Mounted Corporal Killeen.'

This was the first time I had seen Killeen for some weeks. He looked pale but calm, making a good figure in full dress. If ever he had been at all ill with his dysentery, he looked fit enough now.

'Take the Bible in your right hand and repeat after me : I swear by Almighty God ...'

He repeated the oath firmly and clearly. A plausible man. Oily but plausible.

'Sit down in that chair, Corporal. You will address your answers to my questions directly to the Court. State your name, rank, number, and employment in this Battalion.'

In a matter of moments Lovesy brought out Killeen's position in Alastair's Troop and the fact that this Troop had proceeded, on November the 12th, to a position near Glukeia.

'And on the night of November the 16th, how were you employed?'

'I was commanding the picket, Sir.'

'And therefore responsible for the safety of the Troop. Do you recall that anything unusual occurred that night?'

'Yes. About one in the morning, while making my rounds, I thought I heard some suspicious noises in the forest down the hill from our camp. I went to the Troop Commander's tent.'

'And what happened then?'

Glancing towards Alastair's men in the audience, I noticed how tensely they now sat.

'I put my head through the tent flap and saw the Troop Commander, Mr Lynch, in his camp bed. There was someone else in the bed with him. After a second or two I recognised Drummer Harley.'

'You're sure it was Harley?'

'Yes, Sir. I was shining my torch in Mr Lynch's face to wake him up. The other face on the pillow was quite plain.'

'I see. And then?'

'I told Mr Lynch about the noises and he said he'd come and see.'

'And did he?'

'About three minutes later. But we heard nothing more, so after a while he went back to bed.'

'Did he say anything about you having seen Harley in his bed?'

'Nothing at all, Sir. He was as cool as you please.'

Some of Alastair's men smiled, knowingly and with pleasure.

'Well then, Killeen. Had anything occurred before this incident which might have been construed as prefatory to the scene you saw?'

'Sir?'

'Were Mr Lynch and Harley often to be seen together before the incident you describe?'

'Frequently, Sir. Before we left Gikumo for Glukeia, Mr Lynch chose Harley as his runner nearly every day. Then, when we went up to Glukeia, he made Harley Troop Trumpeter—'

'Troop Trumpeter? What appointment is this?'

'No one had ever heard of it before, Sir. But it meant that Harley was moved into Troop H.Q. with Mr Lynch. They were together most of the day. Harley often used to ride into Glukeia with Mr Lynch to see the village Headman.'

'And was this preference for Harley's company noticed by the men in Mr Lynch's Troop?'

'A number of jokes were made.'

'Which did not assist discipline?'

'Definitely not, Sir.'

'Ah. But when you finally saw Mr Lynch and Harley in bed together, did you not think you should tell someone about it?'

A look of disdain appeared on Colonel Grail's face at the right of the Court.

'I mentioned it to Mounted Infantryman Simes, Harley's friend. He said he had his own ideas about it already. Then I got to thinking it was my duty to tell someone in authority. So when I got dysentery and had to go back to Gikumo, I told Captain Duthwaite.'

'And how did he react?'

'The Court,' interposed General Peterson, 'cannot interest itself in Captain Duthwaite's opinions as relayed at second-hand.'

'If the President pleases, I had proposed to call Captain Duthwaite, had the Court so desired, to corroborate this witness. Since both Killeen and Captain Duthwaite were acting, at the time of the interview, in an official capacity—'

'You evidently forgot, Colonel Lovesy, that this affair could call Captain Duthwaite's military character very much into question. We cannot do that while he is out of Court; nor is it desirable to press him in the matter should he appear in the stand as a witness.

I see no reason why Corporal Killeen's story should not stand or fall by its own inherent credibility and by such direct corroboration as you may be able to produce.'

Colonel Grail registered satisfaction. The Judge Advocate nodded agreement.

'As you please, Sir. Perhaps I may have the Court Orderly instruct Captain Duthwaite he is released?'

'You may,' said Peterson with a sign to Sergeant Godawake. 'Now kindly continue your examination.'

But Lovesy had concluded his examination and Colonel Nicholas declined to cross-examine. Killeen's departure was thus something of an anti-climax, and in my view at least the force of his testimony had been lessened by the sudden switch of attention to a different matter – the competence or otherwise of Duthwaite as a witness. Still, Killeen's story had a definite ring of truth; no doubt he had deliberately manufactured an excuse for spying on Alastair in his tent, but none of us disbelieved his account of what he had seen there. Indeed, Alastair had long ago admitted to us the truth of the tale. There was plainly no point in cross-examination.

The next witness was Fergusson the mortar-man. Rather unwillingly, he admitted that one night, about a week after they had reached Glukeia, he had left his tent to relieve himself at half past two in the morning and had seen Harley going into Alastair's tent. That such evidence from Fergusson should ever have become available indicated the extreme thoroughness with which the investigators had done their work. They must have brow-beaten the whole Troop, I thought. Hitherto, I had been inclined to blame James Sinclair for making up an unnecessarily detailed summary. But now I began to realise that he could hardly have disregarded the discoveries so conscientiously made by the S.I.B. men even – and this was unlikely – had he wished to disregard them. Still, however that might be, Fergusson's evidence was plainly true and, in a general way, plainly corroborated Killeen's story. Once again, Sanvoisin declined to cross-examine.

Lovesy had advertised Corporal Barnett as his next witness; but now he remarked that Barnett's evidence was mainly in confirmation of what Simes would say, and that therefore, if there was no objection, he would call Simes first. It seemed impossible to detect any very remarkable forensic subtlety here, and Simes was duly called. He looked clean, smart, honest and stupid. For once in a way he did not look resentful at the presence of officers. Perhaps he had been looking forward to the occasion.

'And what did you know, as Harley's close friend, of his relationship with your Troop Commander, Mr Lynch?'

'They were very thick, Sir, from the time we got to Gikumo. Mr Lynch was always picking Harley for his runner. And then they

154

used to go for walks in the evenings. I used to see them down by the stream. They were at it for hours.'

'At what for hours?'

A titter from a journalist, instantly muffled.

'I don't rightly know, Sir. Just together for hours. It made me mad. I used to ask young Harley if he'd forgotten his mates completely.'

'And this is all you knew about the matter?'

'Oh, no, Sir. Later on, up at Glukeia, I heard a lot of dirty things said. There were sayings about Harley going to Mr Lynch' tent in the night, and then Corporal Killeen tells me straight out he's seen them. So I thought about all this for a long time, and at last I worked myself up and went to see Mr Lynch. And after that I knew it was true – that young Harley was going with Mr Lynch just like he was his girl.'

The Court sat boot-faced. C.S.M. Mole's cheeks were sunken like goblets.

'When did you go to Mr Lynch?'

'Four days before we were attacked. I said was it true he slept with Harley? And he nodded his head. "I thought so," I said; "why couldn't you leave him alone? He's not your type. He doesn't come from college and he doesn't speak with a nice educated voice. He doesn't know about all these foreign places you tell him of, nor yet about the fancy ways you've picked up there. Why did you have to fill his head with that? Why not leave him to his mates? And then on top of that you have to take advantage. He's only eighteen, but you have to put your gentleman's hands all over him, soft, white hands, I can see, but as dirty as hell for all that. You dirty, rotten, ——ing sod," I said, "why couldn't you leave him alone?" Then I said a lot more I can't remember properly, but it all came to the same. That Mr Lynch had done wrong by Harley, that he was there to protect him and make a soldier of him, not to teach him filthy habits and paw him about like a paid whore. And Mr Lynch just nodded and said nothing. Then, when I'd said all I could think of, he just said in that cool sneering way of his, "When you're older you may be more tolerant. And now you'd better go." '

'So you went?'

'Yes, Sir. I went straight and told Sergeant Royd what I thought of his precious "Mr Alastair", and then I went to Harley and told him I knew for certain now what he got up to. I said he wasn't fit to look his mates in the face. I said a lot I'm sorry for now, that he was just a nasty little pouf, a randy little girl sniffing round men's trousers, things like that. I wish I hadn't.'

'What did Harley do?'

'He looked rather sad, Sir, and went away. I'm sorry now for what I said. I'd give a lot not to have said it.'

'But did you discuss this matter again with Harley?'

'Yes, Sir. Two days before the attack Harley came to me and said he wanted to talk more about Mr Lynch and what I'd said. He'd been thinking that over, he told me, and—'

'It is clear,' said Sanvoisin rising, 'that the witness is speaking in the best of good faith. Nevertheless, I must ask the Court to caution Colonel Lovesy against allowing Simes to repeat anything that Harley may or may not have told him on this occasion. It is hearsay of the most elementary nature.'

'I concur with Colonel Sanvoisin,' said the Judge Advocate. 'In so far, Colonel Lovesy, as you intend to refer to this discussion between the Witness and Drummer Harley, you will kindly proceed with the greatest care.'

'As the learned Judge Advocate pleases,' said Lovesy. 'Now, Simes, you must pay strict attention to all my questions and only tell me what you are asked to tell me. Above all, you must not attempt to repeat anything your friend, Harley, actually said to you.'

'Why not?'

'Because he may not have told you the truth.'

'He always told me the truth.'

'Mounted Infantryman Simes,' said General Peterson, 'I appreciate that you wish to do your duty by your dead friend. Please believe that the best service you can do for him and for all of us is to answer with the greatest care and exactly as Colonel Lovesy has told you.'

'Sir,' said Mounted Infantryman Simes.

'Well then,' said Lovesy, 'you say that Harley came to you two days before the attack – two days, that is, before he was killed.'

'Yes, Sir.'

'Who started the conversation?'

'Young Harley did.'

'What was the subject?'

'He was on about Mr Lynch. He said—'

'Never mind what he said. You both talked about Mr Lynch?'

'About what Mr Lynch and Harley did together.'

'And in what way was the discussion conducted?'

'Quiet like,' said Simes, 'quiet and friendly.'

'And Harley told you how he felt about Mr Lynch? And how he felt about your own disapproval of their . . . connection?'

'He did, Sir.'

'And how did you feel when the conversation was over?'

'Glad,' said Simes, 'real pleased I was, because I thought—'

'Never mind that. Were you pleased for Harley or for yourself?'

'I was pleased for myself, Sir, and right happy for Harley. And as for Mr Lynch—'

'That will do, Simes. The conversation was quiet and sensible, and it pleased you for your own sake but even more for Harley's. Did you ever discuss Mr Lynch again before Harley was killed?'

'No, Sir. That was all settled.'

'What was settled? That you shouldn't discuss the matter again?'

'No, Sir, but what was to be done. It was all settled that Har—'

'The Court will question the witness,' said Peterson, 'after which the Prosecution will drop this topic.'

Lovesy looked nasty but held his tongue.

'Simes,' pursued Peterson, 'did you make any suggestions to Harley, or did you merely hear Harley express his own intentions?'

'He expressed an intention, Sir, to—'

'Just answer my questions. Harley expressed an intention. Did you approve this intention?'

'Yes, Sir, I did.'

'Very well, Colonel Lovesy. You will now pass to the remainder of this man's evidence.'

'As the President directs. Now, Simes, you will fix your mind on the day of the attack. I am not concerned here with the earlier stages of that attack. Please tell me what happened just before 1400 hours – just before two in the afternoon.'

'Well, Sir, Sergeant Royd called Corporal Barnett and me and Teague and Evans over to the trench he and Mr Lynch was in with Harley. Mr Lynch starts explaining to us that he wants us to get through to Mr Hathaway. He tells us which way to go, and then Harley interrupts him and says *he* wants to go.'

'Was Mr Lynch angry?'

'Not really, Sir. He only got angry later. But this time he shuts Harley up sharp and nasty, and gets on with what he's telling us.'

Sitting on Peterson's left, Major-General Osborne snorted *sotto voce*.

'Was Sergeant Royd still in the trench?'

'No, Sir. Sergeant Royd had gone off to warn everybody about the covering fire for our get-away. He got back a minute or two later. Says there's five minutes to go before we have to start. So Mr Lynch finishes up his orders, and we sit there waiting for the word to go. But then young Harley starts up again.'

Major-General Osborne snorted once more.

'And what did he say this time?'

'He says he must go and that he'll go instead of me. He says he wants to show us all he's not just a little nancy like everyone says. It's Mr Lynch's fault, he says, that anyone says this, and Mr Lynch must let him go. Well, it's a bit late for this sort of talk and we're none of us feeling too good, so I try and shut him up.'

'What did Mr Lynch do?'

'He didn't do anything, Sir. But he looked fierce. Really fierce and

157

nasty. I thought he was going to hit Harley or worse. That's why
I was trying to keep Harley quiet. So there we all were. Me calming
Harley down, or trying to, and Mr Lynch scowling like the devil
himself, and the rest listening to me with their eyes half out of their
heads, and then all of a sudden Harley calls out, "I will go. I'll
show you all." Something like that. And before anyone can stop
him, he's out of that trench and running across the camp – the
same way we'd been told to go, towards the slope up to the horse
lines.'

'But he never got out of the camp?'

'No, Sir. Mr Lynch calls to him to stop, but he takes no notice,
so then I try to get out after him. But Mr Lynch heaves me back,
snatches Sergeant Royd's rifle, and shoots him in the back there and
then, just as the poor little ——er gets to the edge of the camp.
But oh the shame of it, gentlemen. Oh, the cruel, wicked—'

'That will do, Simes,' said the Judge Advocate. 'We are here to
enquire into fact, not to indulge in indignation . . . Colonel Lovesy.'

'Tell the Court again,' said Lovesy, 'which way Harley went.'

'The way we'd been told for the get-away. Doing it for us, he was.
And might have got through if that murderous swine hadn't—'

'Silence,' shouted Peterson. 'Colonel Lovesy, you will control your
witness or he will be dismissed the stand. Mounted Infantryman
Simes, you will tell the Court only what you saw and heard. You
will not give your opinions, and you will not insult Mr Lynch, who
is an innocent man until and unless this Court declares otherwise.
Now then, Colonel Lovesy.'

'Did Mr Lynch make any attempt to order fire to cover Harley's
get-away?' Colonel Lovesy asked.

'I must object,' said Sanvoisin. 'The question plainly invites the
witness to a further expression of opinion.'

Simultaneously, Peterson leant towards the Judge Advocate,
Lovesy swung round at Sanvoisin with a bark of anger, and Simes
began to shout at the top of his voice with terrific speed :

'Of course he didn't. He could have done and he didn't. Shoots
him down instead without—'

'Simes,' thundered Peterson.

'Sir,' screamed Simes.

'If it were not for the fact that Harley was your friend,' said
Peterson evenly, 'you would already be starting a severe sentence
of imprisonment for contempt of Court. As it is, I will give you one
more chance. There will be an adjournment for five minutes. During
that time you will pull yourself together; and you will return before the Court prepared to answer, in a proper and courteous fashion,
the proper questions' – a glance at Lovesy – 'that will be put to you.
Court Orderly, march the witness out.'

Everyone remained seated during the five minutes' break. Peterson beckoned Lovesy up to the bench; and Lovesy evidently didn't like what was whispered to him there. When Simes returned, Lovesy started questioning him again with an almost humble demeanour.

'Well then, Simes. Did anyone say anything after Mr Lynch had shot Harley?'

'Only Mr Lynch himself. He's stopped looking angry now and is sneering all over his face. Cold and sneering he is. And a voice to go with it. "Now you know what happens," he says, "When people disobey orders in action".'

Brigadier Godfrey, on the extreme left of the Court, looked impressed.

'I see. And then?'

'Well then they start up with the covering fire and Mr Lynch sends us off.'

'And did you get through?'

'No, Sir.' And Simes told how the enemy had immediately fired on the get-away party; how Teague and Evans had been killed; and how the prompt action of Fergusson with his mortar had enabled Corporal Barnett and Simes himself to return safely to the position where Alastair had called them.

'And so, despite everything, Mr Lynch's plan for a break-out failed completely?'

Brigadier Godfrey, plainly a 'team-spirit man', now looked almost cheated.

'That it did, Sir,' said Simes with relish.

'Thank you, Simes. Colonel Sanvoisin is now going to ask you some questions. You must not allow the fact that he is defending Mr Lynch to make any difference to you. Nor the fact that he is your commanding officer. You will answer his questions in the same truthful and sincere way as you have answered my own.'

'Sir.'

Sanvoisin, I knew, was relying mainly on his cross-examination of Sergeant Royd and on Alastair's own testimony to bring out what he wanted. But there were one or two admissions that could profitably be extorted from Simes, and these he set about obtaining straight away.

'Mounted Infantryman Simes, you have testified that you were a close friend of the deceased man, Drummer Harley?'

'I have, Sir.'

'You have also said that "it made you mad" sometimes when Harley spent long periods with Mr Lynch. Why was this?'

'Well, I was wanting to see something of Harley myself. Mr Lynch had his own friends among the officers. And then I thought that the things Harley heard from Mr Lynch weren't ... well, suitable. They were things for Mr Lynch and his kind, not for Harley.'

'So you resented both the extent of Mr Lynch's influence over

Harley and the amount of time Harley was away from you because of Mr Lynch?'

'I did, Sir.'

'In short, Simes, you were jealous of Mr Lynch.'

'Jealous, Sir?'

'Yes, Simes, jealous. You were "mad" because Harley spent so long with Mr Lynch?'

'Yes.'

'And you thought the things they discussed "unsuitable"?'

'I did, Sir.'

'And when you finally realised, at Glukeia, that Harley and Mr Lynch had a sexual relationship, you were very angry indeed?'

'So would any decent man be.'

Brigadier Milner sitting on the right of the Judge Advocate, smiled like a demon welcoming a soul newly damned.

'Decency is not in question. You then proceeded to insult both Mr Lynch and Drummer Harley in the most vile terms?'

'Certainly I did, Sir.'

'Why?'

'Because I liked Harley and didn't want him to go wrong, and I thought Mr Lynch was sending him wrong.'

'Exactly. You liked Harley; and you didn't like Mr Lynch because of what you thought he was doing to Harley. You were, in fact, jealous of Mr Lynch.'

'If you put it like that, Sir.'

'I do put it like that. And I suggest to you that the whole story you tell of Mr Lynch's conduct during the attack is warped by this jealousy – warped and twisted and perverted by jealousy on the one hand and your natural grief on the other.'

'I've told the truth.'

'You have also called Mr Lynch a "murderous swine". But can you swear, Simes, that Mr Lynch didn't have a perfectly sound and indeed very pressing military motive for shooting Harley?'

'I can't swear, Sir, but—'

'Who would be the better judge of what the military situation required? You or Mr Lynch?'

'Mr Lynch, I suppose.'

'That is very condescending of you, Simes. Tell me, when Mr Lynch gave you your orders for the get-away, did he leave you in any doubt at all?'

'No, Sir.'

'What did he tell you?'

'He said our best chance was to nip up the slope using what cover there was while all the lads let off everything they had to keep the wogs quiet. We were to go on round the horse lines, split up, and make like hell for Glukeia.'

'But in the event you were spotted. Teague and Evans were killed. You and Corporal Barnett took cover, and then the mortar man knocked out the enemy post that was firing on you?'

'That's right, Sir.'

'But after that, why didn't you get on towards Glukeia?'

'Mr Lynch called us back.'

'Just so. And a good thing, wasn't it? Because just after he did so a large party of the enemy appeared on the slope – just where you would have been had Mr Lynch not called you?'

'More or less.'

'So you probably have Mr Lynch to thank that you're here today. And this is the officer whose military judgement you "suppose" is better than your own?'

'Sir,' said Simes.

A vindictive look from Mole in the audience.

'So I take it that you are now less than ever prepared to swear that Mr Lynch could not have had a perfectly good military motive for shooting Harley?'

'That's as may be. But there was a lot had happened up at Glukeia; and I'm telling you that just before that shot was fired Mr Lynch looked angry enough to shoot his own mother out of meanness. And after—'

'But can you wonder Mr Lynch was angry? With thirty-odd lives on his hands, and a get-away party about to go off for essential help, and Harley grizzling away at him? It would have tried anyone's self-control.'

'I know that, Sir. But Mr Lynch's anger seemed more than that somehow.'

' "Seemed"? "Somehow"? To you, perhaps, with your idiotic jealousies and petty-minded spite.'

As Simes started to yell out his answer, the Judge Advocate seemed about to claw the table-cloth away. But at an appealing glance from Sanvoisin, he sank back quiet.

'That's not fair,' shouted Simes. 'I liked Harley every bit as much as Mr Lynch did *and* I was a good friend to him *and* I should never have mussed him about like a bloody girl. What I felt for Harley was what one man ought to feel for another, respect and friendship and glad to have him with me because he was a fine, good man, brave and loyal and fair and kind, not because I wanted to gush on him and call him fancy names and play about with him when I had nothing better to do. And then Mr Lynch gets hold of him like he did and it made me sick. Sick to my bloody heart, do you hear?' he screamed across the Court.

'Very well, Simes,' said Sanvoisin quietly. 'Both the Court and myself will appreciate what you have said.'

He looked at Lovesy, who shook his head.

'You may go, Simes,' said Sanvoisin. 'Whatever has been said here this afternoon, no one has forgotten, or will forget, that in many ways you behaved with great courage on the day of the attack.'

And despite the scowl with which he received this, Simes left the Court with a look of pride and pleasure on his face.

CHAPTER THIRTEEN

THE PROSECUTION HAD now only two more witnesses to bring – Corporal Barnett and Sergeant Royd. Barnett came first. He too, he said, had seen Harley going into Alastair's tent very late one night when he had been in command of the picket. Lovesy then brought him on to the day of the attack. Point by point he confirmed, as Lovesy had said he would, everything that Simes had told the Court : the summons to Alastair's trench, Harley's brief interruption during the briefing, Alastair's sharp response; how Harley had spoken up once more when Alastair had finished his instruction; how Alastair had indeed given him a look of fury ... But it was not the first time I had heard all this and my attention began to wander; until finally I ceased to hear what was being said in the Court Room and fell to considering what impressions the evidence so far produced might have made upon the Court.

General Peterson had been poker-faced throughout. I remembered how he had reacted to Harley's drunkenness on the guard of honour, how he had finished his inspection looking neither to right or left, stiff, indifferent, no longer indicating by so much as a twitch that he acknowledged anyone's existence at all. I wondered whether he associated 'the deceased man, Drummer Harley' with the boy who had breathed beer fumes at him on the parade ground. Very likely. Harley's name had been mentioned on that occasion ('Arrest Drummer Harley'), and Peterson, they said, forgot very little. But however that might be, his demeanour now was much as it had been then – save that something in the tilt of his head showed that he was paying the most minute attention to what was going forward. Since Peterson, as President, had seen the summary of evidence, he must have known fairly well what Lovesy might be going to say. But to judge from the intent look in his eyes, you would have said he was learning it all for the first time, without surprise or emotion certainly, even without interest, but with intense determination to resolve with clarity a boring and squalid set of circumstances to which only duty compelled his attention. But then to Peterson duty was all. I felt confidence in Peterson; confidence that impartiality and intelligence and an exact comprehension of his own function in the Court, these attributes and these alone, would dictate his interim decisions and his final judgement.

For different reasons, I felt confidence in the Judge Advocate. For all the predatory, hawk-like movements he made with his hands, arching his fingers over the table like claws as he spoke, it was plain

163

SIMON RAVEN

that he did not desire to scratch people's eyes from their heads but
rather to dig out, as it were, from the tablecloth in front of him,
the least vestige of doubt, whether in fact, law or procedure, upon
which it was his duty to comment. Judges advocate, I thought,
though not in the first flight for ability, are chosen very much for
their sincerity and extreme reverence for the law – a reverence so
profound that only second class minds could harbour it. I once con-
ceded that Keyes was typical of his employment – and everything,
from the time he had taken to robe himself to his precise and faintly
self-important manner, showed that he was typical – then there need
be no grounds for apprehension. For this day and for as long as
the trial lasted, our rude tent would be the tabernacle of the law;
and no influence within or without would cause the learned Judge
Advocate to overlook one particle of what was written in the tables.

Major-General Osborne and Colonel Grail, being respectively of
the Guards and the Dragoons, were showing the upper-class detachment one might have forecast. As for these two, I had little doubt
that Alastair's bearing, manner, record and background would dis-
pose them in his favour, whether they allowed themselves to be
conscious of this or not. And quite apart from their reluctance to
convict an old Harrovian, I could not imagine that either of them
would be unduly dismayed by the idea of a homosexual liaison –
they were surely above middle-class prejudices of that kind. The
trouble was that Osborne at least might have severe notions about
'disloyalty' to one's regiment or the Army in general; and if he construed Alastair's conduct with Harley, not so much immoral, but
simply as flagrant disloyalty to his regiment, class and kind, then
he might come out very savagely against Alastair without any regard to the substance of the case. The fact, then, that Osborne and
Grail might be inclined to think in terms of caste rather than of
justice was not necessarily the asset it might appear at first sight.

However, it was only when I came to the two Brigadiers, Godfrey
and Milner, that I was definitely uneasy. Godfrey, I thought, showed
in his face all the typical signs of minor public school distrust for
what might be called 'Etonian' goings-on : this attitude, a kind of
smug petulance, I had long since come to associate with many
members of poorer regiments, who bitterly resented the amusements
of plush-heeled juniors in smarter sections of the Service. Since the
amusement, in this case, was what officers of the dowdier kind refer
to as 'homosexual vice', I feared that Godfrey might take against
Alastair from the start – whatever the Judge Advocate had to say
about such conduct only being relevant in so far as it might have
affected the circumstances of Harley's death. As for Brigadier Milner,
he was one worse than Godfrey. Bullying, insistent, flat-voiced,
common, he did not even have the advantage of being an ex-ranker,
with all the understanding such experience normally confers. He

164

had proceeded in 1939, I had been told, straight from his employment in a midland factory to a commission in the R.A.O.C., had hung on and prospered after the war, and had now come to represent all the worst features of the post-war Army, in which such as he, with their grubby technical know-how, had of necessity to be retained. Everything about Alastair, his voice, appearance, uniform and mental attitude, was calculated to annoy Milner; and the mention of homosexuality could not fail to be an additional irritant. He had all the makings, to judge from his presence, of a man pathologically inimical to homosexuals and their behaviour; and even if this were not the case, a man of Milner's background and attainments could only view Alastair's affair with Harley at best as the irresponsible and malignant pastime of a degenerate worldling. The only thing I could hope for was that Milner would find the matter wholly incomprehensible. But when I considered the gutter cunning that lay behind his fishy bespectacled eyes, I could not feel this to be likely. Milner knew what it was all about; was scenting the dirt with trained and canny nostrils, was preparing with relish to gather the full, steaming savour.

The clue to so much, I felt, lay in the personal attitude which each of these men adopted to the question of pederasty. I might speculate as I pleased, but people's views in this matter were notoriously difficult to assess, let the grounds for assessment be as ample as one could wish. Take Sanvoisin, for example. One would confidently have expected him to shrug the whole thing off with the good-humoured tolerance bred of an objective intellectual approach. Instead of which, when pressed by Michael for his views some days before the trial, he had delivered a very sharp homily based on practical considerations.

'Anyone,' Sanvoisin had said, 'who, like Alastair, dares to be an *open* pederast must combine a number of very dangerous qualities. He is troubled, you see, neither by his conscience nor by the practical question of getting his livelihood. This almost certainly means that such a person is not only intelligent, sceptical and arrogant, but that he is very likely inordinately selfish and very rich as well. This in turn means that at this day and date such people are bound to be a sheer bloody nuisance. We have a young and idolised Queen on the throne, whose family life reflects all the virtues of the middle-classes from which she has sprung : how the hell, therefore, can one conduct public affairs through unchivalrous and irreligious men like these? We have a Welfare State – most of our recruits were reared by it; how can one justify the existence in our Mess of someone as blatantly arrogant, as openly selfish, as unashamedly rich as Alastair? We have a democracy in which human rights count for more than brains; and now what about Alastair's aristocratic scepticism, his subtly educated intelligence?'

'But this is absurd, Colonel,' I had told him. 'You're merely taking a whole string of qualities – many of which you yourself possess – and stigmatising them as anti-social or undemocratic.'

'Many of us possess these qualities,' Sanvoisin had replied. 'I myself am rich and, I hope, intelligent. You and Michael are both sceptical. And so on. But that is not to say we flaunt them. We use them for our convenience and pleasure, quietly and without fuss, and so give as little offence as possible to a democratic world. But an openly practising pederast not only possesses these qualities but is universally and inevitably *seen* to possess them. For they are the very things most evidently inseparable from the conduct of such a life. By being an open pederast, a man is *openly* arrogant, openly rich, openly sceptical. And hence the offence openly given to Mrs Smith of Birmingham, to our "young and lovely Queen" in Buckingham Palace, to trades' union leaders, to good-form conservative politicians – to everything and everybody in the Mediocrity State. The open homosexual, however likeable to you or me personally, is just a pure bloody nuisance in the sort of world in which you and I are forced to live and run an army. And if you want a prime example of his nuisance value, just take a look at this mess of Alastair's now.'

All of this might have been true enough, but I had not expected to hear it from Sanvoisin. If he – a man I knew very well – could suddenly come out with views like these, it was plainly futile to speculate over much as to what thoughts about homosexuality might be working beneath the frozen upper-class exteriors of Osborne and Grail, the Tom Brown façade of Godfrey, or the porcine features of Milner. I would do better, I thought, to limit myself to more general considerations. On balance, then, one could count Peterson and the Judge Advocate as strict but fair.

For the rest of the Court, there was less cause to be sanguine. For while there was no reason to suppose that any of them was unduly concerned with legality or justice, two of them were likely to be prejudiced in Alastair's favour for class reasons (which might well prove double-edged) and two more might be actively hostile from combined reasons of envy and distaste. An uneasy distribution. Again, however, a lot of things had yet to come out that were much in Alastair's favour. The full story of the attack was bound to make a good impression on Osborne and Grail at least; and it was to be hoped that Sergeant Royd, with his evident experience of active service, and Alastair himself, with becoming modesty, would make the best of this. The Court, in fact, had heard the worst; but even so, I was far from happy as I jettisoned my personal reflections and began, once more, to pay attention to the proceedings of the Court.

Corporal Barnett had confirmed, during the examination-in-chief, almost everything that Simes had said about the incidents which surrounded Harley's death. He had, however, refused to agree that Alastair's remark, 'Now you know what happens to people who disobey orders in action,' had been made in a cruel or vindictive fashion. Sanvoisin had elaborated on this during the cross-examination. Barnett agreed that Alastair was very angry when Harley started whining out his request, but, prompted by Sanvoisin, insisted that he had then calmed down. The remark in question, he said, had certainly been coldly made – and he for one was very glad it had been; for he had noticed how calm and cool Alastair seemed after his furious looks of a few moments before, and had thought to himself how necessary it was for him to be calm if he was to maintain his authority. Then the remark had been cold but not vindictive? Yes, that was it. And had Mr Lynch maintained his authority? Certainly he had. And it was certainly true that Mr Lynch's prompt recall had saved both Simes and the witness from being killed during the get-away. Sanvoisin then elicited a few incidental expressions of admiration from Barnett for Alastair's subsequent conduct; but he did not spend long. Lovesy declined to re-examine, and the last witness for the Prosecution was called.

'Mounted Sergeant Royd, take the Bible in your right hand...'

'...address all your answers to the Court. Kindly state your name, rank, number, and employment within this Battalion...'

'...and so you have been Mr Lynch's Troop Sergeant for about eighteen months?'

'Sir.'

'Now what, Sergeant Royd, did you know of Mr Lynch's relationship with the deceased man, Drummer Harley?'

'I knew Mr Lynch fancied Harley, Sir. And later on, up at Glukeia, I reckoned they were sleeping together.'

'You were, after Mr Lynch, responsible for the welfare of the Troop. Did you not feel it your duty to do something about this state of affairs?'

'I was worried, Sir, certainly. But Glukeia was a tricky place to be, even before the attack, and it was no time for making a complaint that might get Mr Lynch sent away from the Troop.'

'But surely your moral responsibility was quite plain?'

'Look, Sir,' said Royd, 'I had other things to bother about in Glukeia beside moral responsibility. Rain and wogs are more real than moral responsibility when the one comes pelting down all day and the other may appear screaming blue murder at any minute of the night. Harley or no Harley, the lads knew and liked and trusted Mr Lynch, and none of us wanted a new troop commander with new ways of going on just then. Things were quite bad enough without that.'

167

'So you knew of this deplorable situation and allowed it to continue?'

'I had my doubts but I left things as they were.'

'Very well, Sergeant Royd. Now kindly fix your attention on the day of this attack. You were in the same trench as Mr Lynch and Drummer Harley?'

'I was, Sir.'

'Tell me about the arrangements for the get-away party.'

'Mr Lynch and I cooked up the idea, Sir. Then we chose our men. Tough boys we wanted for this do, so Mr Lynch suggests Barnett and Teague and Evans, and I says we'd better send young Simes as well. Then Harley stuck his nose in and says not to send Simes, Simes being his mate, but to send himself instead.'

'This was before the party had been summoned to hear their orders?'

'Oh yes. Harley said his piece later on in front of them as well. But this time it was only to Mr Lynch and me. Says the same thing both times, mind you. Says Simes is his mate, so don't send Simes – and anyhow, he wants to show them all, he says.'

'Show them all what?'

'Well, that he's not just a soft-faced little punk but capable of doing his bit.'

'He said nothing about showing them he wasn't a "nancy boy"? Or about it being Mr Lynch's fault they thought so?'

'Yes, there was a lot of that. But I'd got enough to do without listening to that sort of carry-on, so I left Mr Lynch to deal with it.'

'I should warn you that you are speaking on oath in a court of law. You would do well to be more exact in your answers. Was Mr Lynch angry at Harley's request?'

'Not this first time, no, Sir. He just said that Simes and the rest were the kind we wanted for this job, and then he had me call them over. Then I went over to the other trenches to fix the covering fire for when they tried to get off.'

'And after that?'

'I fixed up for the covering fire and then got back to Mr Lynch when there was about five minutes to go.'

And once again we went over the familiar ground, Royd confirming all the facts as deposed by Simes and Barnett, among other things that Alastair had been very angry when Harley made yet another request to go instead of Simes.

At this point Lovesy asked and received permission to treat Sergeant Royd as sufficiently experienced to give military opinions. Yes, Royd said, Harley *might* have got through ... Yes, Mr Lynch *could* have given Harley covering fire and then sent the proper party right off after him; but it would have been a raggy affair if he had ...

Yes, there was no doubt Harley was taking the same route as Mr Lynch had told the others; it was a genuine attempt to get through all right, and all credit to Harley as far as that went; but whatever Colonel Lovesy might say, Harley was just making a complete piggery of the Troop Commander's plan, and that was the size of it. Yes, Mr Lynch had said something about 'this being what happened when orders were disobeyed in action.' A bit unnecessary, Royd had thought, but it was true enough at that, and he'd been glad to see Mr Lynch so firmly in control . . . Yes, the get-away had failed . . . Yes, the lads had been a bit unsettled for a time, but Mr Lynch had pulled them together.

'Thank you, Sergeant Royd.'

Sanvoisin rose to cross-examine.

'Sergeant Royd, Colonel Lovesy has questioned you as an expert on minor tactics : and indeed, no one knows better than I how much action you have seen before coming to Pepromene.

Almost imperceptibly, Royd glanced down at the medals on his chest. There was a Military Medal there. There were campaign medals. There were 'N.A.A.F.I.' medals and 'up-with-the-ration' medals. Leave the war alone, his chest showed that he had since been in Korea, Kenya, Palestine and Malaya. There was a Coronation Medal. There was even some kind of Belgian decoration.

'Yes, My Lord,' said Royd, 'I have been in action before coming to Pepromene.'

'Mainly with young officers?'

'Generally speaking, I've served with a troop rather than back with company or battalion H.Q. This means the front line, Sir, as you know. And the front line means young gentlemen in charge.'

'So that you have seen and judged a lot of subaltern officers in battle?'

'I have that.'

'Good. Now we will get on to the events of November the 26th, the day your position was attacked and Harley was killed. By the time you'd got through to Captain Duthwaite at Gikumo, things had settled down fairly steadily?'

'They had, Sir. Of course the wireless then got knocked out, but at that time we didn't reckon to need it again. And I dare say we should have been all right but for all that ammunition being spoiled. There was all your trouble for you. First we find we've got 8,000 rounds less than we thought, and the next thing we're being rushed all round.'

'What did you do then?'

'I went wet with fright, Sir. I've never been charged with bayonets before in all my service. If Mr Lynch hadn't thought of those grenades, some wog would have had my guts for a pennant.'

'Describe Mr Lynch's action.'

'He shouted "Grenades all round and close in", something like that. So the lads lobbed them over the edge and the whole lot went off ten yards out from our position. Caught the wogs as they ran over them. That finished their game – that and the brens.'

'And it is fair to say that these prompt orders of Mr Lynch's saved the Troop from being overrun?'

'Mr Lynch's orders, Sir, and the lads being cool enough to do as he said. Which many I've known would not.'

'I see. What happened next?'

'Well then Mr Lynch and me falls to thinking about all this ammunition we haven't got. Nor no wireless either. He says someone must get through to Mr Hathaway and bring him up to help. "There's two companies on the way," he says, "but they'll not be here till God knows when with all the mud this ——ing rain has made. If we're careful, we've got enough ammunition to last till five. We want Mr Hathaway here before then." So we made a plan to get a small party out. "It's a narrow thing," he said, "but if only one of them can get through ..." '

'And you agreed with the general idea?'

'I did, Sir.'

'And what about the actual plan for getting the party away? Did you approve of that?'

'Lord love your Lordship, I helped to make the plan. Not that it was much of one, but there wasn't nothing else for it. All we could do was try and keep the wogs quiet and send our boys out where there was most cover. Then it was each man for himself – to hell or Glukeia.'

'So then you chose your men. Now you and others have all told us very plainly what happened after that. But there are one or two points I want to clear up. Firstly, then, you say, as an experienced man, that had Mr Lynch let Harley continue, he might have got through?'

'Might. But there was only one of him and the covering fire hadn't started. Much more likely he'd just have been seen and shot and given the whole show away.'

'Did you ask Mr Lynch why he had acted as he did?'

'Yes, Sir. After the party had set off and then Barnett and Simes got back again, things settled down a bit once more. "What did you do that for?" I said: "poor little bastard." "For two reasons," Mr Lynch said. "Because he was disobedient under fire, and because if he'd got out of the camp he'd have drawn the enemy's attention to the route Barnett and the rest were to use. As it is," Mr Lynch said, "it was probably him running that way which alerted the enemy and got Barnett's lot shot at so quick." '

'How long after he shot Harley did he tell you this?'

'About five minutes.'

'During which time the get-away had tried and failed, and the survivors, Barnett and Simes, had returned to your position?'

'That's it, Sir.'

'So that now, with the get-away having flopped, things looked very bad indeed?'

'Black, Sir, really black. But Mr Lynch gets the lads back to more or less normal, considering what's happened, and we carry on as before. Firing just enough at where we knew the wogs were to keep them quiet. But after a bit Simes starts up and yells out something about Mr Lynch being a murderer.'

'So what happened,' said Sanvoisin, 'when Simes called Mr Lynch a murderer?'

'Mr Lynch said he'd have his chance to say all that later. But Simes keeps it up, so then Corporal Barnett knocked him on the head and that was the last we heard of him for a bit.'

'And then?'

'Well then, Sir, the afternoon goes on and everyone gets lower and lower. And if it hadn't been for Mr Lynch, I don't know what would have happened at all, because it was him kept them going and not much else, good lads as they were. Round all the trenches he went, bandaging and chatting and swopping cigarettes, and from the way he behaved you'd have said the only thing wrong was the boredom. He made them forget that there was precious little ammunition and help not coming till no one really knew when and a crowd of blood-thirsty niggers just waiting for our last bullet to go off. Then he got them to singing to cheer them up, and then suddenly I think to myself that the wogs haven't been firing at us lately, and tells Mr Lynch. So then he goes out for a look and there's nothing there, only bodies and empty cases and cigarette butts . . . And that's it, gentlemen; end of the battle, end of the day.'

'Thank you, Royd. Now one more thing. You have given us a clear account of an unpleasant and even critical situation, and you have described the steps taken by the Troop Commander, at various times, to deal with that situation. In the light of what happened, and in the light of all your experience, in action under officers similar in standing to Mr Lynch, what judgement would you give of his conduct on this occasion?'

'Brave, my Lord. Brave and cool. It was his first time in action, and like enough to have been his last, and everything to make it as bad as it could be. The surprise, the forest, the ammunition, the wireless, young Harley – everything. But for all of that he got us out, and there's not one of us but knows that and thanks him from the bottom of his heart.'

There was a low murmur of approbation from where Alastair's men were sitting among the spectators. Peterson looked up but said nothing. Then there was silence. After a clear minute, Sanvoisin said:

'Very well, Sergeant Royd. Unless Colonel Lovesy wishes to re-examine, you are dismissed.'

Lovesy shook his head. Royd saluted and marched out.

'This concludes the evidence for the Prosecution?' asked Peterson.

'It does, Sir.'

'The Court will reassemble at half past nine o'clock tomorrow to hear the case for the Defence. The Court will now adjourn.'

And we all went out into the damp evening.

CHAPTER FOURTEEN

THAT NIGHT, JUST after Alastair and I had finished dining alone in his tent, C.S.M. Mole came to pay a visit.

'Nice of you to call, C.S.M. Drink?'

'No, thank you, Mr Alastair, not now. I just popped in to wish you all the best for tomorrow ... They should get it finished by tea-time,' Mole added gloomily.

'It's not going so badly,' I said.

'True enough, Captain Andrew. And I dare say Charley Royd's little piece will have done no harm. But when that Colonel Lovesy gets round to his final speech, he's going to say a thing or two – and very nasty it's going to be. He's going to say that Mr Alastair got that worked up, what with what happened before the attack and all that Harley said during it that he upped and shot him out of temper. That's what he's going to say.'

'And I,' said Alastair, 'am going to spend most of the morning saying just the opposite. I'm going to say that nothing whatever happened before the attack and that though I did get angry during it I didn't stay angry for long. And that Harley had to be shot because he was endangering all our lives by spoiling the plan for a break-out.'

'I suppose so,' said Mole, giving Alastair a sharp look, 'though which of you they'll believe is more than I can say ... Anyhow, here are some messages I was given to tell you when we left Gikumo this morning. First of all, as I expect Captain Duthwaite will have told you, Major Berkeley and Mr Robin send best wishes. They would have come, only what with Captain Duthwaite being a witness, and you and Mr Michael being here anyway, someone's got to look after things at Gikumo.

'Then there's best wishes from the Sergeant's Mess too. And Mr Sach said he'd try to get down to see you as time went on. And that's the lot, except for the lads that are down here with me, who asked me to tell you their best respects.'

'Thank you, Moley. Are you *sure* you don't want a drink?'

'No, Mr Alastair, and thank you very much. But I'll just give you this before I go.'

He passed over a grubby envelope.

'I want it back, mind, tomorrow evening. It comes from Ireland, and I don't look to be going there again before I die.'

And then C.S.M. Mole gave one of his rare salutes and left us.

'What is it?'

'Alastair opened the envelope. Inside, pressed between two sheets of ruled note-paper, faded and yellow and looking as if it must turn to dust at a touch, was a four-leaved clover.

'Funny old Mole,' said Alastair. 'I wonder how on earth he came to find that.'

That night, after I left Alastair, I thought much about Simes and the evidence he had given. Hitherto I had known almost nothing of Simes and wanted to know nothing. Even when Sanvoisin had warned us how important his evidence was going to be, I had somehow pushed the man himself into the back of my mind, regarding him as a kind of mechanical mouth-piece who would speak and depart, leaving the Court to believe or disbelieve him as it chose. But now that I took leisure to consider some of the things I had heard about him, to review some of the actions credited to him (quite apart from his astonishing performance in Court that day), the ludicrous complacency of my earlier attitude to Simes was very clear. It was Simes, I remembered, who had persuaded Harley to visit a brothel the night before we left for Gikumo; 'young Simes' who had made tent-floors out of branches for Alastair's men at Glukeia; Simes who had 'carried on like Hamlet with his bloody mother' about Alastair and Harley, who had played an honourable part in the attempted get-away, who had subsequently accused Alastair outright of murder and had denounced him to Duthwaite and me the evening we had arrived at the camp. How could I have been so blind as to think he would just mount the stand and give a colourless account of the mere facts, leaving his friend to be avenged or not at the whim of five glittering and la-di-da officers? The man who had been clubbed by Corporal Barnett rather than hold his peace when told was not going to let the President of a Court Martial stand in his way. Nor had he. Simes had certainly said his bit.

But apart from all his dramatic and even hysterical accusations, who was this Simes? What was the man, and how had that man really stood with Malcolm Harley? I tried to remember the judgements that others had passed from time to time. Sergeant Royd, for example, had regarded him as a loud-mouthed nuisance who was fundamentally loyal to his friends. Alastair, originally, had just conceived of him as tiresome and unruly : liable, Alastair had said, to lead Harley into further bad habits – by which, however, he seemed to mean nothing more than beer and riot. But it was now plain that Simes had adopted what was really a protective attitude to Harley, and had received affection and trust in return. I could appreciate, then, that Simes would have regarded Alastair's influence over Harley with suspicion and jealousy, and that his discovery of the sexual relationship between them would have been a bitter shock –

the more so in view of the paternal and possessive rights he clearly wished to assume.

But then again, had he acted, in his interviews with Alastair and Harley, purely out of concern for Harley's moral welfare? or with a selfish desire to break up something which was an obstacle to his own intentions? And what were they? For avuncular as Simes' initial protection of Harley might appear, there was no knowing whither hope, unconscious or perhaps half-formed, might have been leading him. All in all, and remembering the few times I had seen them together, I inclined to think that the relationship between Simes and Harley was of a kind quite common between private soldiers a long way from home. It was a strong and apparently innocent bond between lonely men, but with passion and sexual inclination ever present though ever unacknowledged : inevitably unacknowledged, because the upbringing and prejudices of such men made it unthinkable to them that two soldiers could conceivably be more than 'mates' to each other. Their position was mathematically simple : no women, no sex. You went to the cinema or got drunk with a mate; but whatever unaccustomed impulses you might feel on the way home, you said 'good night' and went off to your own bed. I had known many pairs of men who thought of themselves merely as friends but who were in fact lovers *manqué* – lovers who were too unsophisticated to know that their love could even exist, let alone reason about its morality. On occasion, impelled by some unusual tension or excitement, even perhaps by despair, they did indeed find out the physical desire that lay between them; but this knowledge did not give them happiness for it was beyond their scheme of things. Whatever the reality beneath their affection, to themselves they were, and wished to remain, just 'mates'.

If the relationship between Simes and Harley had been of this nature, then two things followed. Harley, though educated by Alastair to tolerate love between men, would sense the incomprehension of Simes, and might feel that to sleep with Alastair was to dishonour his obligations as Simes' 'mate'. And Simes, as the senior and protective member of the partnership, must inevitably resent such a division in Harley's life. How could he let someone whom he regarded in this way stay absent from him for hours on end and make actual physical love to a being who inhabited an alien world? Quite apart from which, it was certain that Simes' moral feelings, once he understood enough for them to become operative, would be genuine. He was, before all things, a genuine man.

All this proved to me that everything he had said in Court was sincere. Angry and hysterical he might have been, but he was sincere. Therefore what he had said was probably true. But were his deductions – for the sake of which he had been so eager to flout the Court's authority – also true? He had given a true account of his last conversation with Harley, and this obviously meant that Harley had announced his intention of giving up Alastair, for nothing else would have satisfied Simes. Further, Simes was entitled, perhaps, to assume that Harley meant what he said. But was he also entitled to assume, firstly that Harley had the strength to carry his intention through, or granted this, that such a thing would have led Alastair to commit murder? For this was plainly Simes' assumption. Would the Court follow him in his assumption? Or would it deduce, as Sanvoisin, when he engineered Simes' final outburst, clearly wished it to deduce, that Simes was unbalanced by affection and grief?

Whatever they deduced, they could not have been unimpressed. For there was something heroic about Simes, about his bravery and above all about his indignation, however raucously expressed, however obviously the product of intolerance and selfrighteousness. Simes, in fact, was a natural protestant, and as long as a breath of wind stayed in his body, he would never cease from protest.

When the Court reassembled the next morning, General Peterson enquired what witnesses the Defence would call, and whether Alastair himself would give evidence on oath or otherwise address the Court. On being informed that Alastair would give sworn testimony and that he was the only witness for the Defence, Peterson remarked that in this case it was provided that the Defence should have the privilege of making its closing address after that of the Prosecution. It was, he added, preferable if not mandatory that Sanvoisin should start questioning Alastair straight away without any preliminary observation. Sanvoisin said he was confident that Alastair would make everything abundantly plain without any preface from himself; and the accused was then called to take the oath.

'Mr Lynch,' said Sanvoisin, 'we have heard a great deal in Court of your relationship with Drummer Harley. You will now kindly give the Court a full account of this, from its inception right up to the time of Harley's death.'

And Alastair, prompted from time to time by Sanvoisin, told his story : the boxing match on board ship, his successful efforts to save Harley from detention, the early days at Gikumo, and the evening on which the relationship had first become a sexual one.

'And this type of intercourse occurred again?'

'Frequently.'

'And how, at this stage, would you describe your attitude to Harley?'

'I should say I was in love with him.'

'And he with you?'

'No. He liked me well enough and was amused by my company.

176

I was able to make things easier for him, and he was grateful for this and for my general interest. But love . . . no.'

'But he submitted to your physical demands without objection?'

'After the first time, yes. Partly from gratitude, partly from kindness. Though equally, once he had made his mind up to it, there was no doubt he enjoyed the physical side of our relationship. He told me so as time went on. "It's not like being with a woman," he said, "but it's not bad at that. And since there aren't any women up here . . ." '

'But did you not feel responsible for leading Harley into a manner of life that might prove injurious?'

'In one way, yes. But then again, I was doing my best to influence him for the better in a number of other ways. Harley was a faithful and brave man, but he was also weak, vain, thoughtless and drunken.'

'And did his connection with you make him any the less weak, vain, thoughtless and drunken.'

'Hard to say, Sir. If he had ever come back to Eirene, I might have found out. I can only tell you I tried to disabuse him of all the stupid notions he had about the necessity to show off his manliness by drinking or he-man talk. I told him, over and over again, that strength lay in being able to disregard the criticisms of others rather than in factitious demonstrations of a falsely conceived maturity.'

This was thin stuff. There was a restless shifting of feet from the audience.

'And yet he was anxious enough to refute his critics on the day he died?' Sanvoisin pursued.

'He had been much upset. He had been cruelly and viciously attacked by Simes a few days before.'

'More of that later. Let us go back a little. Your relationship continued to be the same after you reached Glukeia?'

'Yes. Harley came to my tent most nights.'

'This was hardly discreet in the conditions in which you all lived?'

'No. But as far as Harley was concerned, I wanted him too badly to mind discretion. During those days at Glukeia I was passionately involved with him. No doubt that sounds silly, stated here as a cold matter of fact. But it is true. At this time Harley was everything to me. I was unhappy if he was away from me at all. I wanted to have him with me by day, while I performed my duties, and I wanted him with me in bed at night. This was reality for me. Without him I felt as if I was dead.'

'And did this interfere with your concern for the interests of your Troop?'

'Why should it? Harley was of my Troop. His interests and those of the Troop were therefore in many ways compatible. The Troop's safety was his safety, the Troop's comfort his comfort. If anything, my feelings for Harley made me even more conscious of my responsibilities to my Troop.'

Brigadier Milner sneered openly from the bench.

'But surely, the fact that so much of your time was devoted to him hardly increased your efficiency as a Troop Commander?'

'I said I wanted him with me. That did not mean I attended only to him. Provided he was there, I felt entirely able to attend thoroughly and competently to my duties – as indeed I did. While he was with me, he was not only someone I loved but a living reminder of great power and urgency of the duties I owed to him and to the others in my care.'

I felt the restlessness and anxiety of Alastair's men pass over me and towards him like a wave.

'Very well. Now we get on to something of great importance. Simes came to see you four days before Harley's death. He spoke violently about your conduct with Harley, but you heard him out and then dismissed him?'

'That is so.'

'Simes then attacked Harley with equal violence about the same issue. You knew of this?'

'Harley told me. He was very upset. This was not the first time Simes had raised the subject, but never before had he been so cruel and coarse and full of hatred.'

'But had this incident made any difference to Harley's feelings for yourself?'

'Not as far as I could tell. He was upset and I did my best to comfort him. Our relationship then continued precisely as before.'

'In every possible respect?'

'In every possible respect.'

'Now then, Mr Lynch. It seems that Harley and Simes had yet another discussion about yourself two days after the violent scenes we have just been speaking of and two days before Harley's death. This discussion was apparently originated by Harley, and when it was over Simes was "very pleased" by what had been said. Did Harley tell you of *this* discussion?'

'No.'

'So that you knew nothing of any discussion alleged to have taken place between Simes and Harley two days before the latter's death?'

'I knew of no such discussion.'

'Did Harley's attitude towards you change at this time? Or at any time before his death?'

'No. Right up until the day of the attack Harley and I were on the best of terms. He came to my tent on the night before the attack. He was the same as ever.'

'On the morning of the attack, then, how did matters stand between you and Harley?'

'I loved him as much as ever and was confident that he returned my affection – as much, that is, as he ever could return it.'

'So. Now as to the attack itself.'

Sanvoisin then ran briefly over the events which led up to Alastair's decision to send a party for help. No, said Alastair, he was anything but confident the party would succeed. But he and Royd had agreed that it was their only chance – assuming, as they were then bound to, that the enemy would keep up the attack until relief appeared.

'And you stick by that decision now?'

'Most definitely. The fact that the enemy *did* in the event retire before we were relieved is immaterial. It was my clear duty to assume that the enemy had the ammunition and the intention to stay there until we were helped. This could not be before six: we ourselves had barely enough ammunition to last till five. We had to get help before then.'

'So you planned the get-away to fetch Mr Hathaway's Troop. Now at what stage did Harley first interfere?'

'When Royd and I were selecting the party.'

'And we know that you refused his request firmly and patiently. But why did you refuse? After all, he was volunteering. One usually welcomes volunteers for dangerous missions.'

'I refused him because he was not the right sort of man for the job, or at any rate there were better men available. True, he volunteered, but he did so in a desperate and irresponsible way. He seemed mainly concerned to "show them he wasn't a nancy boy" or something of the kind. Lastly, he had been drinking. There was a bottle of whisky he had found from somewhere.'

'Drinking? No other witness has mentioned this.'

'No other witness saw him.'

'Why did you let him drink?'

'Because he was afraid.'

'You said just now that Harley was a brave man.'

'Brave men are not immune from fear.'

'They conquer fear,' said Sanvoisin, 'without the assistance of whisky.'

'Harley was young and he was weak. He probably *would* have come through all right without the whisky. The fact remains that he had got hold of it from somewhere, and by the time I first noticed him drinking it he had already had a good deal. I judged it wiser to let him continue.'

'Was he drunk?'

'No. But fortified. Over-confident.'

'Anyhow, you refused his first request. He then interrupted you during your actual briefing of the party. How did you react?'

'I told him sharply to shut up. Time was getting short; and I did not want the get-away party distracted by Harley from hearing and understanding myself.'

'Which was reasonable. But now, Mr Lynch, we are getting to the heart of the matter. All witnesses agree that Harley, after you had finished your briefing, preferred his request yet once more; and that he repeated his reasons – which were that he wanted to go instead of Simes, who was his friend, and that he wanted "to show them" that he was not effeminate. Do you too confirm this?'

'I do.'

'And how did you react?'

'I said nothing, but I was violently angry. We were, you will remember, in a critical situation. We were on the verge of trying an expedient which was at once vital to our survival and yet most unlikely to succeed. Harley had already interrupted me twice. Now here he was, whining away for a third time – and accusing me, in front of four of my men, of having made the rest of the Troop regard him as "a little nancy boy". I admit that I was viciously and almost insanely angry.'

'How long did your anger last?'

'Not for long. I realised that I must control myself; and I also reflected that there were still four minutes to go before the get-away party left, and that I was neglecting the one duty obvious to any responsible officer. Instead of occupying their minds for those four minutes, I was just leaving them to sit there in silence and chew on their own nerves. Now, Harley was at least filling in the time for them. He was providing distraction – and this time it was helpful distraction. What he said might be bad for discipline in the long run, but it would not affect the morale of the get-away party, as such, in any but a beneficial manner. It was giving them something to think about other than the danger which they must shortly face. And when Simes joined in to quiet Harley, it was much better. Here was a dialogue for their entertainment. Scarcely elevating, but, as I say, beneficially distracting.'

'Indeed? What was the dialogue about?'

'Who had, and who had not, ever said that Harley was a "nancy boy".'

'I see your point. So you were no longer angry . . . But then Harley, declining the role of mere entertainer, opted for that of hero. He jumped out of the trench and made for the get-away route?'

'Yes.'

'You called after him?'

'Yes.'

'You prevented Simes following him?'

'Yes.'

'And finally you shot him?'

'Yes.'

'But you were no longer angry with him?'

'No.'

'Then tell the Court why you shot him.'

'Partly because he was disobedient in the face of the enemy; but mainly because, had he got out of the camp and on to the slope, he would have drawn the enemy's attention to the slope – and so to the get-away party when it started.'

'So you swear that you shot Harley to stop him spoiling the get-away's chances. For military reasons alone?'

'I do indeed.'

'Now, this remark you made immediately afterwards. What was it?'

' "Now you know what happens when people disobey orders in action." '

'A tactful remark, Mr Lynch?'

'No. Ill-chosen. But I saw a need to assert my authority immediately and firmly. It is difficult to choose words at such moments.'

'What did you really mean?'

'I meant that if they wanted to get out alive, their only chance was to do what I told them.'

'You believed this?'

'Yes.'

'Why?'

'Because in times of crisis only a consistent course of action can bring salvation. Therefore only one man can give orders. They may be the wrong orders, but if followed they at least guarantee consistency. And in consistency lies the only hope.'

'Very well, Mr Lynch. Then kindly summarise, for the benefit of the Court, your present view of the action you took that day. Be your own judge, Mr Lynch: in the light of all you have heard and thought about it since, in the light, above all, of your conscience, deliver judgement upon the death of Malcolm Harley.'

'I judge now as I judged then. It was not Harley I killed. I killed a disobedient man who was endangering the lives of his comrades, in that he was about to spoil a plan to bring them help. No matter what his motives, that is what he was doing : spoiling a plan to bring help. No matter that his name was Harley, this was the creature I killed : a man who was betraying his friends. I was not angry with Harley for any reason. And as for the deluded man who ran across the camp, I was not angry with him either : I simply knew that he must be destroyed; that for all our sakes he must simply cease to move.'

'Your witness, Sir,' said Sanvoisin to Colonel Lovesy.

It was difficult to tell what impression Alastair had so far made upon the Court. His earlier protestations of a wish to amend Harley's character had, I think, given displeasure to everyone present; nor was his claim that his love for Harley increased his regard for his Troop at all well received. But as to the action itself, he had been on firmer ground. Whether he was telling the strict truth, when he said his anger with Harley had vanished almost instantaneously, was open to doubt: the reasons he gave for this assertion were over-ingenious, to say the best: but at least he had given a plain account of his motive for shooting Harley, and provided Lovesy could not upset this, all, I felt, should be well. But I was far from sanguine as I thought of the vicious weapons, minutely sharpened to points of innuendo and coated with the venom of prejudice, which Colonel Lovesy might now be expected to employ.

'Mr Lynch,' said Lovesy, 'you have spoken very glibly about your relationship with Harley. You say, among other things, that you tried to improve his character and disabuse him of mistaken notions. But surely none of this alters the plain fact that you, a man of experience and education, were corrupting a simple-minded boy entrusted to your care?'

'Harley had had sexual experience, not only with women, but with at least one other man before me.'

'Unfortunately Harley is not here to confirm that. But even if you did not actually pervert him, you at least encouraged him in what were immoral and indeed criminal habits?'

'I am not charged with seducing Harley. I am charged with murdering him.'

'And I am cross-examining you as to your evidence-in-chief. Much of this concerned your conduct with Harley – which, as described by you, was immoral and illegal. Or again, let us consider your claim that your ... interest ... in Harley, so far from distracting you from your military responsibilities, made you more acutely aware of them. You did say something of the kind?'

'I did.'

'Very well then: am I to take, as a good instance of the efficiency with which you ran your Troop, the fact that nearly half your ammunition was found, in an emergency, to have been ruined by damp?'

'Everything in that camp was rotten with damp. It had been raining continuously for nearly a fortnight. We kept the ammunition as carefully as possible, and so far as we could judge from the day to day condition of the boxes, it was all right.'

'But why had you not previously opened the boxes for periodical checks of the ammunition inside?'

'It is just as well for you, Colonel, that your duties do not include the care of ammunition. To have unsealed the boxes in that climate would simply have ensured that all the ammunition was spoiled by damp immediately. Though I quite agree that we should at least have known exactly where we were.'

There was a ripple of pleasure in the audience, faintly discernible even in the Court.

'I bow to your superior knowledge, Mr Lynch, but I do not applaud your insolence,' said Lovesy. 'I am not only the Prosecutor in this case, but also your superior officer.'

'Then I suggest that it will assist your dignity if you refrain from talking nonsense about ammunition.'

'Mr Lynch,' said General Peterson, 'you will apologise to Colonel Lovesy.'

Alastair apologised with insouciant grace and received a stern look from Sanvoisin.

'And now,' proceeded Lovesy, 'we might observe another example of your foresight and industry. This whisky you say Harley was drinking during the attack. I understand that your Company Commander had forbidden alcohol in the Troop detachments?'

'I was a Troop Commander, not a customs' official. I could hardly prevent the odd bottle being smuggled in.'

'You could have instituted occasional searches to ensure that your Company Commander's orders were being obeyed.'

'I preferred to respect my men's privacy as far as possible.'

'A pity you did not have equal respect for their persons ... Mr Lynch, you have been at pains to show that I am ignorant of practical soldiering; but I do know that it is unusual for a commander to allow even so privileged a person as his ... trumpeter ... to get drunk under enemy fire.'

'Harley was not drunk. And if I had caught him before he started drinking he wouldn't have been allowed a drop. But as it was, since he had plainly been drinking some time, and since he was doing it because he was frightened, I judged it unwise to stop him.'

'And then, of course, Harley incapacitated by whisky would have been nicely in your power?'

'I beg your pardon?'

'I see I must be plainer. Had both of you survived this attack, then ever afterwards you would have been able to ... subdue ... Harley by reminding him how he had once got drunk out of cowardice right in the face of the enemy.'

'Harley was not a coward. He was not drunk. And I was well able to subdue him, as you so coyly put it, without reminding him of anything.'

'So you say. But Mr Lynch, we have heard a great deal from Simes of a conversation he had about you with Harley – a conversation started by Harley – two days before the attack. Simes was pleased by this conversation and evidently considers it to have been important. And yet you say Harley told you nothing about it. He told you soon enough when Simes attacked him on the same subject a day or two earlier. But you know nothing of this obviously significant conversation which happened two days before Harley's death. Or do you?'

'Beyond what I have heard for the first time in this Court – no.'

'I suggest you are lying, Mr Lynch.'

'You have no right to.'

'I have every right. *I suggest you are lying.* I suggest you know very well what Harley and Simes discussed two days before Harley's death. I suggest you and Harley were having a serious difference as a result of what Simes had said separately and forcefully to both of you, that Harley would have nothing more to do with you, and that he did *not* come to your tent on the night before the attack.'

'That is not true,' said Alastair calmly.

'Isn't it? Then why did no one see him coming to you?'

'Why should anyone? Harley was often clumsy and noisy, but he didn't advertise his visits to me. As you yourself say, they were immoral and illegal.'

'Plenty of people saw him on other occasions.'

'A few people saw him on a few occasions. But the occasions were many.'

'So you, in your vanity, would have us believe. Let me just leave you with the reflection that it is *inconvenient* for you that on that last night of all nights no one saw Harley come to you. We now have only your own word – and it is not the word of a disinterested person – that there had been no estrangement between you.'

'I have yet to hear it alleged, save by yourself, that there *was* an estrangement between us.'

'What else, if not an estrangement or the prospect of one, could have pleased Simes so much?'

'Simes is an honest man but not a clever one. He may have read too much into his conversation with Harley. He may have misinterpreted its significance.'

'Then you admit it was significant?'

'Every conversation signifies something – only it is not necessarily the truth.'

'That is for others to judge,' said Lovesy. 'The question at issue is what this particular conversation, the mere fact of its having taken place at all, inevitably signifies. And what would you say that was?'

'Once and for all,' said Alastair, 'I do not know. I know only what Simes has sworn to in this Court; and that is that he and

Harley discussed me, at Harley's invitation, some two days before the attack on our position. Whatever Harley did or did not tell Simes on this occasion, my relationship with Harley remained unaltered up to the morning of his death. Harley slept with me on the previous night, in the same affectionate and immoral and illegal way he always did, and I'm only sorry there was no one under the bed to prove it.'

Sanvoisin glanced very sharply at Alastair, who deliberately avoided his eye.

'Very well,' said Lovesy, 'here are a few more things for you to be flippant about. I refer now to events which happened during the attack. Sergeant Royd has testified that when Harley disobeyed you and made his break he might have got through. Why didn't you give him a chance?'

'Sergeant Royd has also testified that he was very unlikely to get through. The covering fire hadn't started yet, you must remember. Weighing the odds, I thought that Harley's chance was not good enough to discount the grave possibility that he would simply draw the enemy's attention prematurely to the get-away route.'

'Then why did you not do as Simes suggested in his evidence? Why did you not order the covering fire to start up straight away? And then send the other four men off after Harley?'

'The Troop was not yet ready to give the covering fire. To give covering fire at the concentrated rate required, it is necessary to make preparations. Bren magazines must be filled and checked. Clips must be made up and distributed. Mortar bombs must be primed. A thousand details must be attended to unheard of, Colonel Lovesy, in your philosophy. They had been warned to be ready at two – and given none too much time as it was. There were still several minutes to go, and they were not ready.'

'You seem to have thought of a lot in the time it took poor Harley to run forty yards.'

'That is what I was being paid to do.'

'Then what about this anger of yours? You were not being paid to indulge that. You admit you were angry when Harley repeated his request to join the get-away. You then have the impertinence to tell the Court, that your anger gave way to relief because you thought Harley's remarks and Simes' rejoinder would provide a "beneficial distraction" for the get-away party. What sort of story is this?'

'That, Colonel, to borrow your own words, is "for others to judge". I must repeat. I was no longer angry with Harley and therefore did not shoot him out of anger. In any case, it was not Harley I shot. It was a man, any man, who was endangering my Troop.'

'Another neat sophistry. In a court of law we are interested in

185

the truth, not in intellectual conceits. I suggest to you, Lieutenant Alastair Lynch, that for a variety of reasons you were viciously angry with Drummer Harley. You were angry because of his devotion to Simes and because of his wish to prove he was not the effeminate thing you had made him and wished him to remain. You were angry because he shamed you by saying as much in front of your men. Above all, you were angry because he was disregarding your possessive and jealous wishes to keep him safe in your trench. And I suggest that when this disregard turned into active and open defiance, your anger rose to such a pitch that deliberately, with malice aforethought and guilty intention, you shot him in the back – what time he was making an heroic bid to save his comrades by going out alone to face danger and find help.'

'Your suggestions are false,' said Alastair, 'and I repudiate both them and yourself with contempt.'

Peterson opened his mouth to speak; but Lovesy waved his hand nonchalantly and returned to his seat.

'That,' he said, 'will be all.'

After a damp and dismal lunch, Colonel Lovesy started his closing address.

He must invite the Court's attention, he said, to the following series of proven facts. Alastair Lynch, a man in a responsible and honourable position, had become infatuated with Drummer Harley, a boy of eighteen. Having taken great trouble to have Harley transferred to his own Troop, he then so far lost control as deliberately to cultivate the boy's company far more than duty required or discretion allowed; and finally, as he himself had told the Court, he had seduced Harley physically.

This relationship had continued on all levels, including the physical, after the removal of Lynch's Troop to the confined space of the camp near Glukeia. The matter had been an open scandal within the Troop, and had caused understandable resentment in some quarters. The Court would judge for itself of the character of an officer who could so far forget himself and his responsibilities as to continue such a liaison so unashamedly in such circumstances. Finally, Harley's friend Simes had remonstrated in violent language firstly with Lynch himself and then with Harley, to whose interests Simes had clearly been devoted in an honest and comradely fashion. This had been four days before Harley's death.

Simes also swore he had discussed the matter with Harley two days later – two days, that was, before Harley's death – at Harley's own invitation. This discussion had been quiet and sensible; Harley, as the President of the Court had been at pains to elicit from Simes, had expressed an unprompted intention of which Simes had approved; and so, at the end of the discussion, Simes had been pleased and satisfied on his own account and particularly on Harley's. In passing, no doubt the Court had noticed and appreciated the entirely wayward manner in which Lynch had spoken of this discussion. Lynch, in a speech of such effrontery it shamed the dignity of the occasion, had maintained that whatever the conversation was about he had known nothing of it, that he had noticed no change in Harley's attitude towards himself, and that they had indeed spent the night before Harley's death in bed together as was their habit. The Court would consider whether or not to believe this assertion; and would no doubt draw its own conclusions from the fact that the Defence had been unable to produce evidence, apart from Lynch's unsupported word, to prove that he had indeed spent that last night in amicable intercourse with Harley. Now, since the camp was minute, since two sentries were always on guard, and since, above all, Harley had been so frequently noticed going to Lynch on other occasions, it was almost incredible that he should not have been noticed on this. The Court might well consider how vital it was for the Defence to show that Harley and Lynch were still on good terms at this time, and so might perhaps have expected that Colonel Sanvoisin would have made every attempt to show that they were still sleeping together or anything else that might prove an unspoiled affection. But no. Only the defendant could or would speak up to this effect.

'And then, gentlemen,' pursued Lovesy, 'we come to the events of the attack. I shall say nothing of such misfortune as the sudden discovery that half the ammunition was useless, or the unnoticed presence of a bottle of whisky in a supposedly "dry" position; though I shall just remind the Court of the heedless and insolent manner adopted by Lynch when these questions were raised. What I would invite the Court to consider most earnestly are the following anomalies :

'Firstly, Lynch's refusal of Harley's request to join the get-away. Why refuse an able-bodied volunteer for a dangerous task? If the drink had put fresh spirit into Harley – and Lynch has testified that the boy was "fortified" but not drunk – then that was one more good reason for sending him.

'Secondly, how was it that Mr Lynch's anger, which everyone, including himself, admits to have been violent, evaporated so swiftly?

'Thirdly, why did Lynch not at least give Harley a chance of justifying an action which, though disobedient, was evidently undertaken in good faith? Lynch himself told Sergeant Royd later on that he thought Harley's race across the camp, even though he had not succeeded in reaching the slope, had probably helped to give the show away in any case. If this was so, then plainly it was one more sound reason for letting Harley continue.'

Lovesy then repeated what he had said earlier in the trial about the law which governed murder. The essential ingredient in murder was a guilty intention. This intention could be formed and carried out, they must remember, in a single instant. The learned Judge Advocate would also confirm that evidence to prove such an intention was, for obvious reasons, normally of a circumstantial nature – similar in kind, that was to say, to the evidence which he himself had produced before the Court and which concerned Alastair's feelings towards Harley.

'Let me conclude, gentlemen,' Lovesy said, 'by suggesting to you three possibilities. In the light of the proven facts, I invite you to consider that Harley's death might be explained in one of three ways. Firstly then, the Defence will no doubt assert that Mr Lynch shot him as an unwilling duty which was forced upon him by the extreme nature of the circumstances. To this I reply that the circumstances, so far from compelling Mr Lynch to shoot Harley, provided many excellent military reasons for letting Harley continue.

'Secondly, you might think that the facts of Mr Lynch's anger and the general confusion obtaining indicate that Harley's death was not the result of unwilling yet dutiful action, but the result of bad organisation, ill temper and panic. Whether this would constitute murder or manslaughter is a nice question and one that I leave to the learned Judge Advocate. In any event, I now invite your attention to a third explanation of Harley's death which, in my view, the evidence here produced confirms beyond doubt as the true one.'

He drew a deep breath, and then moved violently and suddenly to within a yard of where Alastair sat. Staring straight at him, he said slowly :

'This is that Mr Lynch, bemused by a vicious liaison and frustrated by the course which that liaison had recently taken; angered by Harley's interference with his plans, his concern for Simes and disregard of his own wishes; openly provoked by Harley's disobedience to him both as a lover and as a commander; and finally outraged by Harley's disinterested but, to Lynch, totally disloyal action : that Mr Lynch, incensed by all these motives, anger, pique and jealousy being paramount among them, did wilfully shoot Harley in the back with the guilty intention of murdering him. I maintain, in fact, that it is to Lynch's unlovely passions, to the vicious course of Lynch's possessive lust, and to Lynch's violent reaction at being crossed by the object of his foul affections, that Harley's death must unquestionably be attributed. This I claim to have proved in a fashion which, in men of normal tendencies, proper moral scruple and responsible knowledge of the Army and of the world, can leave no reasonable doubt. With respect, therefore, and equally with confidence in the discerning intelligence of this Court, but above all with a most strong desire that justice shall be done, I ask that your verdict be "murder".'

A journalist coughed harshly. C.S.M. Mole emerged in panic from a nap.

'It only remains,' said General Peterson, 'that Colonel Sanvoisin should conclude for the Defence.'

'The Defence has only three points to make,' said Sanvoisin; 'but after the testimony you have heard, I am confident that these points, all of which are dependent, not on speculation, but on fact, will leave no doubt whatever as to the innocence of Alastair Lynch.

'Firstly, then, as to Lynch's connection with Drummer Harley. Whatever else may be said about this, Lynch's attachment was evidently sincere and genuine. Immoral, inopportune, bad for discipline, irresponsible in its fulfilment, perverse in its conception, it was nevertheless a matter of love.

'Secondly, then, let us consider the Prosecution's claim that it was the spoiling of this affection which led to fury in Lynch and his consequent murder of Harley. What evidence has Colonel Lovesy produced to show that this affection had been spoiled? He taunts the Defence with failing to prove that it had *not* been spoiled; he remarks that the Defence has not brought evidence, apart from Lynch himself, to show that Harley did intend to sleep with him on the night before the attack; and he refers to a conversation between Harley and Simes. What proof is here? If the Prosecution contends that Lynch and Harley had quarrelled, it must show that they had quarrelled. But beyond reference to a conversation in which anything or nothing, true or untrue, may have been said, no positive evidence of any kind has been produced to show that Lynch and Harley had fallen out before the day of the attack. If they had done so, it would surely have been noticed by other people quickly enough As the able Prosecuting Officer remarks, the camp was very small.

'Lastly, the attack itself. I defy anyone to conclude, in the face of the sworn testimony of Mr Lynch, supported by others and in particular by so experienced a non-commissioned officer as Sergeant Royd, that Mr Lynch conducted this action in any manner that was not wholly courageous, competent and creditable. Time was when the mere suggestion, in such circumstances, of disobedience such as Harley's would have led to him being shot without hesitation before question or after. This time is mercifully past. But the time has not yet come, and can never come, when an officer is not bound by duty to destroy anything or anybody who unlawfully imperils the safety of his men. Wittingly or unwittingly, whether from bravery, fondness or hysteria, Harley was ruining what Mr Lynch conceived to be his Troop's last chance of survival. Mr Lynch shot him dead before he could ruin it altogether. What man, what soldier, what commander could have done otherwise than this?'

The Judge Advocate summed up with remorseless exactitude and bleak impartiality. Only one thing he said gave me cause for additional anxiety. It was true, he said, that there did not appear to be strong evidence for supposing Alastair and Harley to have fallen out before the morning of the attack. But the Court would of course consider Harley's words, and his demeanour towards Alastair, at the various stages of the attack. The Court would recall that Harley had twice said, not only that he wanted to show his comrades that he was not ' a little pouf' or 'a nancy boy', but also that Mr Lynch was to blame for them thinking this. The Court would ponder whether or not these words indicated any disaffection between Harley and Lynch, and, if they did, what degree of disaffection they implied.

When the Judge Advocate had concluded his summing-up, the Court closed to consider its verdict.

Had it not been for our anxiety, it would have been pleasant waiting outside the tent for the Court to re-open. For at last the sun had come out again; and late in the afternoon as it was, the warm and unaccustomed light was soothing even to nerves as tired and hearts as troubled as our own. Even so, however, only Alastair showed any signs of wanting to talk.

'That man Lovesy,' he said. 'Not a sahib.'

'So you as good as told him,' said Sanvoisin. 'A good job the Court probably disliked him as much as you did.'

Silence.

'If I told you I'd perjured myself,' said Alastair lightly, 'what would you do?'

'Nothing – now. The case could be re-opened, of course. But candidly, my dear Alastair, I'm so bored both with it and with you that I wouldn't have the strength. Besides which, I'm here to keep you out of trouble, not land you in a fresh lot.'

'Well, in a way I did perjure myself. The spirit of what I said was true enough; but the facts were ... well ... rearranged a little.'

'I don't want to know anything about it,' said Sanvoisin, and moved off to talk to Giles Bancombe.

'For Christ's sake,' I said, 'what are you trying to do?'

'Pass the time,' said Alastair, 'and as it happens I can only think of one subject – this trial. In this trial I have, in a way, perjured myself. Do you want to hear about it?'

'Count me out,' said Michael. He too moved away.

'Well now, Andrew,' said Alastair, 'that leaves only you. You at least must hear this. It's very important that someone should. Now, you're a loyal friend and an intelligent man. Am I right in saying that a good deal turns on whether they think Harley and I were still on good terms when he died?'

'You know very well it does.'

'Well, we weren't on good terms. We'd quarrelled horribly. Oh, certainly he came to my tent that last night, as I said. But he came to tell me he'd decided to give it all up. He agreed with Simes, he said. He'd let me comfort him when Simes had spoken so viciously, but he'd thought it over since, he'd talked to Simes again, and he knew that Simes was right. So now he'd come to tell me that though he was happy to be my friend in the ordinary way, he wanted no more talk of love and above all no more sex. It wasn't healthy, he said, and it wasn't right.'

'What did you do?'

'I set about seducing him all over again. He tried to resist, but he couldn't. He was, paradoxically enough, too healthy to resist a direct sexual appeal. So in the end he yielded, and then he was so ashamed of his weakness that he started crying.'

'It was a vile thing to do.'

'I know. But at the time I could only think of trying to keep Malcolm, and this seemed the one way to make good my claim. I see now how clumsy and cruel I was. That's why I'm so anxious for someone to hear about it – the relief of guilt by confession, as you might say, and also the hope that if I go on talking long enough I myself or somebody else may discover means of pardon or excuse . . . But that's not the end of it. When Malcolm had recovered, he turned to me, all bitterness and spite and cold fury, and said I was a rotten, smooth-tongued seducer, evil and corrupt, utterly selfish and God-forsaken, slimy with lust and decay. I should never have thought he had it in him, such words. And what made it worse was that all this was in whispers. Harsh, fierce, hissing whispers. And I myself was now so angry, I answered him back even more horribly. I said he was just a stupid, bouncing, blue-eyed little whore without the guts to think for himself. Happy enough, I said, to be the Troop Commander's fancy boy, all sugar and sweets, but once let things get slightly difficult and he turned as soft as butter and went off blubbering all over his dirty face and whining for pity and sympathy. So then he left my tent, but not until he'd sworn never to talk to me again and to apply for a transfer the minute we got away from Glukeia.'

'I see what you mean about having rearranged the facts a little. But you also told us that the spirit of what you said was true. You'll pardon me if I say that the spirit seems as false as everything else in your evidence.'

'But none of this had anything to do with Malcolm's death, Andrew. I forgot my anger in the morning and set about thinking how to get him back.'

'But you were angry again just before you shot him.'

'Only for a few seconds. I didn't kill him . . . I don't think I killed him because of that.'

'You don't seem so sure after all.'

'I shall never be sure, Andrew.'

'The Court is about to re-open, gentlemen,' said Sergeant God-awake behind us. 'Please return to your places.'

So we took our places for the last time; and Alastair rose at Peterson's bidding and stood forward in front of the Court.

'Lieutenant Alastair Lynch,' said Peterson, 'the Court having considered its verdict in this case, it is my duty to announce that you are found to be not guilty. You may leave the Court.'

But at this two men came forward from the entrance. One carried Alastair's spurs, the other his sword and sash. Corporal Barnett knelt to fix Alastair's spurs in place; and Sergeant Royd fastened the sash and the sword-belt. Then Alastair placed his busby on his head and, in accordance with our custom, drew his sword, that he might salute the Court with the emblem of honour so lately returned to him. The Court stood to acknowledge the salute. Alastair sheathed his sword, turned about and marched away through the entrance.

Outside he paused, waiting for us to follow him. But C.S.M. Mole and the members of his own Troop reached him long before we did. Mole was gasping and tottering with his emotion. The others, many of them with tears running down their faces, cheered and acclaimed him as the hero that to them he truly was, and within a few seconds had lifted him shoulder high to carry him in triumph to the Officers' Mess.

'Magnums,' shouted Alastair to Jones his batman. 'Run ahead and tell them to get ready every magnum of champagne in the place.'

So that, in the midst of the triumph and the confusion, no one had noticed Simes. No one had bothered about him as he waited outside the Court, with so many others, to see what the verdict would be. No one had seen his face go stiff and white as Alastair marched out, fully accoutred and therefore acquitted, to be greeted with the applause of those waiting and to be followed by the rush of his own men who had been sitting inside. No one had eyes for one man in such a turmoil – unless that man were Alastair: no one had ears for muttered curses amidst so many acclamations. No one thought it odd that a stocky figure should be edging and pressing its way through a crowd in which all was movement. So that no one noticed Mounted Infantryman Simes at all – until he lifted a naked bayonet and stuck it into Alastair Lynch's back.

Even then, few people saw what happened or indeed realised for some time that anything had happened at all. Afterwards there was no one, save for the man on whose shoulders Alastair sat, who could have told you the precise moment when he was struck. Perhaps not even they; for they started to march forward, seemingly unconscious of what had occurred, and only halted, after a few paces, when they realised that Alastair's head was between their buttocks and his busby was in the dust.

CHAPTER FIFTEEN

ALASTAIR'S FUNERAL, which took place the day after his trial, was conducted with all the pomp and circumstance which befitted the demise of a commissioned officer of Martock's Foot. A company of soldiers slow-marched at the head of the procession with arms reversed. Then came the band playing one after the other the selection of lugubrious slow marches which they practised, from time to time, for occasions of this nature. Behind the band was the guard of honour; this was the Troop commanded by Robin Hathaway, which had been hurriedly brought down to Eirene the previous evening to be rehearsed in its functions; for these included the provision of a bearer-party, the lowering of the coffin into the grave, and the firing of several volleys of blank ammunition before the final trumpet call – all of which offices had often, by their ragged and nervous fulfilment, given grave embarrassment in the past. The Guard, in turn, was followed by the hearse, a magnificently decked and tasselled affair, drawn by six black horses, which some enterprising Eirenean undertaker had hired to us and which gave an air, so intricately funereal was it, more appropriate to the burial of an Italian mayor. The coffin, covered by a Union Jack (the same one that had hung in the Court Room), was also surmounted by Alastair's accoutrements : busby, sabre-trache, and sword. Behind the hearse came all the officers who had been available to attend, apart from those controlling other units in the column, marching in pairs with Sanvoisin and Sinclair at their head. Lastly, there was yet another entire company. About half the Battalion was involved in one way or another, and I thought what a splendid opportunity this would have made for Karioukeya, had he been forewarned, to break into the territories which these companies, brought to Eirene early that morning, were supposedly guarding. But Karioukeya was still in the heart of the mountains, and the companies would be back in their positions by evening. Meanwhile, this splendid and barbarous procession wound its way down to the Cathedral in Eirene; and in the occasional intervals between the marches played by the band, the clear and single note of a tolling bell was to be heard above the slow shuffle of the men's feet.

The service in the Cathedral followed its appointed course. So there it was, I thought. It seemed quite probable that justice of a kind had been done. For what was I to make of Alastair's remarks just before he had been so triumphantly acquitted? If he had suppressed so much of the truth during the trial, and indeed when talking to us, his friends, before the trial, there was no end to the further lies he might have told, to myself and to all of us, to Harley or Sanvoisin, to Royd or Mole. The fantasy with which he had indulged himself about the soul of Harley coming to seek its body in his own tent: how could he have said such things about someone from whom he knew he had parted in hatred? The tender account he had so frequently given us of the last night which he and Harley had spent together: when in truth he had merely used his charm and power to take hideous advantage of a simple and unwilling boy. But then again, perhaps Alastair had only lied over this one issue, and lied because he knew, as we all did, how vital it was for his safety that everyone should think that he and Harley were friends to the last. Perhaps, indeed, he had even come to believe this himself, until in that final moment of honesty, whether hounded by his conscience or forewarned by some presentiment of his death, he had revealed the truth to me. But what was the point of going over it all? Alastair was dead. If he had not been dead, he would have been compelled to resign after what had been said at the trial about himself and Harley – however much of this was true or false. Either way he was lost to us. And what was the good of asking whether or not he had really murdered Harley? Only one thing seemed certain to me that morning in the Cathedral: whether Harley had been murdered or not, he would not have been dead if only Alastair had left him alone. He would not have been at Glukeia, and if he had he would not have been with Alastair in his trench. He would have been where he ought always to have been, side by side with some friend of his own age and his own standing, as untroubled by guilt as he was unenlightened by Alastair's educated talk. But blame Alastair? Blame Harley for leaving his village to be a soldier, blame Harley's mother for bearing him; blame God for giving away soft limbs and big blue eyes; blame bullets for being hard and the flesh for being weak. Blame the fact of death. For this was all it came to: Harley, whom Alastair had loved like a woman, was dead: Alastair, whom we had all loved as a man, was dead; and Simes, whom Harley in some way or other had loved, would be dead within six weeks. And so might many more of us, before we had finished with Karioukeya in Pepromene.

At the close of the service, Colonel Lord Nicholas Sanvoisin rose to address the congregation.

'Gentlemen of Lord Martock's Regiment,' he said, 'we are assembled here to bury one of our comrades, Lieutenant Alastair Lynch. In a few minutes we shall commit his body to the ground and his soul to Him that shall receive it. But first, since he was not only one of my officers but also my dear friend, I must ask you to hear what I shall say.

'Alastair Lynch had lately shown himself a man of endurance and

195

courage, cool, resourceful and worthy of command. Those of you who know the details of his Troop's action near Glukeia will applaud both the men of this Troop and their leader. Their achievement, although it will be of no account in history and of small importance even in the day to day record of this campaign, will find an honourable place in the annals of this Regiment : so that in years to come there will always be men to say, as November succeeds November, "This is the day when Alastair Lynch and his men fought bravely in the Mountains of Dis"; and for many years, too, there will be men to answer, "Yes, we were there with him on Mount Chalchos. It is a day to remember with pride and thankfulness."

'Let this, then, be one epitaph for Alastair Lynch: Would that there were no other.

'But there is another, and you must all know it. Yesterday, Alastair Lynch was tried for the murder of your comrade Malcolm Harley. He was found not guilty. But you will all know soon, if you do not know already, that many things were revealed at this trial greatly to the dishonour of Alastair Lynch. For he had seduced Malcolm Harley; he had abused the trust placed in him both by those who set him at the head of his Troop and by Harley himself, who thought he was his friend; and with smooth words and ready charm, he had brought Harley to a course of life which, in the end, could only lead to shame and outlawry. It is true that Alastair Lynch did not murder Harley; but had he held in proper regard his own honour and the honour of our Regiment, had he looked to his duty and not to the idle dictates of his fancy, had he but once thought that Harley was his only to receive lawful commands and not to become the spoiled object of his pleasure, then both Malcolm Harley and Alastair Lynch would still be with us now.

'This is the second epitaph of Alastair Lynch, whom we shall now bury.'

The bearers lowered the coffin into the grave. Robin Hathaway drew his sword, and at his command the guard of honour fired its ragged volleys over Alastair Lynch. Then the guard presented arms, while Robin dipped his sword in salute; and the trumpeter, just such another as Malcolm Harley, blew the long sad notes away over the city towards the hills.

Then we filed past the grave and away towards the entrance of the graveyard; until at last only Sergeant Major Mole was left there, watching the grave-diggers shovel in the earth. A lonely, sad old man, with the tears running down his sunken cheeks : a lonely, stupid, sad old man, staggering slightly with drink, and even now reaching into his pocket for a flask and raising it high over the grave, that he might drink and pour libations to the soul of Alastair Lynch.

Hunstanton, June 27th, 1958.

196

Recent literary fiction from The Gay Men's Press:

Noel Currer-Briggs
YOUNG MEN AT WAR

Anthony Arthur Kildwick, born in 1919 to a well-to-do English family, finds the love of his life in a German exchange
student at his private school. When Manfred returns to Germany he is seduced by Hitler's nationalist rhetoric, while Tony
meets the outbreak of war as a conscientious objector. Yet as
the Nazi regime shows itself ever more demonic, Tony decides
he must fight, and is parachuted into southern France to work
with the Resistance. He discovers Manfred is now an officer
with the occupying forces, and their paths cross again in dramatic circumstances.

Based largely on the author's own experience, this fascinating
story conveys a vivid sense of the conflicts of the 1930s, and
the interplay betwen friendship and internationalism, homosexuality and pacifism, patriotism and democracy, that was
characteristic of those years.

"An absorbing account of the conflict between personal integrity and the tyranny of blinkered patriotism" — *Gay Times*,
London

ISBN 0 85449 236 4
UK £9.95 US $14.95 AUS $19.95

Rudi van Dantzig
FOR A LOST SOLDIER

During the winter of 1944 in occupied Amsterdam, eleven-year-old Jeroen is evacuated to a tiny fishing village community on the desolate coast of Friesland, where he meets Walt, a young Canadian soldier with the liberating forces. Their relationship immerses the young boy in a tumultuous world of emotional and sexual experience, suddenly curtailed when the Allies move on and Walt goes away. Back home in Amsterdam, a city in the throes of liberation fever, Jeroen searches for the soldier he has lost. A child's fears and confused emotions have rarely been described with such depth of understanding, and seen as it is from the boy's viewpoint it invites total empathy.

This novel by the artistic director of the Dutch National Ballet appeared successfully in hardback in 1991, and was made into a prize-winning film.

"A beautifully chronicled document of wartime life"
— *Gay Times*, London

"I was filled with admiration for the way in which Rudi van Dantzig has transformed a difficult and unusual autobiographical theme into a compelling literary work" — *Times Literary Supplement*, London

ISBN 0 85449 237 2
UK £9.95 US $14.95 AUS $19.95

Rufus Gunn
A FRIENDSHIP OF CONVENIENCE
Being a Discourse on Poussin's "Landscape With a Man Killed by a Snake"

The place and time: London 1956. The friends in question: Sir Anthony Blunt, Surveyor of the Queen's Pictures, and Joe Losey, film director and refugee from McCarthyism. Their meeting: the National Gallery, in front of Poussin's disturbing metaphor. Into this landscape, Rufus Gunn introduces a cast of celebrities: Vita Sackville-West, Arthur Miller, Anthony Eden, Ben Nicholson, in a plot where fiction blends effortlessly with fact, as the US intelligence services press the British government to take action against the homosexual peril. Brilliantly evoking the political and intellectual life of the high Cold War, *A Friendship of Convenience* recreates a world where the appearance of politeness and civility covered up a reality of cynicism and betrayal.

"It is a novel of ideas, an intellectual comedy... Gunn forces us to scrutinise the ideas according to which we conduct our present lives" — *Literary Review*

"A thoroughly good book, the travel-fiction-love stories mixture is managed very well, and it's funny and interesting" — Iris Murdoch on Rufus Gunn's first novel *Something for Sergio*

ISBN 0 85449 244 5
UK £8.95 US $12.95 AUS $17.95

Thomas Boggs
TOKYO VANILLA

Not just another "Westerner-looks-at-Japan" story, this is an insider's view of the secretive homosexual underground of today's Tokyo — written by a half-Japanese writer who has spent most of his life in Japan's capital. College student Fumio awakens to his own sexual nature in a traditional society where homosexuality is still seen as a dirty secret best hidden away. Introduced by his straight fellow-student Tatsuya to the "host clubs" where good money is to be made, he is torn between his unrequited passion for his schoolfriend and the comfortable life of a kept boy he is offered by a rich professor. When the professor proposes that Fumio marry his daughter, the web of deceit grows steadily more complex. Influenced in style by Tanizaki Junichiro, this finely written début offers a unique literary insight into Japanese gay life.

Born in Japan, Thomas Boggs was educated in the United States and served in the US Navy. Now based in Tokyo, he is active as a writer in both English and Japanese.

ISBN 0 85449 255 0
UK £9.95 US $14.95 AUS $19.95

Martin Foreman
THE BUTTERFLY'S WING

Andy McIllray and Tom Dayton are a well-matched gay couple in their thirties, still happy after seven years together. Andy
has a high-flying job with an international organisation, while
Tom has given up his unrewarding work in catering to look
after the smallholding they bought in Berkshire. Disaster strikes
when Andy's work takes him to Peru, where he is kidnapped
by the Shining Path guerrilla movement. Tom has to take new
and unaccustomed initiatives, seeking out every possible av-
enue in the struggle for Andy's release.

This ambitious new novel by Martin Foreman is cast in the
form of two diaries. The torment into which both Andy and
Tom are thrown forces them each to face hidden truths about
themselves and their relationship. Exploring the strengths and
tensions of gay love in the 1990s, the story weaves in major
issues of the contemporary world scene as it unravels towards
a dramatic dénouement.

"Technically accomplished... literate and dignified... deeply felt"
— the *Times Literary Supplement* on Martin Foreman's short
story collection *A Sense of Loss*

ISBN 0 85449 223 2
UK £8.95 US $14.95 AUS $19.95

John R. Gordon
SKIN DEEP

Two young and talented black men, photographer Ray and struggling actor Chris, are best friends in 1990s London. But Ray is only attracted to white men, which Chris sees as betraying his race, while Chris is into a heavy sexual masochism which Ray cannot understand. Their current lovers bring more complications. Drawn into the S/M scene through his relationship with Chris, the heterosexually-identified pimp Clinton is imprisoned for manslaughter; and Ray's young white lover Louis is beaten into a coma by a black street gang.

This ambitious novel by the author of *Black Butterflies* reflects the complex entanglements of real life in a society where racism and homophobia distort the most intimate relationships, yet love and friendship are still possible across the barriers of oppression.

"I was dying to get to sleep but I kept telling myself 'just one more page...' and before I knew it it was all over and I had no choice but to start again from the beginning" — Rikki Beadle-Blair, screenwriter of *Stonewall*

"*Skin Deep* is thought-provoking and funny, subtly erotic and in-your-face nasty by turns; often deeply touching and at times, surprisingly wise" — Larry Duplechan

ISBN 0 85449 246 1
UK £9.95 US $14.95 AUS $19.95

Jeffrey Round
A CAGE OF BONES

Warden Fields, an ingenuous college student from Toronto, is discovered by an Italian model agency and persuaded to work in Europe. He begins to find the love and affection he desperately seeks, but the glamorous and frenetic world of the fashion houses in Milan and London makes it hard to maintain a relationship. Warden's boyfriend in Italy is drafted into the army, while his adventures with an English lover draw him into illegal political intrigue. Sensitive and subtle, this fine new novel weaves together tragic and comic themes into a moving and delightful human story.

Jeffrey Round is a director and award-winning dramatist, and an associate of *Pink Triangle Press*. He has drawn for this novel on his own experience in the fashion world he depicts.

"A brilliant novel by a writer whose moral vision will surely ensure his place in the world of literature" — Shyam Selvadurai, author of *Funny Boy*

"You can gauge the depth of my admiration when I tell you that my reaction to *A Cage of Bones* was simply envy" — Douglas LePan, twice winner of Canada's Governor-General's Award

ISBN 0 85449 252 6
UK £9.95 US $14.95 AUS $14.95